WINNIPEG
SEP 15 2017
PUBLIC LIBRARY
WITHDRAWN

D1563659

LOST IN SEPTEMBER

a novel

LOST IN SEPTEMBER

KATHLEEN WINTER

ALFRED A. KNOPF CANADA

PUBLISHED BY ALFRED A. KNOPF CANADA

 Published in 2017 by Alfred A. Knopf Canada, a division of Penguin Random House Canada Limited. Distributed in Canada by Penguin Random House Canada Limited, Toronto.

www.penguinrandomhouse.ca

Library and Archives Canada Cataloguing in Publication

Winter, Kathleen, author
Lost in September / Kathleen Winter.

Issued in print and electronic formats.

ISBN 978-0-345-81012-0
eBook ISBN 978-0-345-81014-4

I. Title.

PS8595.I618L67 2017 C813'.54 C2017-900883-8

Book design by Jennifer Griffiths

Cover and interior illustrations by Jennifer Griffiths

Printed and bound in the United States of America

10 9 8 7 6 5 4 3 2 1

For my mother,

who has always loved dogs

I know,
I know and you know, we knew,
we did not know, we
were there, after all, and not there
and at times when
only the void stood between us we got
all the way to each other.

PAUL CELAN

PART III: RED MAN

PART IV: GREEN MAN

JANUARY 2, 2018

SAINT ALFEGE CHURCH
GREENWICH, LONDON
UNITED KINGDOM

Dear James Wolfe,

I wanted to write this book in time for your birthday. Silly, I know, but why not place it on your grave here at Saint Alfege on this day that celebrates your life? That is, after all, what I have tried to do in these pages. Forgive me if I have not entirely succeeded. Try to see my intent. I don't mean to complain, but you gave me no choice except to look for traces of you in unexpected streets, in modern places as well as old haunts. How else was I able to find what you dearly wanted me to know? For I have, dear James, heard you whispering to me at night in the park, or by day in libraries, and in the voices of people I have met while on your trail. And I believe with all my heart that you wanted me to meet a certain representative of yours—that you placed him in my path, so that he might hand me your message directly.

Still, though I listened as carefully as I could, I don't know how you will feel about my rendition of you.

I have come to know a James Wolfe who does not appear in the historical reports of your military strategy, nor in accounts of your siege of Quebec. In those tales, you always wear the same red costume and sustain one aim, which can be boiled down to a sentence: *In September 1759 he took Quebec for the British, and with that victory, achieved in fifteen short minutes of battle, forever changed the course of history, ensuring that Canada would be British and not French.*

What I know is different. I have intercepted a deep-hearted sadness. You have become present to me, in the way of those I loved and whose bodies I have held but are now gone: my mother, my grandmothers, my grandfathers, each of whom has known love and loss and war.

Do souls depart?

You think not, I suspect.

I *remember* you, as I remember the faded presence of departed beloveds. Perhaps memory of a person is one thing, and the real, present person another, like a body separated from its shadow. I am, in your case, flooded by your memory without having touched you. As I walked your death-ground last autumn I mourned a soldier I feel I remember. Not in the flesh—rather, you were a light-body slipping through me.

I miss that light now. These pages are what remain.

Faithfully yours,
Genevieve Waugh

YELLOW MAN

1 Gregorian Chant

SATURDAY, SEPTEMBER 2, 2017.
AFTERNOON.
Gaspé Peninsula, Quebec

"SOPHIE!" I WAIL, BUT THESE barrens swallow my voice.

Behind me recede northern lakes, distant peaks draped with snow. Here come little bridges, fragile fences . . . I check the ditches, always check the ditches, because if I've learned one thing it's that I'm not, in fact, invincible—one minute you're fine then in a split second—fuck! *Elwyn* . . .

Is nobody around?

"Sophie!"

I've got no route-clearing equipment with me here, nothing but my eyes to check the culverts and ravines, that *wadi* up ahead—but no, it's a harmless peat gully—am I back in Scotland, then?

Sophie would know. Far ahead of me, she has probably already pitched our tent. Not in Scotland, no . . . our tent is in . . . Montreal, that's right. It was 1745 when I was in Scotland—god, was I only eighteen?

Here come the birches. I have to keep reminding Sophie that it's easy to wonder where the hell I am, for the birches of Scotland and much of that land are one with this Gaspé outcrop, bitten off the same biscuit of ancient earth.

But Sophie has grown very impatient. Threatens this is the last September she'll work with me. "It'll be our eleventh year," she warned last fall. "One for each day you claim was stolen off you. Jesus, Jimmy, why haven't you come to your senses long before now?"

There is nothing wrong with my senses, especially my hearing. War's din roars in my lugs like the sea in a pair of old shells: Elwyn screaming for me to haul him into our Coyote amid mortars and radio static, you don't know whether the fire's Russian or American, you don't know what you're hearing, all I know is Elwyn's down that goat trail, he's crawled behind the rubble, and meanwhile the head of Ned, my little brother, still rolls in Dettingen like a kicked pig-bladder.

Can a man be blamed for having treasured Elwyn, or Ned—or even Bonnie Prince Charlie and his Highlanders, their bluebird-coloured hats pinned with white roses? It broke my heart back in '45, to see how those Highlanders would gladly draw their swords and beat their drums and skirl their demented pipes to defend that place. We formed our mute English line as those fellows straggled onto the field, starved after their night march and noisy as hell. Easy prey.

But once we slaughtered them, who had won?

A soldier is only a visitor.

Emptied, Culloden heath: crows, distant hills full of birches. Dettingen: mud, rubble, my lifelong horror's tender shoot. Ghundy Ghar: from our new trenches fell bones from old wars over the very same land.

Land, wind and clouds were present before our carnage, and after it they continue to lie, blow, hover.

"Sophie!"

Every year I become seasick trekking over this terrain: it falls away in great troughs then swells against my face in sudden crests, as if a demon ocean has been turned to swamp and stone—always with treacherous rivulets and pockets where the leg of horse or man might break . . .

No, not *horse*, not these days—and now here's the perilous Spout, heaven help me. Each September as I pass its ledge I feel its fantastic tug—sixty feet down to the rocks. But sparkles plash up its hollow. Now a whoosh of barm, a column of brine rising toward me at the precipice, a silver fountain inviting a man to dive on its breast and plunge as it falls, plummet to fucking oblivion below, with the seals, and the herring, and the blessed sway of silent weeds . . .

Irresistible.

"Not now," I tell the Spout again this year, like I've told laudanum, heroin, cocaine. "I've one more chance with Sophie, in the city . . ."

Can this really be the eleventh time I've made this trek? Eleven autumns walking this stretch of coast from Manche-d'Épée to L'Anse Pleureuse, trying to escape seagulls, stones and seaweed? Leaving behind a root cellar full of seed potatoes whose stolons have grown long and white and threaten to strangle me? Sophie's right: I must escape this cycle.

"Come on," the Spout sings, as all the opiates sing. "Come to me, baby—does your Sophie even need to know?"

Sophie certainly *would* know, or would at least suspect, if I dived, but then—I think—on to another soldier she'd move, there being no shortage.

"No," I answer the Spout once more. "Not yet." I remind myself that these barrens, with their chasms and blood-sucking pitcher plants, mustn't swallow me now. Their curtain of fog is my foyer to a better world, where Glory waits to rejoin me as it did on the Plains of Abraham . . . if only I can find my way to those plains again . . .

Glory, do you hear me?

Look—there's the boulder marking the border beyond which I've walked ten Septembers, and now this eleventh, from bog, from stony ground, from that desolate beach where no one but the summer snack-van attendant remembers my name, though she insists on diminishing it to Jimmy.

"*Soph*!"

The only reply is geese heading south in a noisy, honking V, abandoning the lonesome Gaspé, the place Sophie has always urged me to leave.

Likely she's already pitched our tent on Mont Royal and hopped the orange line to the mission. Filled out her seasonal work forms, begun mopping floors, stacking Habitant soup tins, listening to every squeegee kid or drunk widower, every vagabond soldier . . . and quite unable to hear me.

Pure peat surrounding my boulder is easy to dig barehanded, though peat takes two thousand years to form. Compared with that, what's any soldier's puny history?

I retrieve my fanny pack with all my ID cards—expired by now, but vital if I ever try to renew them, according to Sophie. *Update yourself,* she yelled as we parted last September. *Fight for your military pension. Bloody well visit Madame Blanchard and get your ancient papers sorted out! Stop obsessing about the number eleven. Eleven, eleven, that's all I hear about from you, your endless Gregorian chant.* This is how she views my need to recover the time fate cheated from me long ago.

September 3 through 13—that last being the number that marks the very anniversary of my death on Abraham's plains. These are the lost days I hired Sophie, a decade ago, to help me find. At least, that is how I have understood our bargain. But like the birches dotting this Gaspé coast, our agreement now feels ethereal and broken, ready to scatter into bright, white paper pieces.

WHAT SOPHIE DOESN'T KNOW is that last year, near the end of our usual eleven days, I found a great cache of my old letters. I spied an article in the *Montreal Gazette* saying they'd been bought by the Fisher Library in Toronto for a million and a half dollars. Of course, I got on the bus to Toronto immediately. Imagine: every letter I'd ever written to my mother, and a few to my father, and my one plea to my beloved George Warde, ink and paper beautiful and intact. But by the time I arrived, a Mrs. Waugh had installed herself for days, sopping the nuance out of my letters laid in their sparkling cradles of archival sponge. I had to stifle my alarm.

Don't salivate!

Stop cracking my spine!

Treat my letters like the creatures they are: papery skin, insubstantial bone. . . .

I could have whispered every living word of those letters into her ear, though I'd inked my last full stop 238 years before, on the banks of the Saint Lawrence.

I found the head librarian, a Mrs. Heather Forest, and without hesitation begged her to give me my papers back, but one look at the incredulity on her face and it dawned on me that I might be prevented from visiting them unless I hovered unobtrusively over Mrs. Waugh's shoulder with my dollar-store reading glasses perched just so.

"I'm sorry I haven't combed my hair," I told Mrs. Forest. "Perhaps I should've—"

"It's not that. Your hair's quite . . . striking." She looked at me with a glimmer of what I took, with faint hope, to be understanding. Dared I lean forward and whisper the truth into her ear?

"It's hard to remember niceties such as one's coiffure when one is on leave from the battlefield," I began.

Then, in a rush, I confessed to her my name.

I find that even stern librarians are among the more soft-hearted denizens of the New World. Perhaps they feel kinship with my type: antique, forgotten, relegated to history.

"I understand," said Mrs. Forest, her face so grave yet kind that I believed her. Some people recognize truth even when it has been orphaned for a while among this world's bright falsities. I believe that a tiny part of Mrs. Forest took—not pity on me; never pity . . . had she taken pity I'd have fled. No, a part of her, the part that welcomes people who ask to stay in her sanctum and study, to steep themselves in history so that time loses its artificial calibrations and begins to swirl as a single entity, that part of Mrs. Forest took me at my word.

"At least," she said, "I can let you sit here and study some of the non-restricted materials." She gave me bound photocopies that included letters to my father and entries about myself in old editions of the *Dictionary of Canadian Biography.*

I noticed that Mrs. Waugh, the researcher ensconced with my material, had hair messier than mine—how had she the right to my original papers? She nosed through my letters in a cardigan whose elbows she'd patched with bits of other, even more decrepit, attire. I felt both envious and sympathetic.

I overheard her ask Mrs. Forest, "However did Wolfe manage to find that pineapple he gave to the wife of his enemy, Drucour, in Louisbourg?"

Ah! That was a fantastic pineapple, my pineapple of 1758, the summer I ravaged Louisbourg in preparation for my victory in Quebec. It was a delicious, perfectly ripe specimen in a sere and fruitless land.

"I can answer that," Heather Forest said, "since my other interest, outside these archives, happens to be eighteenth-century horticulture."

"Really?" said Mrs. Waugh, with childish delight.

"The British were mad about pineapples!"

"Were they?"

"Off their heads. They packed trenches with manure to make hotbeds, and they grew pineapples in the manure's heat. Pineapples became a symbol of exotic opulence and people presented them to each other with great ceremony. There's a famous painting of King George being presented with a pineapple by his gardener, a man named Rose. . . ."

Dear Heather and the unkempt Mrs. Waugh moved away from the study area ranting about pineapples and I tuned in from afar with the aid of a hearing augmentation cone I made out of my souvenir map of Culloden battlefield; they seemed not to notice me listening in.

I observed that into her battered briefcase Mrs. Waugh had crammed several books about me, written by military historians. They all boasted that painting by Benjamin West on their covers: my battle scene, with me perishing while attended by my battlemates. On my second Montreal September I read in a fat new history book at the Grande Bibliothèque that a literary person called Margaret Atwood claimed West made me appear like a dead, white codfish, and I had to agree. Evidently Mrs. Waugh had acquainted herself with the extinguished codfish: she'd dog-eared the books beyond redemption.

"Unreasonable and odd relationship with his mother," I heard Mrs. Forest say.

"My former companion—an eighth-generation francophone Québécois, a Beauvilliers—told his tante Claudette what I'm up to, studying these letters," said Mrs. Waugh, "and she had a fit . . . *Le cochon! Le maudit chien anglais!* She said Wolfe burned whole villages along the Saint Lawrence. This was at a family dinner with all the Beauvilliers brothers . . ."

"I can well imagine," said Mrs. Forest. "*The dog, the pig, the Wolfe . . .*"

"But after Claudette's outburst the brothers were silent. Ghislain, the eldest, brought up Voltaire . . ."

Voltaire! My scorched villages! My succulent pineapple!

I began to think that perhaps Mrs. Waugh was more perceptive than I'd believed. How sick I'd become of people parading the same tales about me over and over again. You could pretty much make a paper doll in my likeness—a James Wolfe paper doll, I mean—and manoeuvre him on the end of a stick like a child's puppet: have him cross the ocean and float up the Saint Lawrence River and shimmy across L'Anse au Foulon and mosey on up the cliff and fire off a few musket-balls on the Plains of Abraham and get hit three times and slowly expire while ascertaining victory was certain and exclaiming, "Well then, I can die in peace." You could do the whole thing in four minutes.

"Ghislain—they call him the family intellectual—told me Voltaire wrote about why the French really lost the battle," said Mrs. Waugh. "It wasn't because of Wolfe. It was because the government of France had abandoned the people of New France. They thought it more worthwhile defending colonies where there was warmth, sugar, rum. Why should France trouble itself over, as Voltaire put it, *quelques arpents de neige* . . . a few acres of snow? France was indifferent and Montcalm didn't have what he needed to win the battle."

"Yes, it's famous, that quote about the snow," said Mrs. Forest.

"It makes my heart sink a little bit," said Mrs. Waugh. "It makes me feel desolate . . . er, do you mind my asking, who is that man over in the corner?"

"The one with the long red hair? The tall young man?"

"Yes, him, the thin one. He seems to be studying my subject, and, to tell you the truth, I find his face remarkably . . . I mean if you just look at him over there and then look at these pictures, I mean this one in particular . . ."

There was no mistaking it. They were talking about me.

Mrs. Forest put her arm around Mrs. Waugh and led her just out of earshot. They turned their backs and murmured, and seemed to have forgotten that the letters, the precious letters that by rights are mine but which I cannot have, lay on the table. I stole a peep at the topmost one, dated November 13, 1756, in which I beg my mother's forgiveness yet again . . . would my mother and I ever untwine? I the shoot, my mother the vine festooned with deathly trumpets?

But my sad reverie was cut short; Mrs. Waugh was coming back.

If only I was allowed to touch my letters as she could touch them! I longed to finger them once more: my High Street paper fragile, woven and folded, stained pink by my seal and blotched with my notorious ink-spills. Transparent with time, rain, and oil from my own fingers and my mother's—how often Mama folded and unfolded, read and reread each letter of mine, searching for the wound I in fact revealed to her over and over again, the truth she couldn't grasp.

Mothers!

Now my letters sat on their bindings in crazed time-worn layers, 232 of them, enfolding my brother's death, my lost innocence, my picking of those wild, sweet Canadian strawberries so tiny and juicy, my love of dogs, the deep unease with my mother, the arms of my lifelong dearest George, my forlorn ethereal Eliza, yet more anguish with my mother, and my everlasting question of how not to lose my humanity in the ecstasy of war.

Sophie Cotterill knows nothing of these words. But Mrs. Waugh, in the year since I met her at the Fisher, has been devouring them.

Will she find the one thing hidden inside them that I wish the world to understand? Dear Mrs. Waugh, can I trust you to locate it, recognize its importance, and explain it to Tante Claudette?

The injustice of it has, if Tante Claudette wants to know the truth, been driving me mad.

Sophie doesn't listen to what I say. My mother failed to listen, my father couldn't listen, my military superiors had no idea what listening was, or if they did, they didn't care. They did not hear, none of them heard my plea, my cry, my heartfelt question.

Eleven, eleven, eleven. When, for pity's sake, might I have my eleven stolen days returned to me?

What I would have done with those days. Were they truly too much for a soldier to ask?

Had they not been pilfered, the course of my life, and of history, might have . . . well, for a start, dear Tante Claudette, you'd be *très contente*, for the whole of Canada would have remained *French*.

Every river and its tributary, every mountain and hill. Every street in every town and city.

French.

Ah, my beautiful, beloved, lost French world! Can you perceive it, Mrs. Waugh, as you study my letters? Is it plain enough or have you only a glimpse? Wait till we meet again, soon, I hope—I'll tell you about Hotteterre, about La Pompadour, about Montparnasse in the rain studded with *umbrellas*, those graceful apparatuses Parisians knew long before doddering Londoners. . . .

—

BUT DO I YET TRAIPSE the Gaspé? Look at its birches now, reminding me of loneliness, of being lost, of my eternal homelessness.

Partridge, ptarmigan, trout.

Homespun wool, barley.

Potatoes, rhubarb, herring.

Melancholy, eternally mine.

How Mrs. Waugh perked me up last September. Near closing time at the library that day, she went to the washroom and I sidled over for a look at what she was up to. Her notes were a mess. They were not official-looking. In fact, they were covered with drawings and marked to near indecipherability by arrows and asterisks and rough pencil sketches of other library patrons, including a surprising likeness of myself. I had not been in the slightest aware that Mrs. Waugh had been sketching me.

Was it her sympathetic rendering of my face that made me do the thing I did next?

I think so. It was easy to swipe one of her expired requisition slips and make another in her name, ease it into the pending requests box on the counter, and wait to see what she would do when they gave her my most precious possession. It too had been stolen from me, like my eleven days. And now it was entirely forbidden for me to touch it, though it belongs to me, a gift from the only one who loved me: red, pulsing, alive, an animal locked up in the hall of memory and longing.

I went out for a drink at the fountain on the second floor where the water is lovely and cold. When I returned Mrs. Waugh was still at the toilet so I checked to see whether my possession had been delivered to her—but it was still in transit. I noticed that amongst her notes lay a copy of a letter she had written to some handwriting expert in Montreal. It read thus:

Dear Monsieur Choiniére,

I am a Montreal author, currently writing a book about a real person who is no longer alive, but whose handwriting and documents are available to me. I am seeking a psychological handwriting analysis based on a sample of the person's handwriting. I can provide only an electronic or printed duplicate, as the original documents are in the care of archival custodians and cannot be taken from their storage. I understand it is likely that you normally work only from originals, but it would be of great service to my book project if you might consider doing the best you can with the facsimile I could send or bring to you. If you might be able to do this, please let me know your timeline and fees. Thank you for considering this,

Sincerely,
Genevieve Waugh

A psychological handwriting analysis! Dear god, what kind of person was this Mrs. Waugh? I decided I would have a little talk with her. Maybe I'd wait for her on the steps outside, later on.

Then came the clerk with the surprise object. To her credit, Mrs. Waugh did not let on that she had not requisitioned it. And the box is so exquisite, if Tante Claudette herself were presented with it she would, I am sure, not do a single thing to betray the fact that she had not asked for it. She would, like Mrs. Waugh, let it arrive.

"His poem," said the clerk, "is in a box within a box within this box." She lifted the first lid and took out a layer of card, then lifted the second box out and laid it in the sparkling cradle. "You can take it from here."

"Thank you," said Mrs. Waugh, as if all were normal.

The inner box is oxblood red. It has a fragrance: fruity, like dried figs. It looks but does not smell like leather. Inside lies my very own copy of Thomas Gray's famous poem, "Elegy Written in a Country Churchyard." My book is chocolate-coloured and also chocolate-scented: pure chocolate from cocoa without sweetness. From three desks away I smelled the fig and chocolate, felt the plumes rise and disperse in that vaulted pentagonal room with its five floors of rare manuscripts and tomes rising up so very far above us to the distant ceiling. But not without curling first around Mrs. Waugh's torso and hair.

Mrs. Waugh gasped.

We both understood that an animal had had its enclosure opened and we were able to smell its body. Together we inhaled my old, familiar vapours.

Ha! Gotcha, Mrs. Waugh. The vapours have got us both.

I waited outside on the steps for Mrs. Waugh to come out. I gobbled half a cheese sandwich tossed in a bin by some member of the university's extravagant student body, that crowd sprawled down the edges of the stairs—none of them anywhere near as serious as I'd expect: civilian life becomes progressively harder for me to comprehend. Mrs. Waugh slowed when she saw me. I nodded. She came closer, looked me in the eye.

"You do look like him. Like Wolfe."

"I should say."

"Heather Forest explained to me that you—"

"Would you like an interview?"

"I—"

"If you wanted to bring me to your house, I could explain things that aren't in my letters: missing pieces, gaps, in-between things

I wish people understood—you are writing a book about me, are you not?"

"I'm trying my hand at a book based on the letters of—on Wolfe's—I'm a journalist, or have been one, not so much anymore, but—these days I'm, to tell you the truth—it began as a rather personal inquiry. I've studied letters for years, finding connections between mothers and sons—or daughters—who try to understand each other across time and distance but who can never seem to . . . and, when I found this collection of Wolfe's letters to his mother, in which at times he seems so lost . . ."

"Indeed."

Right then and there, on those steps, I tried to explain to Mrs. Waugh about my lost eleven days. "Not just any days," I told her, "they were days I had been granted leave to go to Paris, after many years of asking. They were to have been my dancing days, my hour of learning, my time of freedom from a decade of combat. A golden segment of my youth, stolen as I was about to dance the sarabande in Paris . . ."

Mrs. Waugh regarded me carefully but declined my offer to accompany her home and fully explain. She lived, she told me, not in Toronto, but in a tiny apartment across from Saint Louis Chapel on Montreal's Rue Drolet.

"My apartment is very small," she began, "unsuitable, really—"

"But I visit Montreal every September," I told her. "We could convene at your kitchen table while I tell you about myself and my mother—"

"I don't actually have a kitchen table," she said, "and I—well, I'm embarrassed to say I have a small problem with mice, little black mice who come in from the garden next door once September comes—right after the first one or two cool nights . . ."

"I do not mind mice!"

"Well, I mind them." Mrs. Waugh grasped for a firm reply. I saw she was one of those people who startle at intimacy of any kind. I had an impression she might rather be alone with her mice than have large humans intrude upon her. She wished to examine my letters in the safe cloister of a library, not necessarily to befriend their author. I understood this, and decided to give her a piece of encouragement.

"Here," I took a precious envelope from my pocket, "is a letter you won't find in the Fisher Library."

That fixed her. She read it, then handed it back to me quite shaken. "How did you get this? It's—" She glanced back at the library doors.

"Don't worry, I didn't steal it from there."

"But it's a—it looks like an original document . . ."

"Yes, my mother wrote to the prime minister—"

". . . written by Wolfe's mother, Henrietta—look, you can't just walk around with—"

"My mother! Yes—She wrote this one begging, beseeching, demanding the pension due to her upon my death—look, you can see how angry she was, the injustice of what a government will try to do to cheat a fallen soldier's family—" I held the letter aloft and read my mother's indignation aloud:

> *Am I to sue on bended knees for what should be given . . . and would have been had He survived the Campaign which covered England with Glory. . . .*

Distressed, Mrs. Waugh actually touched my arm. "Look, you have to give the letter back—Heather Forest will be . . ."

"It isn't Heather Forest's letter," I said, spiriting it back into my pocket, where I hold it as one of my most important papers, a testament to everything I am and stand for. "It's my own. It was my mother's—Henrietta Wolfe's—and now it's mine. And I have a lot more to say about what led up to her writing it than you'll find in the archives. But perhaps you aren't interested in words from the horse's mouth. Perhaps . . ." I fixed her with what I believed to be my coolest, most dispassionate expression and, while doing so, backed away from Mrs. Waugh slightly, as if to announce a final parting.

"Wait," she reconsidered. "Perhaps . . . well, it could be that I should . . ." She looked at my hair, my face. "Certainly not at my apartment, but . . . if there was a neutral place, some café perhaps, or—if by the post we could arrange something, once we are back in Montreal—but you say you only visit there?"

"Next September," I told her, "starting on the third for eleven days, you can leave me a message at the Old Brewery Mission on Clark Street."

I did not tell Mrs. Waugh about my tent with Sophie Cotterill in Parc du Mont-Royal. Nor did I mention that the ideal place to leave me a note was to tuck it in a crack of the Mordecai Richler Gazebo in the park just below our tent, between the gazebo's railings and its north pillar facing the park's angel. I could tell her this later, should she choose to contact me. As it was, she gave me a post-box number belonging to one of the little rentable mailbox centres offered by all the Jean Coutu drugstores. Box 444.

2 His Flute

SUNDAY, SEPTEMBER 3.
NIGHT.
Montreal, Quebec

AS I APPROACH, I SEE Soph's silhouette inside the tent. I smell her bean tin brimming with scalding hot Labrador tea.

Everything in the tent is a bit damp: the sleeping bags, the tent walls. Sophie has a cozy little corner set up where, for our time together, she'll commune with her emails between checking Facebook and insulting me. I hope my letter-writing notepad isn't damp. She notices my hand sneak to it.

"Writing to your mama already? You haven't even said hello."

"Maybe." This is a lie. I need, in fact, to get a note to Mrs. Waugh to inform her that I'm here. "Did you get the honey for my tea?"

"Here, pass me your quill and parchment. I'll write that mother of yours a few home truths." She grabs my pen.

"Dearest Madam Wolfe," she announces. *"Sweet Henrietta: Your son, Bigbad, is an unbelievable procrastinator, a real fusspot . . ."*

"I'm not. I'm timely. I don't vacillate and I'm not fussy. Ask anyone."

"He claims he isn't particular, but tomorrow he's going to send me all over the Plateau looking for honey that simply must . . . Where the hell is your honey supposed to come from?"

"I need Minorcan honey."

"He says he doesn't vacillate but he swans in and out of Payons Comptant pawnshop gawking at the poor old flute he claims once belonged to him . . ."

"My flute saved me, you know that. Playing my flute protected me from untold horrors."

Sophie can turn self-righteous and often claims to possess all sorts of attributes far more interesting than I've been able to discern. I mean, when I met her—eleven Septembers ago to this day—what was she doing? Plunging wieners in the deep fryer in Germain Medosset's wagon on the crescent beach, just below Madame Blanchard's house, where I first emerged from my hibernation, shivering and uncertain as to where to turn. She didn't even sell cod or real chips, only corn dogs and prepackaged nuggets and onion rings, and flat Coke. "I'm not interested in having sex with a crazy soldier," she said as I ordered a second cone of previously frozen fries. I had not solicited her at all! She passed me her business card:

SOPHIE COTTERILL
Short Order Cook
Janitorial and Maintenance Services
Wet Nurse
Hypnosis, Talk Therapy, Shamanic Tent

"I thought a wet nurse had to be— Aren't you—"

"Aren't I what?"

"Pardon me."

"What."

"Nothing."

"Too old?"

"I wasn't—" But I was. She had to be nearly fifty.

"That's how much you know, buddy. Have you never heard of Judy Waterford? I thought you said you were British. I've kept my milk going twenty-seven years. I hear from my other soldiers who miss their mommas that it does the trick. Check out my reviews on wetnurse.com."

It was a while before I entrusted Sophie with my September nights.

I hung out by the snack van for a couple of days and discovered she loved a midnight bacon sandwich as much as I did. We ate these on the stones while I talked and she repaired her tent, which she was planning to set up in Montreal once Germain Medosset, her cousin, came back from hospital. "He had nobody else down here," she told me. She'd come from the Magdalen Islands to give him a hand. "Don't get the idea I'm a pushover though," she warned me. "I have my own reasons for getting off the islands and working through the winters in Montreal. What about you? How come you're stuck here in the land of cod and fog, a young man like you in that big old wreck of a house up the hill?"

That's when I started telling Sophie Cotterill about my past. I told her about Cartagena then Dettingen, about losing my brother, Ned, at Ghent, and nearly losing my mind on Flemish battlefields.

"A child soldier," Sophie said, nodding.

I divulged the horrors of Culloden, then the broken promise of my longed-for leave in Paris, where I'd thought I might become free—and I told her about my eleven stolen days. How, on September 2, 1752, England fell for Europe's shiny new Gregorian calendar, and how every man, woman and child among us found

September second followed by the fourteenth, missing out the days between. Portentous interval! The new calendar not only stole my dancing lessons in Paris and all manner of joy, it darkened the very date—September 13—of my death, seven years later, on Abraham's plains. I swear I felt a shadow.

"As it happens, today's the anniversary," I told her. "September second, the day I lost everything."

By the time I finished telling her my story I broke down on the pebbles near that barachois where I'd mouldered, since Madame Blanchard's forlorn departure earlier that summer, without a soul to listen or offer consolation.

"Jesus," said Sophie, "If anyone needs my services it's you. You need to come back to the present, my friend, or you're gonna fade to nothing here, like that starfish in the dried-out rockpool behind you."

She invited me to come with her to Montreal and share her tent while she helped me salvage whatever I'd forfeited in my lost days, though she was clear that I'd have to pay for her services and the space. "Have you got any money?"

I told her about my faint hope of a war pension, which I longed to recover, but so far had not.

"I can help you with that, if you do your homework. Have you no cash at all?"

"I have a little in the shortbread canister on top of Madame Blanchard's spice tin . . ."

"For heaven's sake, give me a bit up front and the rest when we get that war pension sorted out. You're the most pathetic soldier I've ever met."

"I'm not looking for pity," I warned. "I need someone to listen and guide me in a no-nonsense way through the logistics of the modern world."

"There'll be no nonsense about me," she said. "On that you can depend."

"But can you build me up? Rescue me from my doubts?"

"Do I look like a cheerleader to you?"

"You look more like a . . . you're not a succubus?" Succubi had been a problem when I encamped near my battlefields. Between the dryads of Scotland and camp-followers of the British army there had been more nights than I could count when I'd awoken to a woman's exhalations on my neck, her limbs now cold, now hot, now wet, now dry and scaly as cedar bark, chafing or sliming or entwining, leech-like, around mine, smothering and unwanted.

"I can write succubus on my card if you want," she said. "Look, if you want to stay in my tent, be my guest. I've told you what my fee is. But I don't give crazy soldiers any guarantees. Sometimes they perk up and more often they mosey on back to their demented little worlds without having a grain more sense than they had when we met. That's your call, Mr. Wolfe."

LISTEN NOW TO HER SNORE! Sophie's one of those people who're jabbering away one minute and fast asleep the next. I tore an article out of the paper for her on the dangers of sleep apnea but she said silken-arsed wimps like me don't understand how tired a hard-working woman can get. In mid-sentence every night she joins the dead like this, yet she fails to credit me when I explain how a man can linger amongst the living even if he has died—can linger for centuries, trying to make peace with what he has lost.

Mrs. Waugh, might you believe me? I reread the note I'll post to her at Box 444 tomorrow.

Dear Mrs. Waugh,

Further to our little chat last year on the steps of the Fisher Library.

Have you thought any more about my lost days? You would be one of very few. All England had protests in the streets, but who in power ever cared about workers losing eleven days' pay, or about young soldiers called back early from their leave?

A lord or a duke will summon a soldier back to battle on a whim.

What did my superiors care that I'd begun learning Hotteterre's prelude in D on my flute—three minutes of pure and unassuming beauty? Even my failed attempts brought small birds to the door if I left it open. Starlings paid no mind to mistakes in my tune and I only wish now that I had learned from them how to bless and forgive.

Can it be that my wailing has tormented the angels, causing them to relent? Have they noticed that my eleven lost days included September the thirteenth, the day I would eventually die on Quebec's plains? Has Michael, the Archangel of War, taken pity on me? —how else has it come about, this feeling that, with your assistance, I might stumble out of my fog and become the man I might have been were it not for all that vanished with my stolen days of 1752?

All I want, Mrs. Waugh, is for you to understand my plight, and perhaps, if you can, relay it to others. I am staying in my friend's little tent at Parc du Mont-Royal, just up the hill from the gazebo in whose railing you may, if you wish to arrange a meeting, slip me a note, or from whose platform, if you desired, you might witness me try find the ordinary joy of life that has so far eluded this soldier who remains,

Sincerely yours,
General James Wolfe

How Sophie would ridicule this letter. After years of working on my case, she has started advising me to "suck it up" whenever I mention my lost leave. Reminds me I don't believe in religion so can claim no help from angels. Part of me wishes I'd met Mrs. Waugh, not Sophie, on the beach a decade ago, frying corn dogs in a van, although I can't imagine cuddling with her in a tent.

Hotteterre's prelude! When I'm tired like this and lying down, I can hear every note of its tender fallibility, its spaces, its unassuming shape. It meanders like a small country stream of no importance to anyone but young walkers, long-legged spiders, dragonflies and slender ducks. Its emotion is an innocent happiness, though not a witless flight of childish primary colour—it remembers all the clear-eyed queries I made, as a serious child, of the river and fields. It suggests botanical exactitude, painterly adherence to precise ochres, chlorophylls and butterfly dyes. The prelude travels—I ride it now—takes modest flight, alights on an ear of wild grass, stays in one place and listens. It paces itself then runs ahead, serious and merry yet never frivolous, weightless yet not sweet. Its rhythms are contained as time contains a line that has no end.

Its line wanders with the unpredictable harmony of a conversation between open minds. Oh Sophie, if only you and I could talk in that way. . . . Its beauty is original and a little bit strange. It lasts only three minutes, yet is not easy to follow, and has taken me forever to memorize, if in fact I have ever truly known it at all.

3 ~~Madame Blanchard~~

MONDAY, SEPTEMBER 4.
MORNING.
Montreal, Quebec

EVERY SEPTEMBER IT TAKES ME a while to reacquaint myself with Montreal's city smells, its colours, the subway lines, its mélange of English and French. Eggs *tournés* or *miroir* or *brouillés*? On Saint Catherine Street this Monday morning, as I slip my letter to Mrs. Waugh in the mailbox outside Ogilvy's, I hear a man hail a taxi shouting old French slang for a chariot—Montrealers mangle quaint, backwoods French with chopped American, yet wield baguettes and bottles of Bordeaux like Parisians. At Casse-Croûte Diane, where we eat breakfast, Sophie critiques my list:

Bread
Figs
Available veg
Pop-up tins tuna or etc. (Not Flaked)
Arm-and-Hammer toothpaste (Not Gel)
The Gazette
Maudite Lager
~~*Madame Blanchard*~~

"Why," she asks, "did you write the *Gazette* instead of *L'Itinéraire*?"

"Isn't *L'Itinéraire* the one homeless people sell on corners?"

"Exactly."

"Won't the *Gazette* have more pertinent news?"

"Are you serious? And how come you crossed out Madame Bee?"

"I don't know, I—she—"

"You know you fucking well need to go see her."

"You're more profane than my brigadiers! You do all you can to make me feel even worse than they did. And this bacon's horrible."

"You've demolished five pieces."

"It's acrid. Tasteless. If only it were a bit of Wiltshire peameal. . . ."

"Quit comparing everything with good old England and stop exaggerating that stupid accent."

"I'm not!"

"You sound like someone drunk at a party translating the Queen's Christmas message. Quit complaining about everything. The bacon, the money."

"But the money feels strange, fuses together . . . what's it made of?"

"Vinyl. Everyone said it smelled like maple syrup when it first came out. City noses. Can't tell petroleum from spruce."

"I wouldn't mind a grilled tomato."

"I've told you, take consolation in all the things that have not changed."

"Is marmalade too much to ask? Is a toast rack out of the question?"

"Poor Bigbad." She hauls her phone out. Her shift starts in nine minutes.

"The sausages contain no sage. At any comparable dining establishment in England or Scotland, even a modest rural inn . . ."

"Soon you'll start ranting about the tea."

"This sachet of dust floating upon its lukewarm pool is not tea!"

"Anglos crack me up. You wear this immaculate layer of don't-touch-me around you no matter how lonely you are or how you ache for someone to love. Get a load of that one." She points at a gentleman working on the *Gazette*'s daily crossword.

I have to admit he looks as if he's planning the annual budget of the Pitcairns. He has brought his special pencil sharpener and sweeps the dust into his cupped hand then drops it in a cactus.

"A colonial Englishman never does his crossword with a pen," she says. "He wouldn't be able to erase his mistakes and therefore pretend he never makes any. He's the only person here besides you, by the way, drinking a cup of tea first thing on a Monday morning."

"They wouldn't have it on the menu if nobody drank it."

"He has a jar in his satchel for putting old tea bags in so he can reuse them. See how he treats his cup like a brother? English people hate getting close to other people so much that their teapots and cups become their companions. Try to talk to them and they glance apologetically at their tea as if to say, *Hold it, old chap, excuse me, but I'm afraid we've been rudely interrupted.*"

She rams her beanie on. "Meet me at the Brewery at noon? It's Habitant Pea Soup Day, followed by out-of-date Sweet Marie bars, and you should claim your bunk before tonight. The forecast says twenty percent chance of freezing rain. Why are you sighing?"

I prefer Sophie's tent to the smelly, overcrowded bunks at the Old Brewery Mission. The moon and park lamps glow through its canvas. I love the old walrus Sophie had started painting on it when I met her and has been augmenting ever since, intensifying the creature's eyes, sharpening its tusks, adding blue to its greyness so it casts blue light on our skin as we lie together. The only reason I ever try to secure a Mission bunk is in case we get bad weather, or Sophie and I fight, or the police harass me, or I desire to receive anything by mail.

Involuntarily I touch my pocket and Sophie winks. "Okay, see you after you write to Mama."

Sophie Cotterill does not remind me that my mother, Henrietta Wolfe, née Thompson, passed away in 1764. Sophie understands about talking to a person you've lost: how the person listens if you speak to them as they did while they lived. But she likes to tease me. She likes to grab my writing pad and scribble postscripts to my mother: *Your son continues to regret the cutting short of his leave in Paris, 1752. That is a mighty long time ago, Henrietta. Could you not teach him any better how to let things go?*

I used to try and explain to Sophie how worn out I had felt, how that lost leave meant everything to me. Ten years of hard soldiering from the age of thirteen. Then, in Paris, a reprieve, ever so fleeting—Sophie still thinks I mean it was a holiday. I never convinced her it wasn't leisure but much-needed leave, crucial to any military man for his cultural development. An enlightened general treats culture as part of his work! He can't get ahead at all unless he knows how to carry himself with sophistication. I wanted to learn the minuet. I made surprising progress despite the curtailment of my leave. I mean, I never learned the steps to great perfection, but at least no one mocked me . . . I even met La Pompadour! But even then, in the glory of being young and up-and-coming, I glanced in La Pompadour's mirror and found myself staring at an ancient, broken man. Two of my visible teeth had broken like biscuits . . .

"Why not just talk to your mother, instead of writing?" Sophie says. "Do you imagine she can't hear you?"

"I'd like to think she can—but . . ."

"You and your mother are odd, Bigbad. Weird. Close but not warm-close, more like frozen together. Can't be pried apart. Totally fucking English."

Out she swaggers—before noon she'll scour a hundred filthy sinks. I wish I still possessed the capacity to love I owned in my early days. I might be a better companion to her and to myself. As soon as she's gone I grasp my pen and pad like someone addicted to the written word, which I suppose I might be. How else is anything to be pinned down or even half understood?

Dear Madam, I begin.

MONDAY, SEPTEMBER 4.
AROUND NOON.
Casse-Croûte Diane. Montreal, Quebec

WRITING TO MY MOTHER HAS always been part duty, but I do feel unburdened by it.

I've always saved special little things for her letters, things that have no place in my letters to my father, or to my military superiors, who wanted to hear tactics, strength, evidence of stern competence and a will to succeed. Never mind that the profession of war demands finesse: it demands time—every day precious—studying our own tactics and those of the French with their precision and grace. Being mentored by my elders, learning the language of my future enemy—did my superiors have no idea what happens to an English soldier in the dark, on the banks of the Saint Lawrence River, who cannot deceive the shadows with his tongue? And my fencing lessons! As with my prowess in riding a horse in Paris I found I somehow, naturally, knew how to fence: with my long arms and longer legs, I had the most extensive lunge of any student my teachers had known. A bayonet became a different instrument once the French taught me how to regard a blade. Yet still I needed more time than I had. One doesn't capitalize on natural talents without practice.

My Parisian studies prepared me for battle but they also nourished my soul—without them, dear mother, I wither. I withered when they were snatched in my youth and because of their absence I rot to this day in that blind, sere land I inhabit between Septembers.

Dear Madam,

~~So help me if I don't claim the fruits of my stolen fortnight this year I'll hurl myself in the Spout, the chasm of sluicing~~

No. A mother can stand to hear a little of her son's anguish, but not too much. I have to continue reminding her of noble things, such as how I spared women and children in battle, or how, despite falling ill and succumbing to despair, I have come back to myself and will, as ever, remain her loyal, obedient son. Then there are the funny little bits, the cryptic parts. I add things no one but my mother would understand, to make the story only we two share.

Our letters electrified one another with that feather whose touch astounds: each jolt intimate, particular, and ours alone, even the fragmentary installments of our never-ending quarrel.

And so, each September I still write letters to my mother and I mail them, as I did in her lifetime, but of course not to Blackheath and not by ship. Sophie torments me about dropping them in the red Canada Post mailbox.

"Nobody does that anymore," she says. "Even my grandma on Grand-Entrée Island uses email."

SEPTEMBER 4TH, 2017, MONTRÉAL

Dear Madam,

In Montreal I have found a place a little like the sanctuary we so much used to enjoy at the Bath . . .

What I've found is, in fact, the Chinatown YMCA.

I've found steam, swirling hot waters of the whirlpool, and penetrating heat of a sauna. And I've found society. I do not think I mislead my mother too far when I describe the society at the pool on Rue de la Gauchetière. It does bear a certain resemblance to taking the waters at Bath.

The *bodies.*

Something soothes me about those bodies, all shapes: indolent, quick, wiry, lard-fat, slow or electric, everyone's guard down. There is one man, blind and dressed in yellow, whose seeing-eye dog waits, ever so patient, beside his glowing pile of clothes while he showers. None of us has to pretend uprightness or strength. I delight in freckles, pot-bellies, undulating buttocks. I loved that about Bath as well. Both places give me uncustomary pride in my own weird shape.

Why is it that, naked, I lose my strangeness among men?

When I wore the red coat, those who loved me found ways to assure me it mattered not that I possessed gangling calves or was chinless. My brother, Ned, and my beloved friend George Warde insisted I appeared not at all like an orange mop on stilts. My mother comforted me all the time about my chin.

At the Chinatown Y, as in Bath, the steam releases our tension. We emerge bright-skinned and lithe, even the blind man slowly pulling his yellow garments back on: sweatshirt, trousers, even his socks are yellow—and the twenty-five-stone man who keeps muttering to himself and lets loose a final howl as if he's experienced a resounding orgasm. I refrain from writing to my mother about these people.

If she were alive I would want her to believe I'm comfortable, even while I suffer my post-battle fears and indignities. Knowledge is healing, Sophie says, but I do not think all knowledge helps mothers.

> My accommodations this September are no worse than they have been previously. At The Old Brewery I have a pretty good bed if I need it. But I prefer my tent after dark, on the mountain, which isn't really a mountain, but a large hill in quite a nice park in the centre of Montreal.
>
> Do not worry about my spirits! A friend has given me a little trick to make me feel more at home here. . . . Not the way I felt at your house, of course, Mother. No place in Canada has the comforts of the room where you lay, or the little parlour where my father and I used to dress.
>
> Nearly everything here is different and I am in an alien world, but this friend tells me I should dwell not on the differences between here and home, but on familiar things that have never changed . . . such as pigeons.

It never fails to lift my heart, seeing a flock of the purple and mother-of-pearl fat-bellied city birds lift, shaking stars, off a cornice in Place d'Armes. They are nowhere near as graceful as linnets, or even starlings, whose nets of choreographed skydance I also love. Pigeons roost in the gutters of every common shop, but I find them uncommon. Pigeons are doves, and have not changed in any place or time, but are the same as ever in London, Edinburgh or Montreal, and—I remember—in the cornices around Quebec City's plains. Pigeons make me come back briefly to my old self. I know my mother understands this, though she always complained about the mess they made in St. John's Park.

> Madam, I'll head down to Montreal's Ruelle des Fortifications again this afternoon. My friend, the one who reminded me to appreciate pigeons—I might have mentioned her name is Sophie and I am far from romantically involved with her: you know I'd tell you if I was. Sophie is a friend to me in the way George Warde was, and you know how I cared for him. You'll be amused to know she challenges me even more than you ever have. She calls it folly to lament my lost days or to examine the fruits of my past actions, but that is why I am here. How else can I see if winning New France was worth losing all I ever loved, including you?

I don't tell my mother that I reimburse Sophie for her services.

Nor do I mention that Ruelle des Fortifications is featureless, not a proper military passage with breastwork or alternating staircases or even the remains of a watchtower. It is covered by glass and by protruding storeys of overhanging offices and hotels. I can hardly see the sky. It, like many historic military sites I have revisited, now has a disappointing, civilian meaninglessness. Its old fort walls have tumbled or been dismantled and now it is merely a corridor. People with suitcases on wheels find themselves in it en route from their hotel lobbies to the subway station.

Nor is it entirely true that Sophie and I are not physical. I adore resting my head in her lap in the tent when she's not on night shift at the Mission. I love her holding my hand as we watch leaf shadows on our lamplit canvas and listen for the park watchman, who found us once. I do not mention to Henrietta that Sophie is in her fifties. She might be sixty by now for all I know. But over the years I have, like many sons, learned to tell my mother what she wants to hear.

> Once I complete my inspection of the fortifications, I intend to walk on the old Iroquois road, to an area just up from the port where you'll be amused and perhaps happy to know they have named a modest but dignified street after
>
> Your devoted, loving and obedient Son . . .

I despise Wolfe Avenue.

If my mother ever saw it she'd lose her mind.

The street is no more than a block and a half long and contains no landmark, no building of commerce or industry, no church and not even a scrap of shrubbery for beauty. It is a street with shuttered doors and heavy red brick over narrow, frowning windows, and it holds a terrible and undefined sadness, especially when in shadow, as it remains for all but a half hour each day. I would rather not have a street named after me at all than see this tiny avenue with my name on the sign at the end, obviously erected with supreme reluctance by the city fathers: an afterthought. There is no joy in it for anyone. My only solace is that next door to it lies a street exactly the same named after Montcalm—not that I wish such melancholic remembrance for him either.

How strange that Montcalm and I lie side by side, in cement and treeless brick, in shadow: each of us dreaming of loves we lost while fighting one another on the desolate plains. Montcalm, I know, dreams of his beloved daughter Mirète. And I am myself tormented over losing Ned, and George, and Eliza, though Sophie claims I did not love Eliza Lawson at all. She claims that with Eliza I had something else going on: yet another reason I must come back each autumn to the land of the living to try and redress what was left unfinished.

I did not save all my mother's letters. I know sons do—they collect them in a drawer to revisit once she has passed on, hoping her letters might, over time, release some yet-unfathomed importance. I never felt that way about my own mother's letters. The only one I keep, the one I showed to Mrs. Waugh and guard in my pocket, is the one beseeching the prime minister to release my pension.

I've recited others to Sophie in our tent at night, despite how impatient she grows.

"Where are the originals?" she demands. I have to explain to her again and again that my mother's letters to me have become caught between the years and I'm unsure whether some library keeps them, or I left them in my desk at Westerham in Kent, or if, in fact, they might be in the upstairs room where Madame Blanchard safeguarded some of my belongings in her little saltbox on the Gaspé.

"The one I need to examine," Sophie says, "is the one about your bloody pension."

"I thought I showed you that one already."

"No, you keep promising me you will but so far all I get is wild stories in the night."

Despite Sophie's attempts to assist me over the last ten years, I torture my soul bringing to mind Henrietta Wolfe's letters. The more I ruminate over them the more terribly their every word inhabits me. Did I imagine time might render them neutral?

Dear James,

I'm in my garden . . .

My mother often wrote to me from her garden, as if her phlox and sweet peas and Canterbury bells and all her other garden entities were accomplices without whose assistance she dared not compose. At times on the battlefield I craved a special trip to that garden so I might tear her bleeding hearts and columbines out by their roots.

> There is a little chaffinch mother laying spider-silk in my pear bush, and her eggs are the loveliest green except for one that glows red with a maroon splotch that strikes me for all the world as the shape of the birth-mark on the small of your back . . .

This reference to an intimate part of my body that only a mother or a lover would know disturbs Sophie. I have not told her how once, when my mother and I still lived together, Mama touched a tender, hind-part of my neck and announced I had a mole growing there, with a coarse hair coming from it, that had not been there before, as if I'd arranged to have it appear on purpose to confound her. My mother's fingers burned me and I flinched, as I flinched from all her attentions.

Her attempt to discourage my affection for my intended, Eliza Lawson, began with a single letter that I now think my mother believed would suffice to end the liaison, though I did not realize her intent at the time:

> Miss Lawson showed up at Mr. Keith's in her grey gown held over from last year but with new ruffles at the neck. The sons

of various families asked her to dance and she appeared eager to comply with every request, so for most of the night I had a hard time watching her at all, so many corners and partitions did she flit behind, for minutes at a time, no doubt entranced by the company she kept.

I knew Eliza loved dancing and hadn't the money to have a gown made every year—her unconcern over such vanities was one of the things I admired about her—so my mother's insinuation took no foothold in me then.

But later, when my mother started sending me letters infected with loneliness, that first one came back to mind with its frantic edge highlighted, and I was surprised to have missed it before. Then came this:

My beloved,

Sadness looms like Blackheath's thunderclouds—suspended unmoving, bright silver-white—it chokes the day. Melancholy is heavier than any cloud. Though to weigh it on Dr. Morrison's scale wouldn't move the gauge.

Does my loneliness have a colour? Red? No. An absence of red: your red hair, your red coat, your blood once part of mine.

Does loneliness weigh anything? It has the weight of a little white mouse scampering over my mattress in the night—a dream mouse that tells me at midnight how many miles you have gone from me. The mouse weighs less than a slice of bread but if he scampers on my heart he crushes it. I wake unable to breathe.

What sound has my loneliness?

It's the long thin needle a curlew flings, that sharp note hidden mid-song. You kill me with that secret needle, suggesting you'll marry the Lawson woman. What became of your way of leaning your neck on mine when you loved me here in the house?

My mother wrote these things as if I was responsible for our intimacy, if that's what it was. Perhaps Sophie is right to criticize. Should my mother not have had more restraint?

When I was with my regiment in Scotland and my father travelled away from home more and more often, supposedly for his work as inspector of Marines, my mother wrote me nearly every day.

My dearest son,

Did you know before you were born I had to lie with my eyes shut for an hour every morning, persuading myself it was all right to be alive? I don't mean I was slightly sad. I mean that waking alone, with you not born, I had a stone on my chest that would drown any other woman if she held on to it at our summer bathing spot.

The stone bore spores from deep underground, that coldest place where memory fails and the future fails and so does any present joy.

Who embraced your mother then? But when you were born, that first time I saw you, I found the warmth others somehow gain from the sun or friends or hearths and pots of supper and candle flames and all the lanterns of ordinary life, lanterns whose light has never touched me.

> I counted on you too much to provide me with some little comfort. You didn't know it for awhile, a very little while. But then you did know it. Everyone around me comes to know it, and considers me, in the end, a drain-hole, a cave into which they can pour any amount of care only to have it twist into ice. I live in a malevolent chill and can't be saved.

I think now that my mother blamed my father for claiming me, even before my birth, for a military life. She said he and his beloved army were like creditors in a magic tale, in which the first-born child is the debt payable upon its coming-of-age.

I remember her entreating me to lie snug against her in her bed where we slept entwined through my youth until well after I was twelve. I remember my mother's scent, her silk night-dress cool in summer against my skin. My friend George Warde's mother did not ask him to sleep with her like that. I know this because one hot day as we took shade in his own little room, I said how nice it was that he had a room to himself.

"Do you not?" he asked me. I told him I slept with my mother in her bedroom, and he said, "In her bed?" and looked so surprised that I answered of course I had my own bed, though I did not.

Now I think what my mother feared most was not distance between us, nor did she fear time—but she dreaded the day I found my own purpose. The thing she resented, and of which she was most jealous, besides Eliza Lawson, was my warrior's sense of purpose and the value—meagre though I know it to be—that king and country assign to an army man. I believe she thought that as long as she kept me close I would be purposeless, as she was:

My dear James,

I lash sweet peas to their trellis . . . the dogs have all got catarrhal fever and Ball has had to be put down, while my evenings are devoted to feeding Caesar and Romp with spoonfuls of milk and cod liver oil . . .

I know you won't understand this, but I sit at the open window all day, as long as the rain falls, looking at my drenched currant bushes. The rain does all the cultivating work, quenching leaf and stem and giving ant and robin a little drink at the same time. The rain (and not myself) brings life to the garden and to the countryside beyond. As long as it falls, no one will discern my uselessness. If only it could keep on raining.

But it won't. I dread being exposed, a dried-up husk of an insect, fit only to be blown into the street by the first warm wind.

Help me, son . . .

What son can fulfill such a claim on him? How can he answer it except by crossing an ocean as soon as he possibly can? What can he do with a letter like this:

When you were born, I imagined you belonged to my world. But this is an illusion to placate mothers. Motherhood is a temporary blossoming. Then we contract again. When you departed my life turned back into a hard little seed, not living this time but dead: the caraway in a cake to be spat out, unpalatable.

I might have escaped being discarded if I'd only continued contracting, into a smallness more infinitesimal than any

seed—a point that intersects with pure zero and then
continues into a different world. A world where mothers
have no fear of being seed-small: they've moved beyond
the smallest, most inconsequential nonexistence and have
entered a space a man can't know.

"You understand," I told Sophie last September during one of these recitations, "my mother kept writing to me after she knew I was gone. She wrote two letters before word could reach her across the ocean—that happens to military families all the time. But this one I'm telling you about now. . . . It was dated December 13, 1759, exactly three months after my death:

My Dearest,

I've had the mantua-girl on St. James Street make me a little visard to shade my eyes so I don't have to suffer anyone noticing their puffiness. It's embarrassing to cry in the park or in the shops and I never know when I'm going to do it. A fan is not concealing enough. The new visard allows me to walk outside without worrying over others' pity.

This is worse than when you stopped holding my hand, all grown up, while mothers with smaller boys felt rapture as their sons clung with fond grabs, kisses and petulant complaints.

I wasn't finished with you. You still live in my second, phantom memory, one in which you and I are younger, or sometimes older, than we are at this moment. I see you helping me choose the leather for the new shoes I'll wear at your wedding, though I can't envision the bride.

Your father never cared about buttery leather the colour of

a cream-brown rosebud. You remember the shoe, don't you, though we have not yet gone to choose it, and now we never will choose it outside our secret world. Your father and I never shared such a world.

You promised me you'd quit the army after Quebec. When your father died just after you sailed, I leapt, thrilled: his and the army's claws would have to release you. Why did you not come back?

Remember walking past Mrs. Torrence's garden twice one morning on purpose, to see her fat lilies ache open by noon? Or us, slow as caterpillars past Drake's on the corner to watch the old baker roll knotted buns in time for our tea?

All the flickering green light your father never noticed or cared about, all the shadows in the leaves—we cared about them, didn't we. I wonder if you care about them now?

"You and your nonsense," Sophie said. "Always going on about trees, and little old men, and things you spy on the street." She crammed into her mouth popcorn she'd scooped for free out of a machine at Jumbo Video—she's always storing free food to eat at night in the tent. "And tell me, where am I supposed to believe you found that letter, since you had died by the time she wrote it?"

"I can't remember—why?"

"I suspected you might be a bit vague about it."

"What does it matter? She wrote it to me and I remember it."

"If, as you say, Henrietta wrote it to you after your death in 1759, obviously you'd not have received it posthumously."

"It must have lain among the papers I retrieved out of our house at Westerham when I went back to England, two years ago, to endure the mock musketry among the watermelons, the so-called reenactment of my glorious battles. . . ."

"So you stole it."

"I don't see how it can be called stealing—anyone could see the letter was plainly addressed to me."

"What about that pension letter to the prime minister, hmm? Why won't you hand it over?"

"Is my pension really all you care about?"

"You should care about it too, Jimmy Bee. Money is power and we had an agreement."

4 Lonely Calèche

MONDAY, SEPTEMBER 4.
AFTERNOON.
Place d'Armes. Montreal, Quebec

I STILL HAVEN'T COMPLETED MY mission and found a baguette—even though Sophie did remind me bread is to be found in the city's second circle of roads, not the first.

The first circle is what she calls this old Iroquois road along the Saint Lawrence River up as far as the cobblestones around Place d'Armes. They aren't, strictly speaking, cobblestones at all, since they haven't come from a beach. But I'd best keep this knowledge to myself, as Soph becomes offended when I correct her.

Looking at our shopping list lifts my vapours slightly. I used to love going to Blackheath Market with a shopping list of my mother's: currant jelly, eggs, bacon. Shopping was always a cheerful prospect after military camp and it still gives me solace here amid the rain and stones of Place d'Armes, where statues preside arrogantly over the square and a lonely calèche horse awaits a customer, nostrils aquiver at the sugar-scent from the pile of wet carrots on his red seat.

I've no umbrella, dammit. I tried to add one to our list but Sophie mocked the notion—an opinion my mother shared. So now my collar wilts in this dreary square and I can't free my heart from the oppression of these statues with their pompous inscriptions.

Every September I come to Place d'Armes to try to understand what has become of my legacy, but am instead compelled to read a plaque extolling the heroism of Paul de Chomedey for slaughtering an Iroquois chief, on this spot, a hundred years before I lost Ned, and a hundred and twenty before I scaled L'Anse au Foulon. You'd think de Chomedey overcame the chief with his knuckles instead of firing his snazzy pistols. And you'd have no way of knowing I ever set foot in Quebec.

Plenty in the square extols how the French wrested Montreal from the Iroquois—bronze nuns tame savage children—is that Jeanne Mance bandaging the finger of a Mohawk child with a scrap of plaster from the chemist? Sergeant-major Lambert Closse crouches behind me, his dog and gun staring down a bronze Iroquois warrior, the most splendid of the bunch. There's no English face among the statues unless you count the gargoyle masks wreathed in fresh-harvested grain, sticking out their grotesque tongues in a bloodcurdling cry of . . . victory? I fancy not.

Where've I seen these masks before?

They aren't English, exactly, not in the way I am English—I suspect they've been added to the monument to frighten any English away.

Sophie would tell me to stop taking things so personally. "Loosen up. Go buy yourself a beer. But not in the first circle. You'll have to catch a bus. Do I have to repeat everything?"

I recall perfectly well her explanation of Montreal's circles. It happened the first year we met, when I went to the Mission to get rigged out with a few clothes. She found me a passable pair of boots in the basement, as not many men can use a size thirteen. From the donations pile she nabbed me a couple of shirts with sleeves nearly long enough, but hats were a different story. No one cared about hats any more. I'd tried proper hats on in the shop called Henri Henri only to find that a single one cost a month's worth of my former pay.

"In the first circle . . ." and here she tossed me a six-pack of socks with the L'Équipeur label still on 'em, "you won't find anything a person really needs. The first circle is for pastel caricatures of your girlfriend made while you wait. Amulets on blankets. Cupcakes covered in glitterballs four dollars apiece and each no bigger than my nose. My brother-in-law's carvings marked up fifteen hundred percent. No bread except in fancy restaurant baskets. No toilet paper, no Dumpsters."

"I did find a *papeterie*," I confessed. What a place. State-of-the-art nibs and bottles of Venetian ink.

"Don't get distracted, new kid in town. Don't blow your wad on dumb trinkets."

Last night I admitted to Sophie I still crave that fountain pen, the vial of ink, the rag Amalfi notecards with deckled edges. But I have hardly any money left, again.

"You're just like all the other ex-soldiers who come to me for help. You find it almost impossible to hold on to money or dignity, let alone both."

Sophie does her best to correct the notions of mine she finds misguided or unhinged from sensible civilian perception because of what she calls my "unbalanced military past." Her advice amounts to quite a compendium. She overwhelmed me with it in our first Septembers together.

"Watch out for fancy *boulangeries*," she reminded me this morning. "Get the baguette on Wellington Street. Take the Metro to Marché Jean-Talon and scavenge a few red peppers out of the Dumpsters."

Marché Jean-Talon is in the second circle bordering the third, where a change in the streets makes it dangerous for me to walk around or find things, though Sophie claims I could fill my backpack using the Costco card the Mission gave her for janitorial supplies.

She insists I buy bicarbonate of soda instead of toothpaste, but demands fancy toilet paper. The Mission monitors quantities pilfered by staff and anyway she doesn't like theirs, she wants three-ply and she wants it quilted, whereas I'm fine without any at night in the park.

"We've plenty of leaves and moss," I tell her. "There's always the newspaper."

"You and your newspapers!"

"I keep hoping to find clues in them about things I've missed. Might the *Gazette*, for example, not address my wonderment as to where I may glimpse the simple domestic scenes that bypassed me during my soldiering years?"

When I go on like this she buries her nose in her phone. "You and your sad little questions."

"Why do I never see windows with curtains and coloured lamps peeping out, or the shoulders of someone buttering a slice of bread and handing it to a son or daughter who has come home from school? Why don't I see anyone practicing a violin or splitting the talon in a game of piquet with his mother? Where do all the mothers and sons live?"

Mothers and sons certainly do not live in Sophie's first circle, where people swarm in suits cut from dark wool, or hang about alleys drinking Hungarian wine, or lay watch chains on the curb with an eye out for the permit inspectors.

"Condos. Down by the Champlain Bridge."

"Those faceless boxes?"

The boxes loom, bordered by miniature walled gardens that promise intimacy but fail to deliver it. Walls around the plants lie low enough to show shrubbery off but not low enough for a child to climb, or for the child's father to sit and fill his pipe or consult his street map. The garden walls stand like boudoir biscuits around a cake, narrower than brick or stone, so narrow that even if they were lower you could not balance your croissant on them, nor a picnic cup. Around the greenery, which is shiny and alienating, run banisters, platforms, and outdoor passageways that purport to be for people to walk through but that are instead full of bitter wind licking round corners like tongues of the tiny northern lizards that hide in cracks in the cement.

"Always wanting picnics," Sophie scoffs. "Is this the Cotswolds? Are we Bill and Dot cavorting around the Lake District?"

I suspect she has no idea what the Cotswolds are like. I suppose Bill and Dot must be relatives of hers whom I have not met.

"A hamper, please," she singsongs, "a checkered cloth, a steak-and-kidney pie and eight hard-boiled eggs—poor little Tool-of-the-Empire wants his cucumber sandwich!"

"But look, why do things here possess a façade, even the vegetables? Nothing seems content to be itself."

"What are you on about now?"

"Even a parsnip has no fragrance under the skin."

"Are parsnips the fat grimy white roots? Didn't you eat them in the Gaspé?"

"I can barely locate a parsnip. But if I were fortunate enough to find one, it should be full of perfume. That's the point of a parsnip."

"What about carrots?"

"You can't inhale them here. There's no sharp intake of perfumed bitterness. No anointing. How is it that North America manages to strip a thing's essence? All that remains is counterfeit external structure. A convincing, robust specimen, but only on the outside."

"*Huffington Post* says people are asking supermarkets to keep the spindly carrots and tarnished produce in bins for snobs like you."

"I wouldn't mind a spindly carrot. But more than that I yearn to see a crumbling wall, or a wall that at least has a chance to crumble in a few years, a wall not full of . . . what did you tell me it was? Styrofoam. Everything is so ostentatious yet unreal: the buildings, the parsnips, the athletic people running along the Saint Lawrence in their clothing that seems to have been made out of rubber pressed paper-thin then overlaid with silver lightning-bolts in case we mistake them for sensitive walkers trying to notice snails along the path, or caterpillars . . ."

"You'd like runners to wear handspun outfits?"

"I'd like to look at a thing that remains itself all the way through and isn't made of chemical compounds that have been solidified and macerated then solidified again to resemble building stones or fabric of any kind."

"You need a drink."

"Parsnips and carrots should emit an unexpected pungent burst . . ."

"It's hardly unexpected if you expect it."

"Nothing can prepare one for the delight."

"But . . . you'd be a bit prepared . . . this would not be your first carrot."

"The sensation of an Old-World carrot can't be held in the memory. It's too particular and animal. It's a small delight, but one such delight builds on another to create one's real life. Which is what I miss."

"You miss feeling like an animal."

"I miss smells. Leather and smoke. Primroses. Lily-of-the-valley."

"You're completely out of it. You and your simplicity and your crumbling walls."

"Out of what?"

"In this century, simplicity's for wealthy people. Who all think they're not asking for much. Haven't you clued in to the fact that only big shots get to have a crumbling wall made of real stone? The rest of us can't even hope for plywood anymore. Do you even know what plywood is?"

"Of course."

"Plywood is too good for us. We might get particleboard if we're lucky."

"Board made of particles?"

"Remember I told you to buy tins of solid white tuna, not chunk light or, God forbid, flaked?"

"You said flaked is the factory floor sweepings."

"Good boy. Particleboard's the wood version of that. It's sawdust that has been reconstituted with glue and pressure to make extruded planks of building material."

"That's exactly the kind of thing I hate."

"I know, but you seem to think people nowadays have a choice. You're looking at it as an aesthetic failure because you have no clue about the cost per square foot. You don't think about the cost per square foot of anything, do you?"

"Nothing could be farther from the truth."

"Really?"

"I've always been aware of bills, and of paying them, and of the humiliation of asking my father and mother to help me make up for the shortfalls of a soldier's pay. . . ."

"For God's sake, don't start crying again. Maybe I *am* wrong. Maybe you're not a privileged little dickhead. Maybe the soulless new world has drained all the flavour out of your parsnip. Or maybe the culprit is your own naturally occurring decrepitude. I mean, according to your own calculations, your taste buds are nearly three hundred years old."

And so Sophie continually berates me, and I continue asking questions of her like an innocent child.

"What about the horrifying third circle, north among the warehouses? Do people live there?"

"What do you even know about that circle—you refuse to go."

"And why are you so judgmental about the second circle right around our park? I like all the blue and red and gold doors. The spiral *escaliers*. The cupolas and wrought-iron railings."

"Gentrification."

Sophie is strange about money. She wants and doesn't want it. She's one of the few Mission staff given her own room separate from the dorms that house hundreds of homeless men, but she refuses to sleep there unless it's twenty below outside. She recoils from people who live in park-side apartments with elegant balconies overhanging the boulevard. Yet woe betide me if I'm a day late with her rent. Over the past ten Septembers she has kicked me out of the tent early more than once, due to my precarious funds.

In the eleven autumns I've known Sophie, I have slowly come to suspect that my own destiny in New France might be that of a street person, much like her: constantly on the move, sleeping where the daily battle warrants, forever dreaming of stealing a fortnight in a proper bed, yet—if that opportunity approaches—realizing I've become fit only for our ramshackle nest under the sky, which she reminds me I'm lucky to have.

I fear being homeless might render me aimless like the men

slouching on the Mission steps, smoking Pall Malls they buy from Kahnawake.

"How can they hang around so purposeless?" I once asked Sophie.

"They're like the pigeons you're so fond of. Hanging around the sidewalk, letting time go by. And hopefully they make it through the day."

"I can't see how they can stand it. Surely it's a misfortune not to have an employment or a profession of some kind or other, to fill up the intervals of our time. . . ."

"Spoken like a real military man."

"But . . . to live merely for the sake of eating, drinking, without the prospect of any business, or of being useful. That, in my mind, is a heavy condition."

"Isn't that attitude precisely what gave General Wolfe all his troubles?"

Sophie has an unerring instinct for magnifying every misgiving I have ever entertained about my life's work. She holds my military career up to me as if it were a mirage that I now have a chance to see anew. And even as she does this, she gets so impatient with me.

She says I refuse to gain perspective, that I'm too invested in my crimes: still needing to make sense of them, to justify my butchery.

"You can't see the forest when you've torched all the trees," she taunts.

If only it were just trees we burned.

Dear Mother,

We set fire to so much more . . .

—

GOD, I NEED TO GET out of Place d'Armes—the place makes me depressed. But . . . to journey to the third circle!

Must I go?

Catacomb of alienation!

Still, Costco at least boasts a section where a man can find sausage in a bun. I'll admit Sophie has a point when she claims every Englishman is constantly on the lookout for a sausage. Costco also sells a cold brew *sans* alcohol but with a sharp fizz like new beer, sweeter than Parisian lemonade, in paper cups the size of tureens one can refill at no charge.

Have I remembered Soph's Costco card? All right, Jarry Station, here I come.

I labour once again to master the eye-avoidance people practice in subway cars. The Montreal trains are full of passengers who are not white or who are too young or too old to own cars. I seem always to be the only tall white man on the train.

I end up wedged next to a black woman weeping unobtrusively, her tears sliding in silent streams down a face otherwise expressionless, even serene.

I depart the car to transfer at Station Sauvé.

Hello bus 121, pilgrimage through cathedrals built of strata and substrata of expanded polystyrene covered in glass fibre mesh embedded in crack-resistant polymers replete with cracks and groaning bulges and peaks and valleys of synthetic stucco stretching endlessly to the new world horizon.

Why did I not even lay a hand on that woman's arm, to comfort her?

5 Costco

MONDAY, SEPTEMBER 4.
AFTERNOON.
Costco and environs. Montreal, Quebec

THE REAR BUS SEAT IS EMPTY! I plonk onto its wild velvet pattern as we sway around traffic islands, past Walmart and fly-by-night computer repair outlets.

That which is, already has been. And that which is to be, already has been. And God seeks what has been driven away. . . .

Ecclesiastes always strikes me as the only reasonable part of the Bible. It supports my belief that if you arm yourself with philosophy, you can be master of whatever befalls you. As Montreal's charmed balconies peter out and warehouses abound I find Ecclesiastes more comforting than I did in any pew with my mother, or at wartime devotions, or by candle in my billets and camps.

Our driver lurches in and out of her stops. I know nothing of those who board, nothing of these outskirts' shopping centres or parking lots. I ride anonymous in their sprawl, waiting for the crater that might jolt me properly into being in the present instead of floating in the past. They call Montreal's copious potholes *nids-de-poule*—chicken nests. I need our bus to bump in and out of a giant one of those, maybe an ostrich's home instead of a chicken's.

The English painter J.M.W. Turner had an exhibit two Septembers ago at the gallery near McGill University—his images glowed at me from billboards on Sherbrooke Street—I bought a ticket and marvelled at the man. He was born sixteen years after my death but might have been my brother. From his paintings I saw he must have been perpetually in a condition like the one I inhabit every October through August, the time when I am not with Sophie. He dwells in pure atmosphere: air, fire—*vague* like the French word for a wave in the Atlantic whose heaving waters never failed to sicken me when I sailed with the fleet.

I read how Turner lashed himself to a mast and painted his silver fury of storm and spindrift. His work evokes the frightening mist to which I return once my September leave is done. Standing in front of his paintings I felt understood for the first time. Sophie called this ridiculous. "He was very short-sighted," she said, "and so are you. The thing you have in common is that you're both half-blind."

As I bump along on the bus now, I find it dispiriting that no one in this city ever recognizes me. Even when I put the red coat on, people don't know who I am. I have to confess, I expected many difficult things, but not anonymity on my return to a French-Canadian city. And I miss combat. As long as I lift no musket, shoulder no cannon, shout no order nor hold council of war with men—even men whose disdain weighs more on me than the other tasks combined—my heart hurts more than it did in battle.

I yearn back, crane forward: I look with impotent compassion upon the soldier I was. I rage against that soldier's time lost to dreary encampments with their filth and noise: damp fires where we devoured our dead brothers' rations and scanned the hill in case a brother was not dead or had somehow revived and might crawl back to us even if, like my beloved comrade Elwyn, he now possessed only one arm.

Civilians imagine we soldiers need to recover from the horrors of active duty, but it is the white-hot ordeal of a soldier's inactive waiting that gnaws him from the inside out, starting with a walnut-sized cluster of dusty brown worms in his brain, and for me those worms are not done feeding yet.

I wish I could write to my mother at this moment—but on the bus, my knees jiggle and the minute I look down the motion sickness starts. Writing even a few lines to her would make me feel less aggrieved by how the fragile haunts of earth—so humble and ordinary for civilians—elude and torment me. Even the print on the fabric of the bus seats reminds me of certain glorious fireworks.

AT COSTCO YOU SIT AT A TABLE with your knackwurst and as long as you can produce a membership card no one accuses you of loitering, even if you sit writing to your mother all day.

I always rummage in the Lost and Found to see if anyone has left something I can use. Last September I found a scarf woven in the Scottish borders. So far no one has left me an umbrella.

This place, dear Madam, I write as a woman hollers into her phone near a pyramid of paper towels: "Arnold! Where'd you disappear to?"

> This place from which I write to you now is in need of attack by French fire-ships: I know you feared those more than any other weaponry at my Enemy's disposal, but I thrilled to their conflagration. It was so easy to quench them that I deliberately let them float toward us longer than necessary . . .

"I'm over here by the Bounty. Did you get Jasper's food?"

I know my mother does not want to hear how the approach of Montcalm's fire-ships thrilled me at night on the Saint Lawrence. One flame-lick to our vessel and molten oakum would rain fire on my hair. I loved how the fire-ships lit the embankments, unleashing smoke and turpentine from the spruce overhang. The incense filled me with lustful purpose.

"No! I read that one has ground-up tumours in it. Get the Kirkland."

I try not to write to my mother about mortal danger, nor erotic thrill, nor my days of meaninglessness and despair. How many letters have I begun to her, only to crumple and fling them in the fire?

This place is crying out for a conflagration now. . . .

Around my Costco table, which has been bolted to the floor, the walking dead appear. They move slowly, heavily, and have lost all animation or verve. Are they French? English? Was it for them my blood poured out of three ragged holes?

Where is the splendour I envisioned?

Mother, remember when I said I believed there would grow
a people here, out of our own little spot in England, to fill
this space and become a vast Empire, the seat of power and
learning?

The man named Arnold rejoins his vocal woman. Together they wheel an enormous cart. It holds dog food, chocolate, marshmallows, bottles of Pepsi and crates of electronic equipment, a fifty-pound bag of Yukon Gold potatoes and eighteen loaves of sliced bread in cellophane. It holds fatty meat ground up and crammed behind film bulging over foam trays. The meat glitters under the lights in this echo chamber of disparate and towering imports.

> It is as if England has had a nightmare in which the Empire's crowning achievement has been to inflate the size of material goods: every chicken leg, every shirt, all the grapes and loaves and boxes of tea, even the people, their bodies sluggish and distended. Madam, if you thought me thin in England, then I am emaciated here.

"Remember the Kirkland made him throw up all over Amber's beanbag chair?"

> Dear Madam, if I am not careful, someone—a guard, for this place employs beefy guards—might have to send for a doctor and have me removed to hospital. . . . I am beset by an overwhelming panic.

Sophie warns me I need to stop hunting for the fruits of General Wolfe's labours. She says they cannot be arrayed like corpses on a battlefield: four hundred French vanquished here, ninety Savages laid waste there, and over here twenty Canadian prisoners . . . *whose wives, I promise you, Mother, we have not harmed—in fact we have offered the wives, as well as all the old men and babies, decent boats and shelter. . . .*

No such calculation of wartime accomplishments occurs in peacetime, Sophie likes to remind me.

I've told her I'm well-used to the shock of peacetime, its boredom and lack of passion—I've experienced it many times and know it takes months to acclimatize to the loss of adrenaline. My fear is not the fear of stasis: waiting and inertia are a soldier's everlasting companions. My fear is that I see no evidence that our lives in peacetime have any direction at all.

New French Britain is extremely frightening. I don't see how any soldier returning here could want to do anything except slit his own throat.

Sophie claims this is not the fault of the place. The fault is mine. I need to be rehumanized.

And she says I have to do it myself. She hasn't time to help, the way I have time. She's got too much other work to do, too many other soldiers to shelter. All she can do is direct my vision.

"Get your ass out of Montreal to Quebec City," she says. "Search its bloody Plains of Abraham. Look under every bush and examine every blade of grass—until you see that what you lost in the past isn't there."

MONDAY, SEPTEMBER 4.
EVENING.
Mont Royal. Montreal, Quebec

EVEN SOPHIE HAS TO ADMIT I'm pretty good at building our clandestine campfire on the mountain. While I prepare the draught for my ailment—it involves boiling snails, from an old recipe of my mother's—I try to describe my day, including Dogfood Woman and Arnold.

"This new letter to your mother is maudlin and useless," Sophie declares.

"But I must tell her of the overpasses, the cement pillars, the lots twinkling with cars. How there is nobody walking, or if anyone does walk he's in mortal danger of getting stuck at a curb until the end of time waiting for the light to change. I often predicted to my mother that our colonies might become tinged with the vices of England, but if ever I had envisioned Costco . . ."

"You're coughing again."

"My lungs are worn purses Dick Turnip might have slashed to ribbons, finding them entirely useless!"

I smash my snails with a rock to steep overnight among bits of willow in my medicine pan.

"Turpin."

"What?"

"The eighteenth-century highwayman who robbed your neighbours was Dick Turpin, not Turnip. Nobody's called Turnip. Did you get the bread?"

Sophie has surprising nuggets of knowledge. But I have forgotten the bread! "Sorry."

"Baking soda?"

"Colgate."

"For God's sake. What about the Dumpsters?"

"Covered in disgusting tomato pulp." In fact, I did not get around to the Dumpsters.

"And Madame Bee? Did you at least make arrangements to see her?"

"I did nothing about Madame Blanchard."

"I'm asking about her for your sake, not mine."

"I got distracted."

"Don't blame me if you wait too long. She is not getting younger."

Sophie hauls up our sleeping bag. It's not really a bag any more, more a tattered blanket. I found it in front of a pizzeria sign whose salami the sun had bleached green.

"I need you not to be on your phone just now."

"Yeah-yeah."

"I'm paying you to listen . . ."

"You haven't paid me anything yet."

"I gave you nearly all the money I earned in Westerham."

"That was two years ago, and you didn't earn it—that money was the measly bit left over from the government cheque I helped you—"

"Sophie, I need to talk about today. . . . I was thinking on the bus. . . ."

"Hang on!" She's lit Facebook-blue. This is far from the kind of listening my mother provided, but it's all I have.

I can't always recall what happened in combat at Dettingen or in Culloden or at Quebec or anywhere else. Events have become entangled: all my wars now transpire in a single battlefield during one timeless period—darkness cut with spears of flame in whose light any instant of my soldiering might have played out. Sophie is supposed to help me disentangle the years. That has been our arrangement, from our first September to this one.

"Please?"

"Okay, shoot."

"On the bus today I remembered flames, fire, all the times I made things burn, or made people burn, or when other people burnt things. . . ."

"Forget about what other people burnt."

"I never burnt anyone on purpose."

"Okay."

"Did I? Not directly . . ."

"You burnt people indirectly?"

"I see them scream and burn—but—I was not barbaric."

"Weren't you?"

"The *enemy* were the barbaric fiends."

"Which enemy?"

The answer to this is always hard to remember.

Sophie wants me to separate out every point of combat. She wants me to draw them on a timeline. But I cannot always remember who the enemy was, or where or when.

"There have been a lot of enemies in a few well-chosen hell-holes."

"Which one are you talking about tonight?"

". . . Montcalm?"

"Are you sure?"

"The French lit the fire-ships . . ."

"We've been through the fire-ships."

"We have?"

"We did the fire-ships last year and the year before. The fire-ships get you nowhere."

She claims the French fire-ships are a story I repeat to distance myself from remorse. She says I project them over blasts I have myself inflicted, not only on soldiers but on civilians, even on children. I can hardly credit this.

"French fire-ships never frighten you for a second. You have total control over them. You know that as soon as you tell me the part about sending a man on a raft to nudge them with a rod, they'll float ashore and burn like chandeliers on a Shakespearean stage. You'll whoop at your post, best seat in the house."

"I already told you about the raft?"

"You're the one who raises or lowers the curtain. You decide everything as far as fire-ships go. I don't want to hear about them again."

"What do you want?"

"To look at my grandbabies on Facebook, then nibble your belly and stuff my snout in your gingerfuzz armpits to keep warm."

"You're supposed to keep me warm, that's our deal. And I meant what story do you want? I need you to listen to at least one tonight."

"You never finished telling me that interesting one about the dragonfly girls."

"Why do you only want to listen to things that make me burn with shame?"

"You want to sulk? Go right ahead. Get mired in fire-ships for all I care. C'mon, nuzzle in."

She clamps me in her thighs and rams her face in my side, licks and bites my nipple so it stands up straight in the canvas-and-maple air. My cough retreats into its lair. After all my mother's disapproval of Eliza Lawson, after all my efforts to please Mama, I've taken up with a janitor who has four grandchildren and is twice my age. If ever I'd imagined sleeping with a fifty-seven-year-old woman in my early days, I'd have forecast dry skin and uninviting horrors. Not in a million years could I have foreseen the heat and salty-sweet of a grandma named Sophie Cotterill.

> Dear Madam, fifty-seven's young! Fifty-seven grabs my buttocks, reaches for my cock and grasps it with the expertise that I'd have thought belonged only to a man who has out of necessity pulled his own cock alone at night on a succession of warships. She has a way of snaking her arm around me so it feels I'm doing the thing myself, or that it is being performed by Elwyn, or George. Her arm is muscled as an eel. If ever she chooses to rescind her rule that I'm never to penetrate her body, I might almost feel like a husbandly consort.

I cannot imagine Sophie in a dove-grey gown like Eliza's, nor does Sophie carry rouge or a handkerchief. She shoves her bison-hide wallet in her jeans and reams her nails with the pocket-knife hung on the key ring in her belt loop. With this knife she also lifts Portuguese sardines to her gob out of tins, slices hard skin off her heels, and digs out splinters. I've whiffed the sardines on her at three in the morning.

"Well, General Wolfe?" Sophie prods me with her sharp elbow.

"Well what?"

"On with your fire-ships!"

6 Fire-Ships

MONDAY, SEPTEMBER 4.
NIGHT.
Mont Royal. Montreal, Quebec

"BRAVERY, SOPHIE, IS A CAST of the dice. And I gamble, but only if I'm wearing the red coat. Without that coat you'll find me cautious as the next man, soft and passive as a slug—don't judge! When I put on the coat it is a costume and I'm a player, a man who'll jump to court the dice. If a soldier chances nothing he might as well go to war in his bedshirt, clinging to a biscuit dipped in milk. You think me a mama's boy? I won't argue with that or even resent it. Brigadier Townshend, that fine artist and soldier, cartooned me as a spineless coward, but he did it because he couldn't tell the difference between soldier and man.

"Superstition engulfed the French in June of 1759, as did grey ghost-ribbons of rain hung in shreds and shrouds in the nearing squall. The French fell on their knees and kissed crucifixes and their priest gave out stale cake and pickled wine to thank their god for the wind rattling our ships hard enough to block the Saint Lawrence with splinters. But the luck of the dice has its own power and I find that it cooperates with a general who won't take his own life too seriously. I mean, I was gaunt, seasick and plagued with the gravels, with dysentery and bad vapours. I'd no reason to fear for my health—it was ruined already. The storm that welcomed us to Île d'Orléans worried my men but I told them to consider it background music to what we would, ourselves, unleash.

"That little snot Vaudreuil must've driven Montcalm crazy—as soon as we reached the island their defectors ran to us, sick of Vaudreuil stuffing himself with goose legs and capers and hoarded sweetmeats while his militia subsisted on the black-hearted turnips they were obliged to count as wages. They told us that Vaudreuil, with his coxcomb's sense of theatre, had prescribed fire-ships be sent toward us on our first night, to finish off what the storm could not. Fire-ships! No modern army took them seriously any more. That man must have been sleepwalking in history, imagining himself fighting Spanish and Turks in ages when fire-ships were a force in which one might still believe. Now they were no more than stage lighting or fanfare for a royal wedding.

"'He's counting on no moon,' said one toothless defector as he wrapped his joyful gums around a crackled pig's ear, releasing a runnel of slaver down his chin. It was difficult for me to make him out, between his atrocious accent and the gnawing and smacking. 'He's made a dozen fire-ships with Delouche in command.'

"'Is Delouche the one with the ludicrous moustache?' I asked Pig-Ears. I thought I'd seen Delouche in Paris, dancing a gavotte with an overconfident frothiness.

"'*Oui.*'

"Flies swarmed straight from hell and we had to slather ourselves with lard to fend off the numbers bulging with our blood, which they sucked through stingers fine as pins in my mother's sewing box. The process would have been fascinating had it not covered us in itchy welts. My men ripped their coats, slashing the red skirts and tearing off epaulets and fastenings and anything that might snag on the stumps and pricks of the twigs and bush all stunted and broken aslant. I did not modify a thing on my own coat, but would eagerly have done so had I not been bound to set a good example.

"As dusk fell we smelt sap and dog-roses in the marsh and heard plaintive notes of white-throated sparrows and eerie snipe. Quebec towered before us and all I could do was glare at Montcalm's encampment that straggled all the way up from our deafening water-cascade at Montmorency through Beauport to the Charles River at the city's back gate. Beyond Montcalm's redoubts and entrenchments loomed the natural cliffs, and on these I kept my gaze.

"The storm-rinsed sky glowered then cleared, as Pig-Ears had promised, without a moon. Vaudreuil was an idiot for thinking this meant we'd have no light to discern his fire-ships' approach: we had a sky crammed with stars dusting the river surface with their influence. Their quiet light gathered in the water and magnified, and the rain-bulged waves sifted luminosity back into the air where it hovered over the whole river before us.

"But Delouche was sailing into an undifferentiated darkness on our isle of Orleans, a blackness that obscured from him my sentries and our artillery—I knew he saw nothing but a silhouette of spiky night trees rising against the Milky Way.

"An hour before midnight my sentries spied looming shapes drifting toward us blue and violet against sky and river. Lumbering and stacked high with relic cannon and loaded muskets, Catherine-wheels and mortar-bits and cast-iron hollow-shot, they lurched and floated toward us like phantasmagoric monsters.

"Delouche sailed like he danced—confident at first, but when the real intricacy of the music began he faltered, though he would not admit it: instead he blazed ahead, mis-stepping, to his partners' chagrin, rather than retreating to study the matter further so that he might proceed with any kind of knowledge.

"Now, as before, true courage did not come to him; a false bravado made him give the order to ignite his fuses too early by half an hour, and with that, his men in their nearby fire-ships also lit the works far too soon for their purpose. Fire spilt up their masts and lit their sails in a lurid glow that illumined the banks and painted Montcalm's tents orange.

"Explosions blew molten holes agape in the fire-ships, and great booms and cracks obliterated the waterfall noise that had at first been so insistent. Grapeshot clattered amongst the birches, staccato like monstrous hailstones, and there was a lightning-bolt followed by thunder that we thought must be the storm returning, but it was a cluster of bombs and grenades catapulting sound and light into the departing clouds. Ribbons of fire lit up the stonework of the fortress and cathedral spires of Quebec so high on its rock I teetered looking at it.

"I tell myself again and again that the main job of a general is to persuade his men to hold fire until we are close enough to finish the enemy. I'm surprised by other men's inability to remember this, and Delouche had forgotten it now.

"He managed to burn alive his own best men and incinerate his boots: my men saw him leap on a raft to rescue for himself a pair that had fused on the melted leg of one of his sailors.

"By the time his fire-ships came close they'd nearly burnt themselves out. My men easily heaved grappling hooks over them and swung them into the reeds where their flames dwindled to embers. By dawn the ships were frail charcoal sticks tinkling as they leaned and collapsed on themselves, reeking that sad stink of burnt houses. For a ship is, like a house, a sort of dwelling, even if it is a temporary one and even if it floats like a houseboat or like the frail, bright dream of a burning dragon."

—

"ARE YOU ASLEEP?" IT WOULDN'T be the first time Sophie has let me tell stories while she conks out. I often wonder if she's heard a word I say.

"I'm listening. Delouche and the burning dragons."

"Hold me? I'm chilled. I feel my old cough deep down."

"General Wolfe," she declaims, turning to address the walrus painted on our tent wall, "has no idea what true cold is."

"I'm uncommonly susceptible!"

"Nor does he understand heat. He swans in here every September and has no clue about our stifling July, and he especially knows sweet fuck all about our brutal winters."

"I get the shivers. I've told you it's why I need to get up so early and walk. All my life I've broken camp at daybreak to get moving—the cold seizes my nose and fingers. It distresses me considerably. . . . What are you doing? Can't you stop that? Always getting that thing out and staring at it."

"Hang on, hang on . . . listen." From her phone sings a man in the Québécois cadence that bears no resemblance to any French I learned in Paris.

"Who's that?"

"This man knows more about Quebec than a British general can ever fathom. Everyone in Quebec knows this song!"

In the white ceremony where the snow
marries the wind—

"Is he singing about winter?"

"It's Vigneault. No one knows his exact intent."

"Voltaire!"

"No. Vigneault! The famous fisherman's son."

"But he's saying the whole of—of New French Britain—isn't—"

"New French Britain!"

"Well, what am I supposed to call this place?"

"Em . . . Canada?"

"Does he even call this Canada? Listen—he says his country isn't a country, it's snow and ice—nothing but winter—that's exactly what Voltaire—"

"Vigneault, not Voltaire."

"May I talk to him? Here, give it—hey!"

"I'm hardly on the phone with Gilles Vigneault. Shut up while I put him on repeat."

My chorus is not a chorus,
it's a gust of wind . . .

Half-awake, I attend the *chansonnier*'s wedding where the snow marries the wind. It's a cold night. I try conjuring warmth from my fire-ships story, but Vigneault has ignited his ceremony of white fire instead, into which I slowly drift.

"Quit thrashing."

"Sorry."

"I'm feeling your military nightmares here."

SUNRISE—TIME TO CRAWL OUT AND STRAIN my snail juice into a bottle containing salt and the night crawler I snatched when I wriggled out for my four-o'clock piss. With each sip I command my cough to arrest itself, as I gaze at the trees facing our camp.

Do I recognize any of the tree spirits I see? Sophie professes I dream them. But they whisper on Avenue du Parc's grand sweep downtown toward the Saint Lawrence. The first tree, crammed with women frozen in frenzied dance, seems unconcerned about my perusal.

Is one of its captives my beloved Eliza Lawson?

I can neither attain nor decipher the women in the trees . . .

"Eliza, my frozen nymph!"

No wonder Sophie ridicules me.

An elm across the avenue intertwines his thighs, plants his roots in solid support of his body with its lewd orifices. His nipples, his tormented face—he makes me ashamed of myself for he draws on my cock and hardens it on this cold morning before I've found a cup of tea.

Women trapped in the western trees have arched away, leaning toward their mother, the mountain. And the cars! Police vehicles flash lights red and blue; buses, and endless New World engines with their monotonous drone and their violent purr of rubber wheels, drive on a thin biscuit of pavement under which the trees' roots gyrate. I sympathize with bicycles gliding toward me then gliding away—they alone proceed quietly, peaceful as gulls riding a thermal.

Elms low on the avenue swerve ribbed and hairy: undulating, tormented beings, sexual, entrapped. A wailing woman hangs bound around a trunk in supplication and anguish, flailing to break free, her wail apparently inaudible to everyone but myself.

My day begins.

7 Gay Village

TUESDAY, SEPTEMBER 5.
MORNING.
Chinatown. Montreal, Quebec

IT'S BEEN A YEAR SINCE my last visit to the hot tub at the Chinatown Y, and I forget what time it opens. There's nothing worse than having to hang around an institution's locked doors. Sophie, of course, insists the Y is not in Chinatown but in the Gay Village. But the village is a bit farther east. She accuses me of visiting it regularly. She spent our entire first autumn together on a line of investigation into what she called my repressed gayness.

I tried back then to brush her off. "You're like the Inquisition."

"You talk a lot about bodies of young male soldiers, whether they were well-made or not."

"It is something a general is bound to notice."

"You go on about someone named Elwyn in particular."

"Who?"

"Elwyn. You moan in your sleep about Elwyn and how beautifully he was made, as if he were a purse, or a saddle or a hat from Henri Henri. . . ."

"You must mean George. George Warde is the beloved friend of mine who was more well-made than any soldier in Culloden or Quebec. . . ."

"No."

"Yes. George Warde, my boyhood friend in Westerham."

"Okay—you loved George Warde?"

"I did."

"You were physical with him."

"We were very close."

"I mean were you intimate?"

"We were as intimate as any two people can be. But I think you mean a different thing than I mean when you say intimate."

"Why are you talking like an idiot? I'm asking what kind of love you have for men like George Warde."

My body language betrayed me. There was no refuge from her questions. Even in silence I let things be known. I said only, "Anything I admit to you about George would fall short of what we had."

The truth is, the words Sophie used were inadequate. Her version of my love for George had me peep through a door ajar, slip one toe on a vestibule tile, when in fact I had dwelt in an innermost chamber of the building.

"How long were you lovers? Was it only when you were soldiering together?"

At moments like this I was tempted to scan the street-corners for someone else, anyone other than Sophie, in whom to confide. Though, as she sometimes had to remind me, her job was to insist on the truth.

"Yet," she went on, "you were engaged twice, to women."

"I was."

"And the first one you say you loved."

"I adored Eliza."

"And your mother put a stop to it because Eliza had no money."

"Eliza had nearly twelve thousand pounds a year."

"Not enough for Henrietta. And your so-called fiancée, Katherine Lowther, whose portrait you carried to Quebec and had set in rubies and topaz to the tune of five hundred pounds, you never loved."

"Not in the same way."

"But you agreed to marry."

"Everyone knows that. That's not news. Why do you insist on going over the same old—"

"But why, exactly, does everyone know?"

"You're exhausting me."

"Everyone knows about Katherine Lowther because your mother used her to shush the story going around about you and George."

"Nobody else has said that. I've never heard that anywhere except here in your tent."

"Katherine Lowther was a cover-up story, like the marriages of gay men to respectable women since time immemorial."

To test her theory, Sophie took me to a couple of Montreal strip clubs that first September, one on the Main and the other in the Gay Village. We took seats in a place called Stock Bar and watched a parade of young men dance around a pole. When the second fellow began to dance, Sophie said, "I like his physique better than the first one."

The first man had been muscle-bound, substantial, and completely uninteresting to me, but not because of his body. He wore tight shorts that he never removed entirely—he simply pulled the backs down so his haunch jutted out. He did this as if casually, as if he was alone in his bedroom getting ready to put his pyjamas on and therefore needing to take the underpants off. But lo and behold, halfway through removing the underpants he was reminded of something that made him pause—a misplaced note from a lover? A lost coin—where had it gone?

He circled the pole and looked quizzically into an imagined half-distance that stopped short of our eyes. Meanwhile his pectorals shimmered, his buttocks—round and concentrated—orbited with the beat of his music.

This second dancer was far more agile. He bent like a sapling but the beauty was all in his body—none flowed from his mind, which he kept from us, guarded, behind a mask of boyish innocence, and I did not blame him.

We were early and there were fewer than thirty men in the room, and only one spectator had gravitated to the stools hugging the catwalk: a dignified old man in a good wool coat and a cravat—his gin-and-tonic at hand. He had the air of a man who frequented the opera, had a Persian cat at home, and came to the bar in a fit of reminiscence about what it had been to be young and splendid in body—he had not fallen into despair because he had not succumbed to any fallen idea of himself, but remained glorious. Perhaps he read a lot, or was an academic, respected and perhaps once loved but bereaved of that lost and cherished and good love. He had fallen on solitary times yet did not seem to mind. He did not mind being the only man who had pulled a stool up close to the dancer, and he did not appear to lust so much as reminisce. I had the impression that if one were to check his pulse, it would not have quickened: it would indicate nothing but a slightly melancholic reverie.

The third dancer was the first one returned, this time with no underpants, his cock at a kind of half-mast that appeared sustained with the help of a metal object, part of which I perceived glinting behind his testicles. I have seen similar contraptions at Smithfield market on beef cattle waiting to be bought and killed.

"That contraption," I told Sophie, "reminds me of the failure of all cosmetic falsehood."

"Stop putting on airs."

Even in that first September, Sophie knew all about my five months of dissipation in London after Mother forbade me to marry Eliza. Sophie also knew of my whores and my opium and my syphilis. I'd told her about the night I nearly died in the Thames after renting myself to the poisonous descendant of the first Baron of Wigmore. She knew I'd woken more than a few mornings in face-paint and a stythe of civet and musk. But I do not think Sophie understood how the cock-ring on the dancer disturbed me. Its constant violence produced only half an effect: his cock bobbing halfhearted as a forced hyacinth in a cruel April gale.

Sophie had already brought me, on a previous occasion, to a place on Boulevard Saint-Laurent, similar to Stock Bar save that women licked the pole, crawling up and down it pretending themselves in heat. I had felt little then, and I did not feel more now.

It was raining outside and Stock Bar's door hung open. I watched silver stripes pelt past the lamp posts on Saint Catherine, rose-coloured balloons strung up and neon-lit the length of the Village.

A few city saplings lowered their gowns and as I watched their leaves drip and smelled ozone shift in the night air, and as street air swirled in to us carrying its fragrance of drenched sidewalks, Sophie said, "Your pupils just dilated a bit."

"I love the rain," I said. "I'm charged by wet bark and shining leaves. By a wet street. By the thought of getting out of this sad place and walking down that street alone."

"No, you're having a response here, with men, that you never had when we went to watch women."

"You are not correctly observing the evidence."

"I'm trying to get you to admit something about why you're clinically depressed and why you can't even begin to function in the real world. Did you or did you not hire me to investigate?"

Sophie and I watched the next dancer whilst turned away from each other with our arms folded. I liked this one least. His face wore an expression I found irrelevant to his movements, incongruous. He had an agenda outside this room, beyond this world, but I knew as I watched his face that he'd never reach a place where he might fulfill that agenda. He knew it too, I think. He hated every last man of us in the room.

The old man at the front took this in. He was interested. He had been similarly disillusioned, but long ago. Love, or beauty, or tenderness, or whatever it was, had gone. The old spectator now blew the dancer a kiss and laid a hundred-dollar bill on the boards. Some entity had replaced the thing he had lost. A new animal had replaced it. I knew that animal. I knew it from London. I knew it from back rooms of certain houses that I had visited during my worst vapours. They were rooms to which I'd vowed not to return.

"You find men well-made," insisted Sophie, "but not women."

"Women's bodies are less firmly held together," I admitted. "But how many times do I have to tell you it is not these dancers' bodies I find informative or arresting? Can you not decipher their faces? What's real up there now, with that one? His anger or his innocence? Are both true? Is one a fable? Has any of us ever owned innocence? Help me look at him and decide—the constant changing of his face fascinates and unsettles me—who is he?"

"You want me to read his face?"

"Yes! I'm trying to . . ."

"You've been looking at the dancers' faces this whole time."

"Yes."

Sophie took a swig of her screwdriver and thumped back in her seat. "Jimmy B, no one cares about their faces."

—

IT WASN'T AS IF I'D NEVER had a lover. Still, I have never found a way to explain to Sophie how dead the strippers seemed to me. The body of the one she liked best was bright and unblemished but emanated no energy. Waxy, it held in light for itself and would not share that light. His cock bobbed and nodded, no more alive than a silicone cock on the wall in one of the sex shops down the block. My teeth have more life in them, broken as they are—at least they quicken when I run my tongue over their enamel.

Paid dancers are nothing like Elwyn. Elwyn's lips were cut plums, bruised against his white teeth. Elwyn trembled like an aspen. His hair lay like wrens' breast-feathers and his skin was a sheet of water entrapped with flecks of gold.

Everything about Elwyn was latent, poised and infuriating, an eyelash away from a trigger I never found.

Elwyn was tantalizing yet had no sharp centre, no wick. None of this was a function of his body, although his body and face, his eyes and his dark hair, were of great beauty.

Whereas I am ugly and pale-bellied, a beanpole, and not a bit erotic.

Saint Catherine Street beyond that club door reminded me of Elwyn.

The street at night is a place for me to hide, a mystery to visit and never plumb. It poses no obstacle to the soul. The street has a body but it quivers, full of glimmering night. It shares the glimmer and every mote sings. The spaces between the motes are vast, and in those spaces I love being lost.

Was the way I loved Elwyn due to his being a man? This is the thing Sophie insinuates. But I am not convinced of its remotest relevance.

People are so eager to annihilate the divine space that makes up the vast, greater part of love.

8 Doppelgänger

TUESDAY, SEPTEMBER 5.
STILL MORNING.
Chinatown. Montreal, Quebec

"Regarde l'homme maigre, Maman," cries a little boy to his mother on the avenue.*"Il est comme un squelette!"*

It isn't easy to describe me, thinner now than I ever was, hard as that is to imagine. The little schoolboy's right; I've become a shadow, a skeleton in motion. I have to admit my reflection in Super Dépanneur La Cité resembles a fishbone with a flame on top, wavering and insubstantial. Could I lift a stone, tie the simplest knot in a bit of string? Or am I a wandering fish-flame incapable of leaving even a breath-bubble or singe-mark behind?

"Je suis desolée. . . ." The boy's mama has gone pink.

"Pas du tout, Madame—your son is correct. *Regarde!"* Beyond the gyrating trees looms McGill University's hospital. "I'd make an excellent subject for surgeons to use while instructing their students about anatomy. Not a morsel of fat would obscure their view of my muscle, bones, or internal organs."

The woman's hair is the tan of whipped chestnuts, like Eliza Lawson's. She'd have startled me with her resemblance were she slightly taller. Sophie says my own thin, tall body attracted me to Miss Lawson, who was taller than all the women around her and very slender. Sophie calls this lovers' narcissism—says it happens all the time. Couples do mirror-service to each other in the name of love, or what they mistake for love. Love is not love at all, Sophie says, if you're only admiring yourself in a glass.

The mother continues to chide her boy far too much, and I hasten to persuade them both I've not taken offence. "If I suffered every time even beloved friends comment on how thin I am I'd be perpetually aggrieved! Besides, I've never been vain."

I'm an idiot. What could be vainer than professing freedom from vanity? "What I mean is, it takes a particular sort of shame to cause me grief. . . ."

God help a general who starts worrying how civilians might judge his decisions. I've rooted such sensitivity out of myself. But personal shame over moral matters is different. Real shame stems from dishonouring a mother or a lover or a friend—I dread that kind of shame more than I love life. . . .

Where has the woman gone?

Is that her on the far side of the street? Is that her little boy running ahead of her to the Australian pie shop? And am I mad—talking to myself again about the difference between a soldier and an ordinary man?

"The personal, smaller shame is really the larger," I explain to the number 80 bus, whose engine drowns my argument as it labours uphill. "A soldier has a uniform to identify him. He has flags and drums, dye and hide—boisterous, deafening! We had red coats not only because red dye was cheap, but to make us forget how delicate we were; the faint blue of a young man's veins."

Was there a poet among us? Had one of us made harpsichords in his village? Did we harbour a tapestry-weaver? Was I a flute-player who loved dogs?

No. None of us was any longer the man he had been.

But now, I see the opposite impulse everywhere: such aggrandizement of personal sentiment. Does no one understand larger duty?

IF ONLY I COULD PLUNGE this minute into the pool I loved at Bath. Scorch me, water! Wash away my self-recriminations. On the shortcut to the YMCA I pass tea shops, chemists, fashion outlets full of asymmetrical hems, the window of the store called Archambault, advertising musical recordings—but wait. I see through the glass a clerk with half his head shaved. He looks slightly familiar and I pop in, ask him about the fisherman's son who sang a winter storm all last night in the tent.

"Who?"

"The famous Quebec singer."

"Ben là!" The clerk has piled what remains of his hair into a luxuriant top-knot. "There are a lot of well-known singers from Quebec."

"This one is—he's beloved."

"Do you mean Leonard Cohen?"

"I'd remember the name if I heard it again. . . ."

"Rufus Wainwright?"

"No—the name is French."

"Jacques Brel? Charles Aznavour?"

"I mean he's from Quebec!"

"But you said French. Brel is Belgian. Aznavour was Armenian but he was born in France. . . ."

"I mean he *sings* in French."

"Is that all you can tell me?"

"He is a fisherman's son. He sings a song about how this

country is not a country, it is wintertime. He's old, but not as old as Voltaire. . . ."

"Then he is Gilles Vigneault. But you must not make this his only song you know. I can let you hear others."

The clerk speaks of the fisherman's son as if he's a king.

How have descendants of Quebec fishermen, whose livelihoods I smashed in the name of England, come to be paramount in this land today? No matter where I search in Montreal for remnants of British conquest I find little. It makes no logical sense.

"Vigneault is the soul of Quebec." The clerk looks even more familiar if I imagine him shorn of his radical hair. He hands me some headphones. Have I seen him before? His tattoo—a word, I see, though I can't decipher it—is it Arabic? "You're wrong about him being old."

"I heard—"

"Yes, he is nearly ninety but has never become old. Do you know why he became a socialist and a poet?"

"I haven't—"

"Vigneault was going to university. He was—how old are you? Late twenties? Early thirties? He was a few years younger than you. He went down to Quebec City from Natashquan and saw cod for sale, fifty cents a pound. You know how much his father was getting for those fish back home? One cent a pound. Okay, he said, maybe the package and the label cost seven cents . . . but who's getting the rest?"

"Is this in any of his songs? I wouldn't mind hearing one if—"

"It's in all his songs. Cod made Vigneault a socialist. Listen." And with that, the clerk presses a button and—headphones are amazing! My ears fill with sound.

—

MY FATHER AND I KEPT the distasteful parts of soldiering from my mother.

I didn't want to ruin her health by telling her warmongering details. But my father had a professional ear and I told him about slashing in ribbons the nets of those fishermen the summer of 1758, the year before the Heights of Abraham. Every day for five months I convinced myself I was part of a big endeavour, for the greater good of England. As if England served some overarching, abstract lord who might make noble use of the food we confiscated from Vigneault's forebears along the Saint Lawrence. But no one could eat that fish, salt-stiffened, full of maggots, and so tough we bundled it to make shelters and fascines.

I look for that greater, abstract man everywhere—that phantom king of England.

Not the human king, none of the Georges, and not a queen either—I mean where is the king behind the king? How glorious he'd seem if I could find him—not a creature but a concept—more powerful than godhead or angel.

When I went in my soldiering youth to any seashore and saw clouds piled and sunlit I looked in those clouds for the phantom owner of all glory, the glory for which I have fought. No one could look upon his face without being blinded, and he had no name.

Did I really believe he lived?

I invoked him when my men carried off a fishwife who had smashed one of their skulls with her cast-iron pan. The men dragged her into junipers where I could not see what they did to her though I'd forbidden them to rape anyone.

"Marie-Yvette!"

It helped that all the Canadian women were named a variation of Mary and all the men were Joseph, so to me they became all one

Joseph and all the same Marie. As we dragged the Josephs down to our ships they called for their Maries over the tips of their tenderly pruned damson bushes in great, sobbing, manly carillons.

We kicked every cabbage out of every kitchen patch until cabbage heads rolled down the stony banks. We tore laundry props supporting wretched woollens knit from our future mutton. We splintered with men's own tools the sheds and stages where they dried their fish.

For my soul's preservation I invoked that phantom glory of England and saw it reflected in cod on the wharfs. Mirrors, the cod-eyes glittered, as reproachful glittered the eyes of Marie-Yvette's nine little girls and one boy screaming *Maman*!

I invoked my king behind the king—honour of England. I imagined him glowing down on me from the silver clouds over those farmsteads. I was not invoking a heavenly father. I believe one of the greatest perils to a man's soul is the unseemly adoption of dramatic and irrational spiritual beliefs.

But I did write to my earthly father:

Dear Sir,

If you could see this shore and its desolate bogs and stones, you'd ask yourself the questions I ask. You know I never plunder, but we were forced to seize the dried and salted cod that would have seen these families through the winter. We were instructed to let nothing remain that might reach and help sustain the fortress at Quebec.

I tried to help the fishermen and their families. I offered to let them keep their boats so they might retreat. I gave explicit command that their women were not to be harmed. But who

can guarantee the effectiveness of such a command when
one's men are barbarians and their actions easily hidden by
these wretched fir and spruce trees with old man's beard
dangling off the twigs and smoke from the burning houses
and barns obscuring the whole shore?

Our clothing was worse than unsuitable—our breeches where mosquitoes burrowed and sucked, our insupportable hats, our shoes whose leather fell sodden even as we approached the man-eating bogs. Our white leggings blotted our own blood from flies' bellies as we slapped and squashed them too late to prevent itching welts. I said nothing of this to my father—we never whined to one another about personal discomfort.

Our shorthand for the destruction of the fishing families in 1758 along that part of the river was "great exploit." My father and I had both done the same on other coasts. We knew that in the British army, "great exploit" is a fine headline for Britons to read in the *London Evening Post* over their black pudding, though we soldiers perceived no greatness in our campaign.

And yet: today Vigneault sings to me.

The fisherman's son reminds me it's not quite true that my father and I did not whinge.

My father complained loud and long. "Britain produces shiploads of money," he lamented, "but all of it for Sweet William, the king's son, and for all sorts of dreary German nobles, while here I must badger treasurers like a beggar to see a penny of my salary years after I'm owed it."

Maybe there's a smaller difference between a Quebec fisherman's family and my own than England's kings might wish its soldiers to believe.

What's Vigneault singing now? Though my French is good I find his poetry almost too elusive to catch:

When you die of our love,
I'll plant in the garden a morning flower
half metal, half paper,
that will cut my foot just enough
to let a stain of blood fall to earth
and become its own flower . . .

As he sings, that phenomenon occurs where I become certain I glimpse a person whom I've loved, but who is dead.

I have seen George Warde and Eliza Lawson many times since they passed, and also my brother, Ned. It has happened, as well, that I've seen a person who has not died but who should be elsewhere—I once chased George Warde in Paris, where he could not possibly have been, as I'd just received a letter from him addressed from his mother's house in Kent.

People have doppelgängers, or the displacement of travelling makes resemblance seem more startling than it is, or the mind and heart miss a person so greatly that they superimpose the loved one's features and gait and whole mien over an unsuspecting other person, in another country, and, in my case, another time.

I have run after Eliza twice in London when even had it been Eliza, she'd have refused to speak to me, having already said she would not love me through my mother's disdain.

And Ned, my brother—though his horse and I rode as one dejected beast after we lost him at Ghent, I saw him alive again the following year at Culloden, and then lighting his pipe outside the tavern in Vauxhall Gardens, though Ned never had a pipe. I saw him a third time—and in this case I believe it really was him—calmly firing his gun among Kennedy's men on the Plains of Abraham.

Now, as Vigneault's stain of blood becomes a flower, I glimpse through Archambault's window Eliza, breezing through the crowds on Saint Catherine Street.

I lurch after her with the headphones on—and had the clerk not kept his eye on me, I'd have yanked the sound equipment off its shelf.

He touches my ear with his lips, his grip strong. "Do you not know me?"

The beloved Lawson curls float out of sight. I know it can't be her but I want to run after her double. I crave that finality when the face dissolves from its illusion of being the face I've lost.

The clerk's grip takes me back to wrestling in the grass with George Warde. He's muscled for someone so slender and smells like something I remember, something from a moment of abandonment or brotherhood. I feel comforted by his scent and do not fight him. I've no wish to attract shop security. They might summon Montreal's strange police, who saunter around in unconvincing garments that appear to me like mock uniforms but with real guns strapped on.

The clerk's release is abrupt: he lifts a ceremonial hand toward Archambault's exit, giving me back to the street.

9 Little White Words

TUESDAY, SEPTEMBER 5.
NOON.
Chinatown. Montreal, Quebec

WHY HAS SAINT CATHERINE STREET no Café Bouleau, a sanctuary where I might find a confidant, a person who can understand? I know from experience that given the right combination of shade and comfort, even a so-called enemy will lend a sympathetic ear.

Everyone says, Oh, Montreal's the place for that—full of wonderful cafés!

Not this strip in front of Archambault's.

How I wish now for my spot where the Marquis de Montcalm and I confided in quiet.

Montcalm named our place Le Café Bouleau after the old birch at its tranquil centre. He would lay his cloak on a patch of ground softer than the tight roots woven all around, where Vaudreuil's ten-year-old Indian slave had been buried the previous summer. On his cloak he set brandy and demitasses of strong coffee he brewed on a brazier the size of his hand. Our homesickness abated the moment we smelled the dark roast.

He esteemed me more than did my brigadiers Monckton, Townshend and Murray, being of my rank and with the same to lose. The nature of our mutual loss was a mystery that intrigued us both. That goal in whose pursuit we each engaged—how golden it had shone at first, like the pears, so unattainable, in stories we had both heard told to La Pompadour by her smart little attendant in a fern-green dress. We'd been fed, the Marquis de Montcalm and I, on identical fairy-tales.

We reminisced on the extravagant details of these stories in our green shade, in lulls between our musket fire and my house-burnings down the shore. Veiled from carnage we stole an hour and a half here, two hours there, and—one Sunday in the deepest heart of my physical infirmity and Montcalm's grief over the news of his dead daughter—an entire dappled afternoon, in which we settled on our final and most covert pact: inaudible though ants perceived it, invisible yet pulsing in the hot blue of a dragonfly on my sleeve as Montcalm grasped me by the hand.

We neither whispered nor wept.

We believed ourselves unobserved.

But it's true what they say about little birds, and plenty of little birds surrounded us. I don't doubt now, when I see my history written in books so plain and definite, that the birds kept our confidence in their breasts. No telegram or seaway bore our secret, nor later did any highway or railroad transmit it.

Little birds could be trusted, then as now, to keep our down-hearted treachery to themselves, to bear our sorrows aloft, to change and uplift a man's suicidal despair—or that of two men—over the Indian slave's burial place and into a New World: and to render that world hopeful by birdsong, tiny notes sprinkling free of any foul thing mankind might hatch, blowing like pollen, waiting for men below to catch its light and love.

Yet anything Montcalm and I agreed upon at our Café Bouleau was personal and did not undermine our capacity for military cunning. Each general remained the other's most dangerous adversary.

We felt a wind nudge us and we both knew it was the first touch of September's equinoctial gales. Our personal secret floated on the eddies with the fragrance of coffee and juniper. Our premonition of the gales to come swirled beneath our conversation. We knew our pact would fruit only when French or English lust claimed this land, as it would claim our bodies.

Afterwards, I wrote to England warning the Earl of Holderness of the coming gales. Already my anchor scraped across the Saint Lawrence's bedrock. Only the accident of its grappling a ridge of outcrop prevented my vessel from dragging anchor and floundering toward the river-mouth with each ebb-tide that sucked wild at night.

There was a bond between the ebbing river and my failing body. Patch me up, I told my surgeon. I know very well there's no fixing this ruin—just knock me back together in time to gain what England craves, before the gales wreck the hell out of our ships and spew the bits in the gulf.

The difference between the river's ebb and mine was that the river flexed violent and alive and would recover.

I was so run-down I let myself do what I had promised my mother I wouldn't: complain about a circumstance while it is yet ongoing. She always urged me to make a game of restraint: wait until a trying situation is over. Afterward, it is permissible to recount things I might do to prevent the undesirable circumstance's recurrence.

But for Montcalm and myself, the war game occupied all our powers of stratagem so that—I confess—we each complained to the other. I mind very much if people know this.

He complained about the regime in which he found himself compelled to work: the lewd and gluttonous Vaudreuil, who stole more than he ever gave to his people. Bigot, whose name summed him up precisely: a small-minded thief of no nobility or discretion, constantly on the lookout for ways he could personally profit from the misery of his own citizens. These were parochial ne'er-do-wells whose minds admitted not the thinnest crack of enlightenment, or service to one's king, or the simplest human kindness; they were the coarsest rogues imaginable. In his off-guard hours with me at our spot in the woods, Montcalm regretted his place among their machinations.

"When I am gone," he told me, "after you and I succumb together to this war's blessed death, Bigot and Vaudreuil will take over here along with the clergy, and willfully cast centuries of ignorance and darkness over this place like a foul rain carrying all the blight and avarice of Old France over this abandoned peasantry."

"No," I argued. We allowed ourselves three brandies apiece and I had downed my second. "When I am gone, after you and I succumb together to our longed-for oblivion with which this war will so graciously oblige us if we play our cards right, my king will send British governors of far greater acuity than Bigot or Vaudreuil, and they will institute a more merciless and pecuniary English rule than the French will ever be able to fathom and from which no Frenchman can find succor, save from piercing his own heart to end the half-life of England's utilitarianism."

"Nonsense," countered Montcalm. "When I am gone, the second after my body succumbs on the plains, Vaudreuil and Bigot will confiscate all the spoils the British thought to commandeer from our people, and sell it back to them for the price of seven generations' wages, with the right of priests to seize their daughters and sons under fourteen years of age for their beds for the same number of generations with a slice of eternity thrown in."

"When I am gone," I replied, "with French shot in my loins and my scalp dangling in your savage allies' hands, England will establish the finest schools it knows how: every hall and lecturer bound by proclamation to entrench the tyranny of Lord, Earl and King—all tremulous or nascent wisdom and philosophy banished to the insane, the penniless, the homeless wanderer sucking his outlawed drop from the last wild brook. . . ."

And so Montcalm and I continued, our valour cast off, our lamentations studded with forbidden complaints about the bog, the flies, the excruciating loneliness of the white-throated sparrow's chorus, the scrawny, inhospitable trees.

And then we got back to work.

HOW YOU SCALP A CANADIAN is that you jam your hobnails between his scrawny shoulder blades as his nostrils fill with the scent of Labrador tea, which soon mingles, unfortunately, with the stench of his terror-propelled excrement.

You grasp a tuft of his greasy locks and haul skyward till his brow furrows like benevolent English sands at low tide. How I miss those sands!

I miss their soft-yet-hard bumps under my bare feet as I dimpled that shiny blue wetness reflecting a Kentish sky. I miss digging for winkles and boiling them in seawater beside a little fire, picking the meat out with one of my mother's hairpins while I rested my head on her thigh.

There was always an unspoken rift between the son she wanted and the man I am.

Barbarities I never confessed to my mother hang to this day in the air over my battlefields: if she got wind of them she used sleight-of-hand to whisk them into that pouch I sent her from Madame Pompadour's dressing-table. . . . Oh Mother, you loved to hear of the time our ambassador took me to kneel before the French king's mistress, didn't you. You devoured my tales of bows and curtseys and of ruffles that ran down your son's fine shirts in France.

You weren't quite so eager to hear how much the ruffles cost, or how, exactly, your son gained the wages to pay for them, or for his fencing lessons, his dance-master, and all that lustre. You treasured La Pompadour's pouch and the lace hoods I sent you from the shop beneath the studio of my dance teacher . . .

The French in their home country are so enamoured of dainty ornament. My fine presents imbued with this sensibility pacified my mother, and god knows she was hard to appease. The lacemaker had stitched little white words across that pouch: *Honour, Empire, Victory.*

When I came to Canada my mother held on to that sachet, but she never sniffed what she'd hidden in it; she just waved the pretty bag around for show. But in it she had mixed quite the potpourri, poison she knew I must swallow but whose existence she refused to acknowledge: essence of human meat and bone, seasoned with a generous helping of *herbes salées du Bas-du-Fleuve*—salted weeds from the lower Saint Lawrence River.

Once you've sunk your cleats in the savage's back, you knife the crescent that stretches from temple to temple and you slice his bleeding meat off its bone. It's fascinating how layers of meat separate off a skull—I fancy, had I been brute enough to tell my mother the details aloud, she'd have forgotten her feigned ignorance of my affairs and exclaimed, "Bravo—that is exactly how François prepares a hare for our soup!"

"Understand, Madam," I once wrote to her—I occasionally slipped up and lost sight of epistolary decorum after too long away from civilizing influences—"I'd perform this act only on an Indian or on a Canadian dressed like one. . . ."

But I remembered, no matter how long I'd been away from England, never to confess that my Redcoats scalped any Canadian they pleased: Indian, *habitant*, woman or babe.

Honour. Empire. Victory.

The word "victory" has gone out of use. Even my mother preferred to look at it only after the fact, in triumphal *Gazette* headlines, on monuments for the town square, or in a telegram from the king. Now victory has become unfashionable, shameful—never bandied about by the *au courant*.

Here is a letter I did not send:

Dear Mother,

> Surely you admit, despite looking away so discreetly from the details of my infamy, that I was not sent to Canada to participate in some sort of benevolent exercise . . .
>
> Only English civility could save the New World from Spanish barbarity or French foppery or Indians burning us alive piece by piece. England sired the only people by whom real kindness might rule overseas: I don't mean to question that . . . but before that happened, we had to win. I was not sent over the sea to assuage or cooperate.

How long scalped Canadians caterwaul depends on how much blood they lose before you peel 'em. I've seen a yowl fit to wake the Duke of Cumberland's dead father rise out of a completely skinned head. Sound travels slower than death.

For all this, I'm grateful I never had youngsters. After scalping Canadians my men woke camp at night with their own howls, dreaming of their bairns thus slaughtered. It's funny how the mind misplaces circumstances at night. My father was never more right in his head than when he used claret to put himself to sleep. The problem is deciding how much to drink without impairing your judgment the next morning. That difficult balance was one of the reasons I begged my superiors to make me second, not first, in command.

There's a gap at the head of things, always wanting to be filled, and I never asked to fill it.

Clarity has always been an attribute of mine, against my wishes. Because of it I have been entrusted with too much. Clarity sounds like claret, but hasn't nearly the same power of tonic for the mind.

HOW YOU SET FIRE to a farmstead after a fortnight of August rain is that you ignite hay in the barn, then light pathetic sideboards nailed from packing crates and balsam till the tar drips. You fling this abroad in drafty rooms till flankers engulf the curtains and bedding already windburnt from hanging on clotheslines over the turnip rows.

There's clarity, there's claret, and there's bed. I don't talk about the times I had to take to my bed. Some beds, beds in every camp I've known, aren't worth the name—rats' nests made by turning round and round in a patch of stones.

Twice in my soldiering life I've had to take to my bed not for the gravels, not for dysentery, not for bladder-stones that've doubled me over so often—these ailments I can work through: they're only discomforts, though twice they accompanied my greater ailment, the one a successful soldier conceals, the one I have concealed to this day.

One of the most satisfying things I ever ate in my life was a blueberry pie set to cool on a sill in Kamouraska. The woman who made it had fled a mile in the woods before the juice pooled in the collarbone of my grenadier and stained his teeth purple.

How you supply a scurvy-infested regiment with nourishment is that you confiscate the sheep, goats, eggs and cabbages of the enemy. It drives me wild that no matter which century I peruse, men look at my success with either praise or blame. They marvel at my genius or my brutality, asking where I got my knowledge. Whether they think me a depraved genius or a profitable servant of empire, their bafflement is constant and it disturbs me.

Not then, not now, and nowhere in the future, does anyone appear to read anything.

They haven't read Xenophon's advice on guerrilla warfare, so they think it novel when I train my infantry to retreat the instant after an attack, hiding behind any available thicket or dune instead of keeping to the silly English way of parading in formation, as easy to target as a street full of houses.

Nor does anyone seem to have heard of Sun Tsu.

It wasn't yesterday he counselled warriors to plunder an enemy's food. For centuries his advice has been in plain sight for anyone with eyes: one barrow of the enemy's wheat and goat meat is worth twenty of your own because of the palaver, and the spoilage, and the cost of transport. Yet England marvels that I manage to find my soldiers cod, pork and eggs, as if the banks of the Saint Lawrence were populated only by owls. I've eaten an owl egg and I vouch instead for jam in a peasant's larder.

How you get peasants to relinquish their precious winter supply of provender is that you nail a note to their wretched chapel door warning them that if they so much as whisper against our invasion their every lamb chop will sizzle on a Redcoat's spit. There won't be a shrew's head or a barley grain left to nourish them through January. You point out that by March they have a choice of flesh remaining on their bones or cormorants spitting out those bones to turn pocked and green in the estuary. When they hesitate you don't flinch. You send reeking Redcoats to torch every hovel on the riverbank until families stream like vermin from all hope of sustenance.

England did well to choose red for our uniforms: fish-gutting and sheep-butchering peasants are well acquainted with red. Unlike flashier generals, I wear the least fancy, plainest version of the red coat. I find that the hue on its own causes more fright than any buckle or adornment. Where is my uniform now? Oh yes, I remember—waiting for me—why have I not already put it on?

I SENT MEN TO CATCH that woman who made the blueberry pie. They dragged her back with her three small sons and her old father who'd been the cause of their capture, for he'd insisted on carrying his lame old bird dog.

"*Pitou!*" the old man wailed as we shot the animal. He did not glance at his house, or at the barn in flames, nor did he appear to care about my men going off to our fleet with wagonloads of his cabbage and swedes. His eyes never left the dog.

This nearly made me sentimental. But we already had one dead Frenchman's dog for a ship's pet, and it had made such sentimental fools out of the toughest of my Highlanders that I hardly wished to add another softening influence.

The old man's dog made me remember my dogs at home. For a perilous moment I was almost plunged out of my soldier's mind and into that man's. When this happens I force myself to look down at my uniform, and to remember that when it covers my body it also covers my sonship, my loverhood, and any private nature known by my mother, or by Eliza, or by George Warde or Elwyn or . . . I try not to think beyond this.

Those who love me know what a whimsical sort of person I am.

They know how variable I am, and how unsteady—how, like the *habitants* we scorch and kidnap, all I desire after retirement from this soldiering life is a house, a very little one, remote on the forest edge or in a meadow like Kamouraska farmhouses. But this is my younger self, the one who knew no motive other than beauty.

The loveliness of dogs! I couldn't help but think, as we shot that poor half-setter, of my own dog Ball in our yard at Blackheath—me coaxing his belly with a cherry branch to make him stop chasing the Newfoundland puppy of a friend who'd come for tea. How I miss dogs—how good they are at quenching the bitter end of loneliness.

I miss dogs now and I missed them in 1759, and had it not been for that old *habitant*'s dog, or his daughter and her pie with the juice running and the pastry piped to a pretty frill by her hand, I would not have remembered my personal self at all in Kamouraska.

I grew afraid when I looked at that woman and dog: afraid I was becoming warped into a peculiar fierceness of temper brought on by war.

I unfastened my buttons and let the equinoctial wind blow on my chest and reminded that wind to bring me warriors into whose hands I might fall early, rather than be converted by degrees into a barbaric, unholy man; a man who has forgotten his humanity.

10 A Soldier's Exile

TUESDAY, SEPTEMBER 5.
AFTERNOON.
Chinatown. Montreal, Quebec

Don't you know me?

Had Archambault's clerk really asked me that? Where would I have seen him before, or a boy like him? He looked nothing like George Warde. Nor my brother, Ned. A soldier from somewhere . . . who am I remembering? Elwyn? No. Elwyn has faded from me and will not resurface. Elwyn is gone. Was it Ronnie, my Highland drummer, that I saw in the clerk's face? Was it Sam? Maybe Sam Holland?

In the tattooed clerk throbbed Danger and Bliss—my twin lovers from camp, where men flung limbs over one another in a snoring web. If the enemy came, no matter his stealth, we'd waken as one.

This is the regiment's interlocked body: sweeter than paired love.

How I miss it now, alone on Saint Catherine. The exile of a soldier ejected from war is unbearable. I've suffered it before, and will continue to do so as long as I wander in my unease in this city of peace.

Is there no one I can summon to walk with me? Sophie has made it clear that traipsing the streets with me is not part of our deal. And Mrs. Waugh, though I hold hopes of our meeting again, is hardly the confidante of my dreams. Isn't there anyone?

Before I left England in February 1759, I beseeched George Warde by letter to come with me to Quebec, invoking all our old methods of mock dissuasion. I promised dire hazard, extreme disadvantage, destruction of his health and constitution—all the exertions he and I craved beyond sex, claret, tobacco or the harder vices.

I promised him peril and even risked committing to paper my extreme delight over the pleasures of his company.

My only regret is that I could not for national security's sake reveal the location in which our exquisite danger was to manifest. All I could say was that I did not mean the Indies but could promise him a far distant land.

He agreed to come and my heart leapt.

If I'd specified Quebec I believe he'd have extracted himself from his obligations. Had he done so we'd not have lost one another. I wish I had identified my campaign by some oblique code.

I longed for George's company as soldier and man. He was the confluence of my personal and national excitement.

This was long after I mistook that other man for George in France, outside Café Procope. My French lessons had taken place around that corner. This man stood out. He was not like the buffoons of Paris.

I grant that now and then I saw a Frenchman I'd call prettily turned, one who moved with grace. Some had generally good faces or fine hair, but most had bad limbs and were atrociously shaped, especially nobles and men born in Paris. Men from the provinces presented a better figure—the one I mistook for George had no foppishness of the city-bred nitwit in him. His gaze was serious and his posture defiant, nothing plump except the lips. George looked on you as suspect until you earned his respect. This was not caginess or unmerited suspicion but an aspect of his constant exercise of precise judgment.

I've forgiven my mother other things, even her cold treatment of Eliza which I regard as involuntary jealousy. But I do not forgive what she did to George. I specified in my will that he be bequeathed a thousand pounds, and she would not give it. She held on to my inheritance: George would have to wait for his portion until after she was dead. I cannot fathom her pettiness and I try to overlook it.

The man in Paris I mistook for George had his own reason for maintaining his figure—he was a prostitute—whereas George kept his shape out of that carefulness I found so lacking in city men, then and now.

I TRY TO AVOID WATCHING Montreal locals lounge in the undisciplined fashion that dispirits me so. Will a swim at the Y revive me? Should I attempt a half hour on the number four rowing machine, the only one I can fathom how to operate?

Sloth, everywhere! I saw the same in Blackheath and London, and remind myself it has less to do with the utter failure of the New World than with the difference between a soldier's life and a civilian's.

A young man, not seventeen, thrusts his cap out at the approach of an old woman walking with a cane. He possesses many times her agility yet demands her spare change.

She suffers a spinal curvature and hoists a dollar-store bag bulging with biscuits and oranges. She rummages as he waits, no shame in him at all, and he accepts her coins. She gives him a smile whose startling warmth glows, I think, from the false teeth you can get these days. I keep meaning to ask Sophie about the teeth. My mother would've loved them, and my own are in such hard shape.

"You remind me of my aunt Trudy," says the beggar to the old woman.

"Do I?"

"You do! I don't know why. She was a very kind person, too."

He condescends as if he's done the old woman some service instead of the other way around.

I wait till she's gone round the corner. He stashes her cash and gulps his coffee. I'm buzzing from the grip of that tattooed clerk, and the adrenaline, along with the sight of the youth's indolence, wakens the soldier in me.

No trouble to grip that neck. "What sort of a disgrace are you? Pilfering from an old woman. Eh?"

"I need money for my train home!"

"You've got a home? Where? Some shithouse? A whorehouse? Or did you crawl from under a rock?"

"Antigonish!"

Where the hell's my bayonet? I'd love to stick his bowels and fling him in the road. I become aware of voices swirling around me.

"Laisse-le tranquille!"

"My God, he's a kid—you're twice the size of him, look at you!"

Are they hissing at me? I wish the fellow would stop snivelling. And that cat—I hadn't noticed the matted cat tied to his belt. A woman in gardenia scent cradles the kid, glaring as if I'm the shameful one. He's conned her all right. Far abler than he looks . . . I'd love to sign him up right here, have him outfitted and trained and put him to use in my regiment. He has everything I require: youth, a decent form unadulterated by an excess of bad food, even an uncouth charm that makes the gathering crowd treat him like a brother.

"If I could harness these qualities of his and direct them properly," I whisper to the gardenia-scented woman, "he might amount to something."

How lovely is her chemise covered in roses. She spits. I check my person to gauge what might have drawn her disapproval and am aghast to see I am not wearing an ironed shirt, nor have my trousers been recently laundered.

If only she could see the shirts I bought in France—the good ones with the ruffles. I found them fussy but others treated me like a gentleman as long as I had one on.

A pair of police: "*Eh? Qu'est-ce qui se passe?*"

"*Ça va maintenant,*" says Gardenia-rose. "*Mais,* this homeless man was trying to beat up the boy and steal his train fare."

Incensed, I scan the crowd for a face that will verify I'm no vagabond. The policewomen's suspicion softens to weary forbearance and the older one knocks me on the shoulder with her baton: *Effacer. Se perdre! Tenez-vous.*

RUE SAINT-ANDRÉ . . . Rue Saint-Timothée . . . What building is this? The humble little library where I first found the lovely old copy of Beckles Willson's *Life and Letters of James Wolfe.* Thank god for libraries—I can sink in that fat green armchair near the S–W section.

I pick up a magazine about skiing and pretend to read it, only to notice that the other armchairs are occupied by bona fide homeless men whose tatters, bags of filthy miscellany, and outright snores the librarian seems willing to tolerate.

It's bad enough that Gardenia-rose decided I was homeless, but it is something else when you realize that you look, in the eyes of others, more dilapidated than you imagined. And then you find a place to recover—and that place turns out to be full of real lost causes.

It's not as if I haven't been dishevelled in the past, at the height of my serviceability. Washerwomen are hard to find on a soldier's travels and when he finds one he pays her well if he cares at all how others perceive him. Can it be possible I look as wasted and disreputable as the men here at La Bibliothèque Gabrielle-Roy?

Dear Mother . . . My pad is stained with the beggar's coffee. . . . *As you know, the entire world has always been my home. . . .*

But is this true? I do not feel, at this moment, that it's true at all. Can I even picture my mother? I hardly remember her address. How Sophie laughs at me every time she catches me looking for a postbox. Ridicule presents itself all around me.

> I have, by reason of my endless wandering, always loved to hear of your perennials, and of my father's onion garden. I imagine returning to your chives and alyssum, your roses and gooseberries, all the while I march through these strange lanes. . . .

That young lout's cat bothered me. How dare he tie it to his belt, depriving it of hearth or scullery where it might doze in a patch of sun? If a man has to roam, he should limit the discomfort of his family and of domestic animals as well.

> But tell me, mother, to what has this all led? I walk the streets of Montreal and cannot say it has become a seat of learning, nor an example of the English values for which I . . .

For which I . . . what?

The S–W shelves loom behind me. Beyond them, past the tiny XYZ cubbyhole, towers the History section to which I dare not gravitate.

What has history decided about me?

If I succumb, as I have in other Septembers, I can hardly expect comfort from the pages of those books that mention me, nor from Sophie who scoffs at my addiction to "reading my press," as she terms it. If I open any page in the collection concerning my life and times with the aim of checking up on my reputation, I'll reap what Sophie says any eavesdropper deserves. It's no different, she claims, from pressing your ear to a door, behind which you know the servants or your friends and family might mention your name.

"I know you're gonna do it, though," she taunts every year. "You can't resist the lure."

I feel ashamed of losing control with that young beggar. I head for Beckles Willson, the one book that never fails to salve my heart. Here's the very bookmark I placed last year, made of foil from a square of orange-flavoured chocolate.

Oh, my dear, lovely page 411 where I behold the image of George Warde. The picture lacks his robust force, but what painting can possibly contain it?

This fragile old book was written before a soul questioned my efforts to win North America for England. If my fingers sneak toward paragraphs that praise me, surely the librarian nearby on her stepladder, changing a bulb over Robert Louis Stevenson, will pay no heed.

Dearest George, you never married until you were past fifty. What soldier can keep house or family on what we earned then? Who would wait decades for us to return home? No woman would endure it—this we understood.

How strange I find it now that the things we kept secret nibble at the edges of historical record. But other things I want emblazoned across the pages have been completely suppressed.

I wait for the librarian to descend her ladder. I try not to appear impatient. She ducks behind her desk to retrieve a sandwich and is about to leave a sign on the desk when I venture, "Might you please be so kind as to remind me how to find the *London Gazette* for the summer of 1759?"

I've looked at the *Gazette* before and know what I'll find. But I feel compelled to check again. I need to see if anyone has reinstated what my prime minister excised from my reports for fear of disturbing Britons with my cruelty.

The light the librarian changed continues to malfunction, flickering.

The *Gazette* of August 1759 has not miraculously altered to contain the censored details of my Quebec campaign.

Things of which I was proud continue to cause national shame.

Meanwhile, a wrecked denizen by the window intensifies his snoring. His feet smell like blue cheese. This brings on my old melancholia, and I glance for salvation out the window.

All save one pedestrian appear to have agreed on sporting navy blue or black. One man emerges from the drab parade.

I recognize his bright yellow sweater, chartreuse trousers, his every garment yellow or golden. He is the blind man I've seen in the showers at the Guy-Favreau YMCA pool. This man gleams like a sun drawn by a child with a yellow crayon.

There's something odd about the way he hurries east on Saint Catherine—something that won't align with logic. Is he missing something, or has some new power been added to him? Some magnificent strength that I can't pinpoint. Has his brightness seduced me? Or do I need only to escape history's dusty shelves?

I rise off my sorry butt and follow the Yellow Man.

BLUE MAN

11 The Hag

TUESDAY, SEPTEMBER 5.
NIGHT.
Mont Royal. Montreal, Quebec

PARC DU MONT-ROYAL'S MAPLES HAVE PALED and a nearly full moon renders the heavens a heartbreaking indigo. George-Étienne Cartier's angel raises silver arms over me as I tread the lawn, fumble in the gazebo, and find what has been deposited: paper wrapped around . . . is this a playing card? My eyesight's not what it should be anymore. Neither my eyes nor my teeth are of the calibre one might reasonably hope to find in the head of a relatively young man.

Sophie, in the tent: "What have you been doing? Who did you see today? What's that you're shoving in your pocket?"

I quickly conceal the letter. I fear Sophie would not take kindly to my correspondence with Mrs. Waugh. For one thing, she'd be furious that I've exposed our existence here in the park to a journalist. Under the radar at all times, is where Sophie wants to live.

"What is it you're hiding?"

"I've been . . . I was rereading my mother's appeal . . ." I decide to refer to another letter, the one I keep on my person at all times, the sole correspondence from my mother that I still possess. "I've been thinking about what you said, that I need to get serious about my rightful pension, and I was . . ."

"The letter Madame Bee wrote to the department of Veterans Affairs? Hallelujah! Finally, a lucid document. Something that might yield monetary results!"

"Actually, it's . . ."

"Pass it to me, will you? For God's sake, how's anyone to help you if you hoard documents until they fall to bits?"

Carefully, I extract my mother's written plea from underneath Mrs. Waugh's letter in my trousers. The two separate papers feel utterly different to the touch: one new and crisp with the mysterious card wrapped in it, the other soft and worn. It was tricky, but not impossible, to retrieve my mother's plaintive words from the small maritime museum I visited near Westerham during my watermelon nightmare. Despite Mrs. Waugh's horror when I showed her this same letter on the steps the day we met, I believe misplaced objects yearn to be returned to the hands of their rightful owners, that repossession is not theft.

"Be careful," I tell Sophie as she unfolds the paper, whose every word I know even before she reads it aloud:

BATH, 22 FEBRUARY, 1761

Sir,

On reading your letter I could hardly believe my senses at the shamefull betrayal hinted at in the Conduct of the Ministry. Is it credible that my dear Son's glorious death has raised up Enemies who in this fashion seek to strike at a defenceless Woman, his Mother, by with-holding his proper reward which is granted to every Officer of his Rank in his Majesty's Service.

Does any one least of all his Majesty doubt that my Son was appointed by his late Majesty Commander in Chiefe?

I pass over the question of the Commission in scorn and contempt. Am I to sue on my bended knees for what shou'd be given of right and would have been had he survived the Campaign which covered England with Glory. But my pen fails me to describe such unlook'd for Baseness as to rob me of what he so hardly earned—if indeed this is the Fact and not an obstacle merely rumoured to enhance the value of the Services rendered.

I am, Sir, your obedient servant,
Henrietta Wolfe

"Jesus," Sophie throws down the letter so forcefully I am obliged to swoop down and rescue it from the messy tent floor. "You really are a hopeless case. This is the letter I'm supposed to use to apply for your pension? Another useless dream from the distant past? It's not the right one! What about here and now? What about Madame Blanchard's papers? Hers are the documents we need to include if we're ever going to see a penny." At the sound of Madame Blanchard's name I see silvered boards, a clothesline whose garments dance in summer wind.

"Have you forgotten her?" prods Sophie.

Forgotten Madame Blanchard! Her empty house—the scabbed turnips, the useless hoe, the pinhole in the pail—

Is that house one of the hundreds I ordered torched in the summer of 1759?

"Where've you really been today? You were ages longer than usual. You're in a worse state of hauntology than ever tonight, aren't you?"

Sophie insists my problem with civilization, or war aftershock, or even melancholy, is really a problem with time. She says all these problems would fall away and thus end my torment if I could only come to terms with her version of time and abandon mine.

Hauntology! Those scorched fishermen's homesteads merge into one in my memory. Do I over-fondly imagine such a house not burnt, not destroyed at my command but somehow restored into one single saltbox: parlour shaded by a lilac at the window, corner where a returned soldier can sit in a chair and read his book of poems, dog at his feet? I see this house plainly, a simple fisherman's house on the Gaspé, yet not his—it's all mine—where has the fisherman gone? I've burned his traps and filled the place with my books! I've stolen his chair for my reverie. My house, hidden in goldenrod and asters ringed by junipers fragrant with sticky cones pink as a newborn's toes . . .

Was I ever newborn?

Sophie cuts in. "Did you go to Gerard's pawn shop today to gawk at your lost flute? Is that what's the matter with you?"

"I put my nose in for a second." I say this, although it is not true. I should have known Sophie would ridicule my mother's letter. Perhaps I did know it—it's why I've put off showing it to her though she has demanded to see it ever since I foolishly mentioned finding it—she assumed I had found an appeal written by Madame Blanchard and I was afraid to correct her. Sophie's outright scorn saddens me now. In all our time together I'd hoped she understood me, the real James, deeply, as an intimate companion would. Instead she insists on dragging me with her toward a frightening emptiness. . . .

"And?"

"Gerard has a bowl with a cobalt glaze like the one Betty Hooper gave me my posset in when I was little."

"You mean Madame Blanchard, not Betty, who fed the Wolfe-child."

"No, Betty—the nurse my mother hired. Betty had all the time in the world. I've told you, she worked my entire childhood on a waistcoat she was sewing for her husband, Roger, who I never saw. She sang Ned and me a song about sheep and marigolds and a white horse. I loved her more than I loved my mother."

"You didn't go to Gerard's pawn shop today at all, did you? For God's sake, Jimmy, I'm only trying to get you to face up to things as they are now, today. That's all I've ever tried to do. Instead you go on about all the useless past history you claim to have seen. Gallows! Lightning rods! England's first potatoes! I suppose you wasted yet another day today at the library, reading up on The Triumphant Life and Times of General Wolfe. God forbid you should forget any important details."

Sophie alarms me not just with her insistence that I learn how to manage modern civilian life, but with how well she predicts my every move. I decide I'd better say nothing about this morning's dust-up with the busker. I definitely must not tell her about following the man I'd recognized, the blind man in yellow from the changing-rooms at the Y, after spying him through the window of my beloved Bibliothèque Gabrielle-Roy.

"Well, then, what else has Gerard got in there besides your old posset-bowl?"

"He has a horse-head cane. A nugget of pure ruby. A set of wine glasses from the 1988 Calgary Olympics, and several violins."

I announce this with bravado, remembering Gerard had a violin last year and shared with me the outrageous stories he makes up to charm customers: it was handmade by a Portuguese traveller, or it came from a short-lived artisanal German workshop and is made of rare black walnut, or its origin is unknown but possibly from the time of that great Cremonese who died when I was ten, though of course Gerard won't go as far as to say Stradivari made the instrument. He likes, rather, to imply that it came from a secondary talent somewhere in the greater man's orbit.

I also recall how much, last year, I liked hearing Gerard mention that secondary talent. I feel an affinity with an anonymous man who is not a hero, not a famed miracle worker, just a competent tradesman working behind the scenes. No famous museum or stratospheric prodigy covets his work. Instead, it lies unheralded in Gerard's dark little shop around the corner from the street that has been named with such reluctance after myself.

I wish nothing at all had been named after me.

MY BRAVADO ABANDONS ME in the small hours. "Have you fallen asleep? . . . Sophie?"

"Mpph . . ."

"Soph . . ."

"Huh. Now you're the lonely one? I was here by myself all evening pining for a story while you were off someplace. Now shut up and lemme sleep."

If Sophie truly wanted to hear a story, a real story and not just a sensational piece of news about the dragonfly girls, or Hangman Hawley, my brutal mentor whom I'd like to forget, I'd tell her about the river. Isn't it amazing that the same river passing below us now—south of the park and Boulevard de Maisonneuve and Saint Catherine and all the old, cobbled streets of the old Iroquois way—is the very same river it was when I knew it so long ago? In spite of what the river has experienced: every crisis, every freeze and thaw, every passing canoe and every sunken suicide, it remains recognizable. The river's form might have widened a little here, narrowed somewhat there, but anyone who knew it in 1759 would know it instantly now, as I know it, upon sight.

Back then, I battled with the river more than I did with men—I was convinced the river found me unpalatable. It spat me out on its demented ebb-tide—it guzzled rain and swelled its current evermore until my slightest manoeuvre took ten times longer than it should've.

Drizzle infected the banks with unease.

I tried to learn the river's vocabulary but it was scummed with vegetal dust that blew off the alders and bulrushes, and its wide beaches whispered to their small sister-shores commanding them to grow more incoherent the harder I cocked my ear. My incomprehension went on for days. On early autumn mornings the gold straw bore tinkling ice-beads, which I took to be the river warning me: "Watch out, Wolfe—my prettiest ice begins like sequins but soon forms lace that grows, thickens and chokes."

The curse of history is its implication, when viewed in hindsight, that any given day in a soldier's life contains certainty. Whereas, in the moment, the only thing certain about the Saint Lawrence River was that it resisted anyone foolhardy enough to try and conquer Quebec.

The river let me hear what it wanted me to hear. It flung prickles of alienation mixed with brackish mist from its estuaries—the honking of its geese threaded itself among a reek of eel-spawn and bladderwrack while my men grew mute, impatient.

My men agitated to alight on the Heights of Abraham and tear into French ground as if it were bread: they were lustful, battering the French as salt wind punished the few birches along the river, ripping their white dresses. My men wished me to be what I am not: decisive, more cunning than the river, master of tides. Certainty is what they craved, and I excelled in its opposite and still do. Rather than pounce blind, I wait and see. Men loathe this.

When did I first notice the little beach at L'Anse au Foulon?

That was the happy part. The early part. The part where I still had a confidant on whom I could rely. I spied the sweet landing-spot earlier than anyone thinks. I took Sam Holland upriver with me out of frustration at not being told the condition of that shoreline. The navy did not exert itself toward providing the army with intelligence. It almost seemed to glory in my inability to find a way to attack Quebec from upriver. Too much wind and tide, they said. Stony cliffs. Spruce roots to trip your men into dislodging rockslides that will send them flying down the banks. . . .

Meanwhile, my men wanted me to feel hatred for the French. My men's derision and the iron in the land were corrosive. The land and the men stood against me, but one soldier, Sam Holland, was a loyal friend. I sensed early that he was a person who understood there is exhilaration in shifting plans and in treacherous tides. Sam Holland knew the power of a secret scheme of last resort.

Certainly the Foulon beach was all hazard. But a general whom ladies chide as bookish does not discount faint possibilities. He does not think anything is simple or certain. I did not think it would be easy to reach Abraham's Heights, even though we had Abraham's own grandson tied up on our fleet, having tricked him into believing we were French merely by raising that country's flag. How little deception is needed when men believe so fervently in bits of bright cloth. This is what I mean about men's ideas of certainty and how they fail us.

But what I do find certain is that beauty hides in risk.

I have no time for safe military games, tame as a round of piquet with my mother. I pant for a chance to amass elusive scraps of military strategy into a satisfying whole. The longer solutions escape me the harder I thrill. If answers outrun me, if I flounder on a dark shore in an uncertain night, I am home.

I might not be certain in word or in command, but I do not lack confidence when it comes to navigating the loneliest, most dismal stretches of shore known to any servant of the king. Certainty is sustenance for coxcombs who have no affinity for a north wind.

"What are you looking at?" Sam Holland asked me. I knew I could trust him by the genuine engagement on his face. He was interested in the reality at hand, not in his future status or promotion. I find it amazing how thoroughly self-interest prevents a man from seeing. It makes him blind. I never minded having my parents' hopes melted when it came to my military career. Nor did I ever fear finding myself lost in woods or in fog around Point-Levis or the Etchemin River or the Foulon. The soldier in me is used to sensations of loss, of being the stranger. It is only when I'm out of uniform that I mind being unrecognized in a Canada that disdains to know me.

I handed Sam back his spyglass so he too could see the embankment opposite the Foulon, where the pretty river Etchemin glittered. I'd caught scent of smoke from a camp of French and Indians and begged Sam to lend me his glass. I'd trained it on the wisp, coiled and slender, where a few of Montcalm's old men and boys and a couple of Indians smoked a heap of silver éperlans, and I have to admit I went into reverie.

I would have flown to that camp for solace had we not been at war, had I not been a general, had I no responsibility on earth save healing my personal weariness.

"Do you see the women laundering their garments in the river?" I asked Sam.

Their linen blazed. Slender boys paddled two canoes. I nicked my hand clenching the filigree on the locket bearing my fiancée's portrait—not Eliza but Katherine, the one my mother had reluctantly approved. Katherine: sensible—not the French *sensible*—Katherine Lowther was not sensitive or thin-skinned at all, but sensible in the English way. Katherine and I both wanted a home life. We did not need the kind of estate my mother envisioned. Here, through Sam's spyglass, I saw the life that pleases me: sons, my home-smoked fish, dogs, guns, shelter. I needed a roof no grander than the huts over this raw edge of a new and different Europe. Although too rough, in truth, even for sensible Katherine.

On the Quebec side, opposite that sweet river camp, sat the lonely beach at L'Anse au Foulon, the dark north shore rising above it to Abraham's Heights.

THE TWO SIDES OF THE Saint Lawrence are different countries. The north side on which Quebec stands is not benevolent like settlements I marauded along the south. It has none of Kamouraska's golden and pleasant incline, no grasses or dreaming horses. The north is the salt side, the tide-harsh cliffs whose rockface and spruce loom so tight there's no place a husbandman can lie down and read his poem or drink a draught.

When Sam Holland and I turned our backs on the pastoral Etchemin River encampment, I grew cold and felt knowledge drain out of me. If Sam had been of a melancholic nature as I am, I might never have thought a Foulon landing possible. But he was one of those souls whose natural warmth emanates toward the man near him.

I knew Sam had a girl at home who was unlike Katherine—one who craved to fling her thighs round him. Katherine and I had a different sort of ease. If I made it home she could count on me for kind attention and my soldier's wages. Ha! In those days I actually believed that there would be a wage coming to me to reward me for my service. Well, those were the days of innocence, and Katherine was part of that innocence—or should I call it gentle peace? She knew I'd sit reading half the night rather than come to bed. It was she who slipped me my favourite poem as I left England—and for a long time I hid the volume in my bunk so as not to arouse scorn.

Sam and I faced the north side's rock. Hostility suffused the embankment beyond Quebec all down Montcalm's guarded shore. Canadian loathing migrated toward my men camped at Montmorency Falls. It spilled over Île d'Orléans and Isle-aux-Coudres. Terror welled up in the ground, engulfed the soles of my feet and infected me.

Yet the Foulon was perfect.

I trained Sam's glass on it for longer than was prudent, given the necessity of concealing the plan forming itself in my thoughts. When Sam questioned me I told him not to mention to any of my men how long I had considered the seemingly insignificant spot.

So I had a good long look, that first time, at that beach at L'Anse au Foulon. I did not even write to my mother about it. I was alone with the river, and something in that dark little cove called out to me—it was a strange, comforting call of victory and shadow.

When Sam and I got back to our camp at Montmorency the men could sense my departure from their ways of thinking. The more they mistrusted me, the more I wanted to scout around the unguarded and unremarked Foulon again, by myself, to tread its bleak stones with exquisite uncertainty and make a plan.

My men complained about the secrecy of my plans. They thought it was vacillation. Sam Holland told me they likened my indecision to the tide that twice daily helped the Saint Lawrence render our fortunes unknowable. The more I secretly considered the Foulon the less my men believed in me. The harder Brigadier Murray ached for me to send him upriver, the less I agreed, given that the naval support we had up there seemed to be falling apart. I wasn't sure what was going on up there. I did not mind being honest about this. But my men would have preferred bombastic lies.

"What do you reckon are our chances if we attack?" Murray demanded.

"I can't presume to know a sum. Given the wind, the unprofessional tactics of our enemy and their resulting unpredictability . . ."

"Can you not give us a single definitive word?" Brigadier Jim Gibson poised his pen to pin down my answer.

"Infallibly . . ." I paused.

Murray rolled his eyes and Gibson brightened.

I faltered. "Probably . . ."

Brigadier Townshend hauled out his sketchbook and moved around to my side so he could nip in the bud any illusions posterity might spread about the strength of my chin.

I did not muster the strength—or was it the weakness? I can't always tell—to utter these words I hold privately within my heart:

Uncertainty is my mistress.

Risk is her middle name.

And in truth, once I fastened my mind on the Foulon, the Saint Lawrence River altered.

She allowed me to plan and dream, and no longer drowned my thoughts in her flow. She gave me assent. The wind and the river's assent separated me even more from my men. I held no council of war. The river knew I'd go to the Foulon once more, alone.

When I love anything, be it man, woman, or river, I want to make it mine. I want to separate it from the world of all that belongs to others, and hold it to myself. I look on it as crystalline, a vision of the heart that only I can see. I have to do this or my love won't ignite.

Is this a failing? I think some call it insanity. But from childhood I did this: I moved away from the crowd so I could hold my love before me and examine it in precision and solitude, like a cut gem with my vision of the loved one suspended inside.

I did this with my secret beach. After I went with Sam Holland, I returned alone. When everyone thought me too ill to act, I acted. While they lamented ordinary discomforts, shrews in the bread and saltwater rotting their shoes, I took a catamaran and one dripping oar and went back to my Foulon.

"ELWYN?"

Usually Elwyn doesn't come to me unless I've been asleep.

Normally I judder in and out of slumber and sometimes I think I've woken up to find Elwyn armless on the ground, outside the tent, trying to open the flap with his teeth. The last bit of the knot eludes him every time, slippery and tight, impossible for teeth to unfasten, and of course there's nothing I, a sleeping man, can do to help him. I'm paralyzed in the bed.

Sophie calls this recurring nightmare "the Hag."

She has rolled over and missed my story about the river. I wish Mrs. Waugh could hear me, wherever she is, out there in the night. I carefully bring out her letter once again, and, for comfort, try to decipher it by the light of the park lamp shining through the tent. But Sophie stirs—paper is so loud! I shove it back into hiding and await dawn.

12 Dragonfly Girls

WEDNESDAY, SEPTEMBER 6.
MORNING.

Mont Royal. Montreal, Quebec

AS SOON AS THE SUN RISES I examine the letter of Mrs. Waugh—it is slow-going to decipher her spidery handwriting, and I dread waking Sophie.

Dear James,

Thank you for your letter, which arrived this afternoon. Can you believe I spent nearly all day today at the McCord Museum in the company of a piece of Wolfe's—of your—red hair? Here in Montreal, on Sherbrooke Street! They have it encased in a glass circlet bound by green ribbon. I wish they'd let me touch it. Red hair's often coarse isn't it. My mother had it, and I fancy if I'd had a son or daughter—but what I wanted to ask is this: it's about the letter you sent me . . . would you mind, terribly, if I had your handwriting analyzed? You see, I've been in contact with a graphologist, a Monsieur Choinière . . .

I remember spying, on her desk among my letters last autumn at the Fisher Library, Mrs. Waugh's own letter asking this man to analyze the handwriting of "someone who is no longer alive." Her note goes on:

> ". . . whose life's work is the psychological assessment of a person through analysis of his or her handwriting and—forgive me if this sounds in any way disrespectful to your own story, which I believe, I do—I believe you have, in some way I might not yet fully understand, brought General Wolfe, who died on Abraham's plains in 1759, here, to Montreal today. I have shown Monsieur Choinière some of Wolfe's older letters, and I wondered if I might also show him the letter you have sent me. Don't worry, Monsieur Choinière is quite sensitive—he says handwriting is a picture of a certain moment in time: people change, they evolve, they go through crises . . . and he looks for the larger picture. You know, yourself—you told me that day on the steps—history books have hardly told your whole story. Military histories, especially . . . with their concentration on strategy, on the geometry of battle . . . whereas Monsieur Choinière's approach is more a sounding out of the inner man . . . but I would never show him your private letter to me without your permission.
>
> Would it be possible, I wonder, for us to meet tomorrow at noon at the Green Spot on Rue Notre Dame? We could discuss matters further, and I would be honoured to treat you to a smoked-meat sandwich with one of their legendary sour pickles.

Tomorrow? That's today! I glance at Sophie, now stirring as I quickly examine the card Mrs. Waugh has wrapped inside her note. I see that it's not a playing card at all, but has some sort of pictorial significance: it depicts a man of my age, about to become not-so-young, standing in a cloak at a river, his head bent in sorrow. Across the river stands a ruined fortress, beyond a bridge that appears inaccessible. The man has spilt three goblets on the ground—has he spilt blood? Two goblets remain upright behind him. The man does not appear to know where to go or how to move beyond loss.

Yes, I should go for that sandwich. The melancholy card, my sudden hunger at the thought of delicious smoked meat—how is it that Genevieve Waugh knows, so exactly, how I feel in both body and spirit?

Sophie twitches, commences grumbling; "You're not planning on hanging around here all day, I hope? It's already Wednesday."

"I'm aware of that," I say as I conceal the letter and card.

"Better get your act together is all I'm saying. You have a few more nights here with me then I've got my next combat-shattered marauder to deal with."

"Do I know who he is?"

"Why assume it's a he? You're such a BMW." BMW is what she calls big white males. "You should be halfway to the Plains of Abraham by now. But no, Jimmy Bee is scared of the real plains. He prefers to revisit them in his imagination, all blood-stained and heroic. Is that why you're scared of getting your paperwork sorted out as well? That it might fail to reflect your true glory? Have you any intention of getting your ass over to see Madame Bee while she even remembers you?"

"Madame Blanchard is not senile."

"I'm just saying time's a fox, not a centipede."

Right! Mrs. Waugh's strange card in my pocket lends me confidence. Touching it reminds me that it would be folly to tell Sophie about my new developments. Or the Green Spot. Or Mrs. Waugh. Or my pursuit, yesterday afternoon, of the blind man in yellow.

I ran after him through the lower shadows of those impressive buildings that form Montreal's skyline as you approach by the Champlain Bridge: the McGill College peak and the Roccabella tower and the Marriott Hotel and all the others—so friendly-looking from a distance, huddled and inviting—but if one walks near them, they impose on you. They shut you out like a phalanx of giant judges. The man in yellow blazed through this modern urban architecture and I was drawn right behind him.

He hastened, and I realized as I followed him past the skyscrapers and down past melons and lumpy gourds spilling out of boxes in Chinatown, that the odd thing, the thing that had defied logic but which I'd been, at the window of La Bibliothèque Gabrielle-Roy, too self-preoccupied to pinpoint, was that he was without his seeing-eye dog.

I saw as he ducked in Rue de la Gauchetière that we were about to return to our old common ground, the shower room at the Y.

I missed that dog of his.

The fact that he took his dog to the Y had been a warm spot in my wanderings. I liked watching him operate with the dog's help. I loved how the dog waited for him, alone, when he went in the hot tub or the pool. The dog was a beacon of mute loyalty and now, with it gone, the yellow man threatened to become like all other men, walled-off and separate. If, as it now appeared, he could see, then I would not be able to spy on him anymore. I realized I'd liked doing this, much as I liked looking at bodies naked in the change-room and nearly naked in the pool. I liked to think my gaze was benevolent. When a man is blind can he tell you're looking at him? Does he know you're watching and feeling, in that one-sided glance, a connection with humanity otherwise estranged?

Yesterday, on catching up with him in the dressing room, I made an awkward attempt not to look him in the eye but botched it. This happens to me on the subway and on buses, too. Sophie says I have not learned how to live in a modern city.

So, I caught his eye and he caught mine: he was certainly not blind now.

"Hello again," he said.

"Have you seen me before?"

"You've certainly been here before, haven't you?"

"Usually you have been here with a dog that I assumed was a . . . a working dog. . . ."

"Veronica—yes. She's a lovely dog. She's been very good to me, Veronica has."

As he peeled off his yellow clothes he spoke slowly, with a quizzical aspect, as if testing statements out on himself to see if he believed them.

In the shower he felt for his soap with searching hand-pats. He held his face as if gazing across a height into a distance. He felt the taps for degrees of hot and cold and did not look at their red and blue labels.

He bore the appearance of a man on whom heaven had bestowed bliss—I'd noticed this about him before. He stood with his hands raised to the shower in divine rapture like Saint Francis on a stained glass window I saw in the chapel of that Flemish town where I mourned my brother, Ned. Normally I no longer fully felt the pang of losing Ned, but it overwhelmed me now. Something in the blind man—innocence?—recalled Ned, barely fifteen when he left me, though this man had to be thirty.

I was drawn to his sphere of childish delight and when he held his soap an inch from his face and laughed at it, I blurted, "You seem to be having a good time."

He looked at me as if I were a dear friend whose name he couldn't quite remember.

"Yes," he drew the word out while he deliberated on the time he was having. "The bubbles."

There were indeed bubbles, little ones, coursing down his arms like sea-froth.

"I haven't seen bubbles," he said, "in twenty-six years. I'd completely forgotten how lovely they are."

"You see them now?"

His eyes crinkled in wonder. "Yes I do."

"And the dog . . .Veronica . . . you don't need her anymore?"

"Veronica was absolutely dedicated . . ." He trailed off, remembering her goodness. Then he said, "Do you know, I was blind from the age of four until yesterday? And now I can't believe how beautiful everything is. Look at the bubbles!" His voice squeaked. "Purple, gold, green, blue . . . all so exquisitely round, more perfectly round than any of my knitting."

I secured my YMCA towel around me and sat on the hot-tub edge dangling my legs. It's not often I get to sit high enough for that. The chlorine smell scratched my nostrils. I know people dislike its sting but it makes me feel blanketed and undiscoverable. I liked the broken clock above the doorway claiming the time was six thirty when in fact it had to be no more than around two in the afternoon. When time is measured incorrectly I feel doom lift: if time can't reach me then neither can the loss of George, or Eliza, or Ned, or Elwyn.

"What happened to you?" I asked the man. His yellow sweatshirt and pants were in their customary heap on the floor.

Bathers straggled in from the Chinatown apartment complex next door, bellowing to each other in Cantonese and smacking themselves all over in a kind of skin-stimulating exercise with wads of paper towel they'd pulled out of the dispensers. They ignored us. On the walls hung signs forbidding anyone to spit, which they disregarded. Members of an aqua-fit class filed out of the pool dripping wet and stood under communal hair-dryers or spin-dried their swimsuits in a centrifugal force apparatus that sounded like I imagine the industrial revolution must have done. So we had to shout.

He roared, "I was raped when I was four!"

I was glad the Cantonese chatter continued so the men had possibly not heard. I felt such revulsion that had he not screamed in my face I might've sidled out to the locker room pretending I'd not understood. Or I might have responded in some noncommittal way: *Right then—sorry for your troubles* . . . and floated off. Being British has its conventions.

But his volume matched the force of his words.

His shout solidified in the tiled room.

It hit me in the head and sent me into my old shock—flung me back to that first time my father ever took me from my cocoon with my mother at Westerham to the town of Portsmouth. I was thirteen, and had not until that journey apprehended anything first-hand about man's depravities.

HAD NAUSEA NOT, EVEN IN THOSE DAYS, overtaken me at the sight of the ocean, I might not have seen what I saw in Portsmouth.

My father ached for me to volunteer with him against Spain at Cartagena. He'd been waiting for me to pass age twelve so I could become a soldier like him. But I turned into a pale, limp mess even as our ship waited to sail. He had to leave me there with a man he barely knew, entrusting him to see me safely home.

But the man was anxious to drag me to a coffeehouse called the Dragonfly.

We stepped over a woman slumped over her bottle, her infant on the ground rooting for its mother's nipple. We navigated an alley that stank of piss and beer. In it I spied someone—two someones, under a cloak; one straining to get away but the other pressing down . . . they writhed, guttural.

The Dragonfly was lit inside for a party, all men but for a fat woman lifting a tray of pies. I was the youngest and soon the men started calling me Old Soldier. Then I saw other youths at the front, two girls and a boy. My guardian went off to fetch brandy and I became squashed between officers boasting Admiral Vernon's triumph in Portobello and Sir Chaloner Ogle's fleet assembling at Spithead. I felt queasy—I always had a bad stomach even then, and was ashamed to be getting sent home, and the shame made me sicker. I vomited in the pot where an aloe towered behind the buffet that bore slices of boiled tongue and a tureen of coffee.

One of Blakeney's 27th officers lifted a silver platter high in the air as if it was extremely important though it was empty.

He laid it on the table.

I wondered why it had no sweetmeats or tarts on it. It glittered bare for half an hour while the men made a hubbub that stung my head. I threaded through them to see if the girls and the boy would play with me but the fat woman pinched me and said, Leave them to their work.

The fairest girl had hair of strawberry blond, lighter than mine with a glow like sunset on buttercups. The boy was one of Colonel

Halpern's slaves, shorter than me, and dark black. The other girl was black-haired and fair and she picked the skin round her thumbnails when she thought no one was watching. But all the men in the room were looking at her, though I don't think they saw her picked fingers.

The men peeped out the corners of their eyes, pretending not to see the girls or the boy. After a while they glanced more directly, but still hesitant or unsure, as if the youths had come in the wrong door and were here by accident and needed showing out to the sweet shop on Broad Street for a lick of barley sugar, which was where I badly wished to be.

Then the girls and the slave started peeling their clothes off. The men stopped talking and set their coffee cups down and gravitated to the end of the room away from the youths, but none took their eyes away. The farther they moved to the end of the room, the more they stared.

Shadows pooled between the girls' ribs as in wet sand at low tide. Their hair hung down as in a painting my nurse Betty once showed me of mermaids.

The slave took his garter and stockings off and stood in pitiful drawers.

The men made a half-circle.

One officer took that big platter and raised it over all the empty cups and remnants of food and he held it aloft amid the men.

The girls bent and moved at their end of the room, not once looking at the men but shifting their rosebud breasts and small hips and swivelling so all the men could get a good look at what they had. The boy let his drawers slide to the floor so that he had no clothes on, and then the men held their members and swelled them—their faces bloomed redder and redder and they pumped themselves until one by one they ejaculated into the big glittering dish. Then that officer of Blakeney's measured the amount of wet in the dish with a measuring stick and wrote figures down in a green notebook.

I DON'T DIVULGE MY MILITARY RANK to civilians as a rule. But swimming with Harold—for that was the name of the yellow man—was like swimming with strangers at Bath: men spoke their hearts and no one had his guard up. Naked, water lapping around us, our words slipped free.

In the azure echoing pool Harold drew my shame out of me.

I told him things I've never told Sophie, or that Sophie, in the name of what she calls tough love, ridicules or chooses not to believe.

Unlike Sophie, Harold did not cajole me to remain in the present.

He did not admonish me to get real.

He realized exactly who I am in the inner man.

I suppose I stared at his eyes, trying to see how they could have gone from blind to sighted overnight. I was dying to ask but couldn't bring myself to do it. He saw my hesitation.

"I didn't make it up, my story," he said. "I'm not crazy."

"I believe you . . . you had vision before you were four, but not after that. Not until yesterday. I know you're not crazy. But . . . how did such a thing happen?"

"I've been working with a neuropsychologist for years. Yesterday he brought me to a place where I no longer need to block out my surroundings for fear of any horror they hold. He convinced me my surroundings are safe. What I can hardly believe is how beautiful they are. The sky. The clouds. People. Everything is so incredibly beautiful that I don't think anything can ever bother me again. I was down by the river all morning. Have you seen that river?"

Had I seen the river!

How could anyone who had not been with me at Quebec City in the year of my death understand about the Saint Lawrence River's profound migrations of geese, its estuaries, its fire-ships at night?

"I've seen it," I told him. "But mostly miles downriver, a long time ago . . ."

"The geese," Harold said, "and herons! Light on the water—all the willows and flowers! After this swim I'm going to walk to the botanical gardens, have you seen those?"

"I've slept in the First Nations part, with the wild raspberries and juniper and birches, on nights when I'm not allowed to sleep at the place where I stay now."

"At the botanical gardens," Harold said, "I want to visit a particular flower that begins with *B*. I intend to go through the whole alphabet." He spoke with a kind of awe. I sensed he saw a fragile future before him, but a future nonetheless.

After exiting the Y, we drank green tea at Magic Idea in Chinatown while Harold knitted. He said he'd learned to knit when he was blind by the feel of the needles and wool.

I tried not to doubt him.

Had his blindness plunged him into real darkness? Or did neurological blindness mean his eyes worked but his brain refused to decipher what they saw? If the latter was the case, had he really been blind at all?

I confessed to him another secret. "I saw the wraith of my beloved, Eliza Lawson, come to me in a vision at night on the open sea." This was the kind of thing Sophie refuses to believe. Get on with the *now*, she says. But the yellow man weighed my statement, unwinding yarn he'd caught around his button. "Eliza wore a gown sequined with herring-scales," I said. "I wasn't dreaming."

"I know you weren't," he said, his voice full of confidence, although his eyes appeared to entertain a silent question mark.

"We'd left land far behind. We were in the oceanic night." He brightened at the word oceanic.

"It's a well-known fact," he said, "about seaweeds, they don't need a stiff backbone like land plants. Or like us!" This fancy seemed to amuse him, while it made me think of alternative humans floating like eels or sea-horses, undulating and without stiff backbones. "The water supports them," he added.

I told Harold other things. He seemed very interested in the death of my brother, Ned, particularly my recounting of the box of Ned's things I sent home to our mother, the box containing special amulets, his sash, his gorget, books and maps. Then I told him of my aborted attempt, these past few years, to visit the scene of my own death, to see whether I could possibly make any sense out of what happened in 1759, the thirteenth of September.

"The thirteenth," he said. "That's a lucky number. People are far too scared of it. And it's in exactly a week from now. That's seven days. Seven and thirteen are wonderful numbers. They make me excited. If you want, I'll go with you after my trip to the botanical gardens. I know somebody in Quebec City whose couch I can sleep on."

He knit a circle three inches wide out of a tiny ball of wool. He snipped the ends with folding scissors strung to his belt loop. He gave me the circle. I put it in a pocket where it comforts me even now, though it appears to be of no earthly use. Harold's unhurried appreciation of the world imbues the little patch. It makes me feel less remote from some unknown comfort. It makes me feel somehow recognized.

I asked him, "You mentioned the alphabet—you mean to visit plants whose names go all the way from A to Z?"

"Not only plants!"

"What else?"

He thought about this, as if watching a parade of possible answers, and said, "Yesterday when I decided to begin with the letter A, I climbed to the top of Mont Royal and inadvertently caused a small avalanche." He seemed amused by this, as he cast on five pink stitches.

13 Oyster

WEDNESDAY, SEPTEMBER 6.
NOON.
The Green Spot. Montreal, Quebec

"THE DEVIL, THE RAM, THE GRIM REAPER in his crypt, the sharp-toothed lunging beast and the hollow-eyed eroded monkey at the door . . . all these and a thousand other stone entities crowded and overwhelmed me so that I feel their disturbance still," says Genevieve Waugh as she bites into her Green Spot smoked-meat sandwich. She has warmed up, this woman, become somewhat excited, as compared with her former reserve when we met last year. She seems to think she knows me well. Apparently she has been all over the place tracing my steps through history, in order to write about me with something she calls "emanations." She has been, for instance, over the water to Scotland to stay in a half-ruined castle so that she might know how I felt in those bleak winter months of 1753 when I did the same. I am not sure how I feel about her enthusiasm.

"Emanations?"

"Yes, in the same way you feel emanations from living people. I mean the way I feel emanations from you right now, or the way you feel mine . . . it's like a smell, except without sensory shape or impulse, and simply hangs in the air, giving off a heart-feeling or an ineffable but unmistakable energy, the energy of that unique, particular person, and no other. I mean, Wolfe has begun to have that for me, now."

"Wolfe?"

"I mean the old Wolfe," she eyes me quickly, "not—I mean, I don't know him the way you do, I mean he doesn't *inhabit* me, but—"

"There is only one Wolfe. There isn't an old one and a new one."

"Of course, I mean that for *me* there is, perhaps, having newly travelled over the historic places and now, getting to know you a little . . ."

"I don't think you know me. I hardly think . . ."

"I mean that I'm finding out new things about him. Things I'm sure, of course that you already—"

"What kind of things?"

"Well, there was a letter to Henrietta all about his being holed up in solitude and dilapidation, and feeling like a clam!"

"No. Not a clam. I can quote that one to you directly: 'Let me alone six or seven days in my room, and I lose all sensation, either of pain or pleasure, and am in species little better than an oyster.'"

"An oyster! That's right."

"Of course it's right."

"Look, I'm not questioning—"

"I wrote it. I would know if it's right or not."

"Like I said, I'm still finding things out, thank you for correcting me. For turning the clam back into an oyster . . ."

"It was always an oyster. How can you write a book about me if you can't get a simple detail like that correct?"

"It's for that very reason that I wanted to have lunch, and to see how you feel about a few new things I've been researching that weren't in any of the historical records."

"What new things?"

"Well, like information about babies with January birthdays . . ."

"Mine was January the second."

"Exactly. I mean winter babies born in the northern hemisphere are known now to be more susceptible to seasonal affective disorder, or SAD, a depression that comes from spending your first few months on earth in dreary sunlessness—a baby like that is prone to suffer disheartened bouts of inconsolable unhappiness, especially in prolonged grey weather."

"The thing that gives me inconsolable unhappiness now," I interrupt her, "isn't the desolate winters of my childhood, nor even the hateful blizzards on the Atlantic, or the windswept rocky wastes of Louisbourg or fog on the coast during my siege. It isn't the deserts of history but modern-day wastelands that strain me beyond endurance now. Tell me, when you went to Scotland, what was the place like once you left the castle ruins and found yourself in a modern village?"

"Well . . ."

"Because when I went two years ago, looking for Culloden and all my old haunts, I found that the whole of Scotland now has a smell I do not remember it having in the past—manure, slightly rancid butter, hops and malt. It is as if the body of land and heather has become a rather old and decaying person who emits a sickly-sweet odour, from breath, or pores, or sweat, every time they manage to shift position on their bed, to which they have taken themselves some years ago and neither their clothing nor their greasy quilts has been laundered since."

"Edinburgh certainly—"

"To the bus driver I said, 'Culloden battlefield?' and he replied, 'Close enough.' In front of me sat a woman with her hair rived up in black velvet roses and a glittering plastic butterfly. The bus lurched through hair-raising suburbs of Smithton: uniform housing coated in damaged stucco. Then the town of Culloden itself—a village of letterboxes and hair salons, like the rest of Scotland. Then—up, uphill—I felt great relief when the houses died away and the roadside grew greener and inward toward the roadway leaned birches."

"Miserable pebble-stucco housing estates," commiserates Mrs. Waugh. "Rubbish lining the roads. Cadbury purple foil chocolate wrappers I kept mistaking for crocuses. Hedges on whose twig-ends people have rammed pop bottles. And then the castle, which seemed friendly and did not appear haunted at first, began gathering about it a plethora of eyes and souls in its stone, wood and earth, watching and bearing influence on anyone foolish enough to stay. And so I couldn't stay."

"Where did you go? Did you have a tent, such as I had when I went?"

"I followed in your footsteps, and went to Culloden. En route at Inverness I found a bed and breakfast—it seemed promising on the outside. But inside, the administrator, a tough little woman, showed me through a sitting room she'd colonized with her bathrobe, her slippers, and newspaper spread over the couches, and not one but two programs broadcasting: football on the radio and a soap opera on television. My room, number ten, was up narrow back stairs. The key was so big and unwieldy I had to kneel on the floor to unlock the door. Fluorescent fire instructions glowed all night on the wall . . . and I had wet beans and tinned mushrooms for breakfast . . . and there were old people everywhere with walking-sticks . . ."

"And on a plinth behind the Culloden bus stop there's a unicorn . . ."

"I saw that unicorn," says Genevieve Waugh.

"... put there in case one had not realized that behind Scotland's dour stodge there rises something *else*."

"Deer," says Mrs. Waugh. "Primroses. Old women hunched over trowels. Smoked haddock soufflé."

"Gargoyles," I correct her, "ancestral dryads."

"I have a confession," says Mrs. Waugh. "I didn't want . . . at first, before I got to know him. . . . I didn't want Wolfe to be spindly and light. And I didn't want him to fall in love with a woman who was like that—Elizabeth Lawson. Where was the fun in that? The hot-bloodedness? The passion?"

"I'm delicate in health. Anyone who writes about me has to accept that. Delicate not only in health, but in my whole person."

"But when I go back to the letters—"

"*My* letters."

"Well . . . They are clear and direct. Strong. Thoughtful and not impulsive—and in them is repeated a thing I like: Wolfe kept insisting that in at least part of every important decision one must leave something to risk, to chance."

"Of course he did." An unnerving suspicion niggles me: has Mrs. Waugh come to decide that she knows as much, or perhaps even more, about James Wolfe than the man himself understands?

"He wanted to leave space for unknown forces to play a part . . . The more I study the letters, the more I see him as a man not afraid to admit he's ambivalent, comfortable with self-doubt, and frail of mental as well as physical constitution."

"I told you I'm delicate."

"Changeability was Wolfe's friend . . . and he possessed a strange kind of ambition . . . he trusted not in titles or in status, but in his own keen discernment of even the most evanescent opportunity. . . ."

"Look here, I wish I were still that man you describe. But please don't—are you looking at me with pity?"

"I feel," says Mrs. Waugh, "alone with James Wolfe in all the world, as if nobody cares about him right at this moment as I do. I feel, after reading and following and casting runes on his behalf . . ."

"Rune-casting?"

"And drawing that tarot card—have you still got it? The five of cups . . ."

I take the melancholy man out of my pocket and place him between my fork and the sugar dispenser.

"I feel Wolfe has been waiting for me to find him, and talk to him, and help him understand what the hell happened."

I feel uncommonly exposed by Mrs. Waugh's gaze. The woman almost makes me miss Sophie's tactics of argument and neglect. I stare at the melancholy man with the cups. "What's the tarot card supposed to mean?"

"It's a card of loss, there's no doubt. But if I could talk to James Wolfe, I'd tell him—no, I'd ask him—what's in those two upright cups behind his desolate form as he stands on the riverbank? What remains and has not been wasted? Did I tell you I drew you a second card?" She shows me a young man dancing away from the sea in his too-tall helmet, balancing two pieces of gold in an infinite loop of green ribbon.

"The two of pentacles. I didn't give it to you because it seems not like Wolfe at all. Too happy . . . somebody else's card maybe? Do you recognize it? I've no idea what it means."

"Neither do I." Although the happy card in fact does remind me of someone. "What about the rune-casting?"

"I cast Tyr, the sky-god. That rune means leadership, warrior, balance, self-sacrifice, logical thought, rationality, victory—these attributes belong to Wolfe all right. He became a consummate warrior. He overcame his physical and mental frailties by exercising mental balance and fleeing from emotional extremes. He made constant effort to practice logic about all military action, as if he were not a man but a principle or agency working on behalf of his country. The logical outcomc of this stance was victory for his country, and death for the man. . . . Don't look so downcast. You're still alive, aren't you? Oh—" She rummages in one of the sacks she carries around. "By the way, I emailed Monsieur Choinière, the handwriting expert, last night, and this morning he sent this—I printed it out for you. He's funny, isn't he?"

Dear Mrs. Waugh,

I have had a busy spring and summer and I am now preparing to give a lecture at a congress at the University of Wroclaw in Poland with a stopover of 4 days in Paris. Poor me! This was decided almost at the last minute but I am looking forward to it as it is my first time in Poland and Wroclaw looks like an interesting city to visit. It was designated the European cultural city last year.

I'll be back to Montreal next week and I should have more time to discuss the handwriting of Wolfe and that of this other person you have mentioned. His time-travel from the eighteenth century sounds intriguing to say the least.

Hoping that you will have the leisure to spend time on your manuscript in the near future.

Have a nice week-end,
Hippolyte Choinière

"I'll be out of town for a few days," says Mrs. Waugh as she takes up our bill and puts on her rather old-fashioned green wool hat, "as I'm taking the train to Quebec City, to see for myself the battlefield at the Plains of Abraham. If I'm going to do justice to any story of Wolfe, I'm sure you of all people understand that's the place one finally has to see."

I let her exit the Green Spot ahead of me. Through the window I watch her grow smaller and smaller as she walks in the direction of Rue Atwater, along Boulevard Notre-Dame. As she vanishes behind the Middle Eastern grocery on the corner, I wonder if Mrs. Waugh has any idea that her own impending visit to Quebec City makes me feel more ashamed than any admonition of Sophie's. It is high time I had the courage to put on the red coat and go there myself.

14 The Moping Owl to the Moon Complains

THURSDAY, SEPTEMBER 7.
AFTERNOON.

Near Bonaventure Station. Montreal, Quebec

THE RED COAT IS THE hardest part of the uniform to get right. My leggings and shoes and garter and hat are all easy to find, but the coat needs to have the right weight and weave or else I can't abide wearing it. I never did wear the more ostentatious versions of this coat and am not about to start doing so. I want my sleeves rolled and do not want extra buckles or buttons or straps. I've seen soldiers sporting these baubles slaughtered when they became caught in rough terrain. What good are fancy bits of uniform plastered to rock and scrub?

You have to be careful that the red coat isn't made of some modern fabric that melts when ironed. I never iron mine to inspection-worthiness as there's nothing sillier than enacting a battle as if one pranced yesterday from the tailor. But between Septembers I do clean and press my uniform so it won't rot or split in the creases or otherwise suffer disrespect.

I met a rugby coach on the train during my failed attempt to reach Quebec City last autumn, and he said, "I have a riddle for you: What's worse than losing the championship game?"

"Winning the game," I said, "is far more injurious to the soul."

He looked at me anew, taking in my facsimile coat and hat. "Aye," he said, "I guess a soldier would know." He proceeded to recount to me the mountains of dolour and grief from which he had to dig his rugby players each season they were victorious. "They get depressed," he said. "They get to asking what it's all for. Some of the best hang their cleats up for good and I can't stop 'em. It's all I can do not to pack it all in myself and go on the beer."

"My favourite poem is about that very thing," I said.

"Favourite *what*?" He looked the way some people's faces turn at the mention of coriander, or asafoetida, or even excrement.

I hauled from my pocket the page of my beloved poem, torn from a library copy of *Palgrave's Golden Treasury*. He found it incomprehensible. He was a lout, really. He completely failed to understand. I found the man so dispiriting I bailed out at the Trois-Rivières station and caught a Greyhound back to Montreal where Sophie sent me to the Mission, having rented my spot to a Cirque du Soleil trapeze artist who'd injured a meniscus.

I no longer possess any copy of Gray's poem—the Palgrave page soon disintegrated. But I know where to find my red coat.

A hardworking toothless woman charges seventeen dollars and fifteen cents to store it for me between Septembers. Alongside unclaimed uniforms of security guards, satin gowns of bridesmaids and dancing lovers, and costumes of retired acrobats, my jacket and its accoutrements hang in a polyethylene sleeve behind the steam presses at Nettoyeur Serge Daoust.

"I might retrieve my uniform at the dry cleaner's," I told Sophie this morning.

"That's a start."

"And I might go into a bookshop and see if I can get my own copy of the poem."

"You and that poem!"

"The poem has haunted me all my adult life."

"What's it called? 'Whingeing in the Graveyard'?" She started clicking around for it on her phone.

"Thomas Gray's 'Elegy in a Country Churchyard.'"

"From when?"

"From when I was twenty-four."

"Which twenty-four? Yours or the general's?"

"Gray wrote the poem in 1751."

"Nobody'll stock that in a bookstore anymore."

"But it's immortal."

"I don't care if it's got wings and a crown, you won't even find it in a discard bin. I'll order it from Amazon and you can pick it up at the Mission . . . there. AbeBooks, Oshawa. You owe me ninety-nine cents."

"But mine cost only sixpence!"

"Well now, you don't have that one anymore, do you?"

"I have discovered that a library in Toronto has confiscated the edition Miss Lowther bequeathed me before I sailed for Quebec," I say stiffly. I do not want to reveal that I have visited it.

"Poor baby."

"At least today I can go and retrieve my red coat . . ."

"What about going to see Madame Blanchard, too? War brides never get over their love for a man in uniform. You'll be welcomed."

"Maybe, if there's time . . ."

AS I NEAR BONAVENTURE STATION my chest tightens at the thought of seeing Madame Blanchard. I no longer take her on outings to Dollarama for no-name laundry bleach or cat food or her dishwashing scrubbers of multicoloured stripes made in Poland. Nor do I accompany her to her annual podiatrist appointment—I was able to help her with these things only as long as she was well. For quite some time I didn't catch on that her growing imperiousness masked poor health, and even now I find it hard to accept.

Bonaventure Station is cavernous. Automatic ticket-dispensing machines have encroached upon the ticket-seller's relic of a kiosk. He devours a bun stuffed with turkey and lettuce.

"Might you be able to provide me," I ask, "with a flexible ticket to the suburb of Dollard-des-Ormeaux?"

"*Non.*" He lodges his bun on his packet of cigarettes. "It is not possible."

Nothing flexible is possible, he insists, unless I fork out a sum that could practically charter a helicopter to land me on Madame Blanchard's nursing home roof.

Does he regard me with disdain? He wouldn't if I had my uniform on! It is more imposing than his . . . if only I could console myself with Thomas Gray's poem. When it's drizzling and I am lonely and uniformed people confront me who've no idea of my history, I become . . . I was going to say I become like a kitten, but even kittens have claws to protect them. . . .

Have I begun quivering? Does a drop hang off my nose?

"Is something the matter with you?" the ticket-seller asks with a lumpy eye.

"I suppose this station," I say, "being open at all hours, gets its share of riff-raff. But you needn't worry about me. I'm simply allergic to the noise here and I seem to have forgotten my medication. . . ."

Sounds roar: trains arriving underground, defective fluorescent lights, the murmur of passengers snaking to escalators at the Toronto and Halifax platforms, a surround of crashing coffee-shop cutlery.

"I'll improve once we get this ticket arranged so I might visit my . . . friend."

It is untrue that seeing Madame Blanchard might make me less unhappy, but I tell him this anyway. He needs to know that I, like himself or like any normal person in this station, have a human connection with somebody.

He doesn't respond.

"Do you imagine I have no fire in the hearth? No wife? No child waiting to climb on my knee and kiss his papa as soon as I return home?" These blessings come straight from Gray's poem and belong to the self I abandoned the day I signed up to become a soldier. But this petty official needn't know that.

"Sir, you are raising your voice." His hat bears plastic buttons made to mimic metal. He fumbles for his phone and I back off, run outside to Saint Catherine Street and lean on a brick wall in tears, eavesdropping on those who pass: how is everyone so cheerful, with their umbrellas and steaming paper cups and chomped sandwich-ends?

AN AGONY OF CIVILIAN LIFE is the constant need to make small, inconsequential decisions—decisions whose stakes are far from high: goals whose attainment matters not in the least. Non-soldiers stand around nattering as if they care about what, for instance, they might eat tonight for supper. Will it be haddock and should the cook add mustard grains to the sauce, or will we instead simmer the bit of kidney left over from Wednesday in broth? One of the things I like about lunching at the Mission is that these decisions have been made for me. A supermarket has donated tins of Heinz beans and cases of Vienna sausage, so praise god, beans-and-sausage it'll be.

I could never stand it when I'd visit Blackheath and, my mother having gone to Bath for her sciatica, her servant Nelly cheerfully assailed me with complex menu choices when all I wanted to think about was what had gone wrong at Rochefort—why had I not convinced my superiors that my military strategy would bear fruit? And as I thought about these important events, events with historic implications, Nelly wanted to go on at length about haddock.

I suppose I knew I could not expect people like Nelly, or the rugby coach on the train, or the Bonaventure ticket seller—or even Sophie, who claims to understand me—to sympathize with Gray's "Elegy." Gray's rugged elms, the yew-tree's shade where the moping owl to the moon complains . . . these are not what modern people of any age want to talk about. Gray loves a nodding beech tree that wreathes its old, fantastic roots high beside a holy brook where an ordinary man—the man I once was, the man a general can never be—stops at noon from his labour in the fields, and slumbers in the grass.

The drizzle worsens. Montrealers rush past me to shops and offices. Brick buildings hulk like sodden fruit cake. People scurrying under umbrellas can't stop to smell Gray's incense-breathing morn. No beetle wheels his droning flight, no swallow titters from a straw-built shed. Outside Bonaventure Station, still without my ticket to see Madame Blanchard, I watch everyone in the New World rush away from Gray's natural joys as if they, like me, can't face the day.

"There's another man behind the soldier!" I shout at the street. "And I am trying to restore him . . ."

Mix rain with tears and no one can tell. So what if I've no ticket. Even if I had it, I couldn't sit with Madame Blanchard the way I used to at her plain table with a box of cream crackers, luxuriating my toes in Missy's fur, rhubarb out the window bulging and snaking under its mealy seed. Madame Blanchard keeps my letters in an old biscuit tin. She watches *Coronation Street* and hangs my socks to dry on the banister: she can no longer operate the rusty little wheel on her clothesline and asks me to . . . But no, that was when she still lived in the house . . .

How much time Gray's "Elegy" holds suspended in it! Time hangs like a banner of gold dust arcing between Gray's every word over fields of space.

Buskers stay out in the rain. A flautist has claimed the alley to the old Hotel de Ville. He attempts Handel's fourth sonata in G. Is that the first or the second movement? I never liked Handel's pomposity next to the modesty of Jacques Hotteterre. Handel was all for glory and glory is what he got, making a present of his music to the Duke of Cumberland after we took Culloden—I thought that work fawning, nothing like what music should be or do. . . .

But who am I?

Hands that the rod of empire might have swayed . . . Did Thomas Gray mean my hands? "Tool of the Empire," Sophie calls me. Gray says there are humble men whose destiny is obscure, then there are men who read their history in a nation's eyes.

The busker moves under an awning, his hands stiff in gloves with the finger-ends cut off. How graceful a flute-player's elbows are, raised parallel to the ground at tender attention. This one falters over the first bars of—is it Mozart, the boy who was three the year I fell on the plains? Everyone talks of Mozart with a love they can't feel for Handel, who elicits pageantry not tenderness.

I duck behind Pub DeVille. Nobody sits in the courtyard with its ceiling of fibreglass parasols down whose poles the rain cascades. In an alcove covered by ivy I sit on a waterproof cushion I untie from a chair. A grate blasts heat, making this a homeless man's version of

Gray's sequestered vale. I could use a blanket, but I run Gray's poem through my head instead. That poem did not save me when I recited it the night before my fatal battle, but by god, how it has come to my rescue since.

I know that outside Montreal the last country flowers have cooled to blue: vetch, chicory, aster. My ivy curtain moves and I remember the twinkle-shiver of a leaf in a glade when rain hits it. I listen to the flautist and try not to think about that house where I saw plain beauty any time I chose: Madame Blanchard's sill with the glass paperweight, the lilac that tapped and kept me awake half the night; such a nuisance, yet when it bloomed who could resist opening the window and letting lilac perfume all the corners? This was poverty: the lilac's glory, the wallpaper's pagodas on their gold background and rose wallpaper beneath that and, if I rightly remember, a pattern of pale green trains under the roses.

Every book about my Quebec victory makes such a big deal about my reciting Gray's "Elegy" to my soldiers before the dawn of September thirteenth.

"He stole up the mighty Saint Lawrence," these histories say, "toward the little beach at L'Anse au Foulon . . . He instructed his men to such stealth that it would have been a vigilant Savage indeed who perceived the curlew disturbed from its roost, the lone vole peeping, curious, from its tiny hole in the hill below Quebec's fortress . . ."

They crow about Montcalm's redoubts, our numbers of cannon and the weight of their shot. Then, Gray's poem . . .

"Wolfe extracted from his breast the precious volume given to him in parting by his fiancée, Miss Katherine Lowther. He raised its pages to the scant moonlight . . ."

I'll say the moon was scant! Would any decent general have

ventured to take Quebec on a night when a fat moon poured limelight on his men? No, I chose waning gibbous, cloudy sky, perfect tide.

From my fronds I peep out to get a better look at the busker's flute. I discern from the fellow's age and from his hesitant fingers that he must have played as a child and retained his ability with a bodily memory that can perhaps be trusted more than he believes. I crawl out and get a bit nearer. My fingers ache to dance on the holes of his instrument. How I miss my own dancing fingers, my breath shared between openings in silver. What a sweet voice a flute lends a man whose throat has grown hoarse and useless shouting commands of war.

He's finished the Mozart, and, hesitant, I ask, "Might I—hold your flute?"

I can't help reaching.

My fingers remind me of the starlings that beg for crumbs under café tables. Around every Montreal *terrasse* these creatures congregate, a golden lining peeping from their feathers of dun. I always like to dust crumbs off myself as I rise. The crumbs, tiny as stardust, sustain starling flight over the city for days. Crumbs *feed* birdsong—that wild parent of anything written by Handel or Hotteterre or Mozart or any of the new composers whose work I have not learned.

The busker gapes. He hasn't shaved and a stink of urine shrouds him. The velvet of his open flute case is smashed, stained with old rosin, the shine long out of it. But the flute is immaculate. It has been cleaned with fastidious regularity.

But the flautist bares teeth stuck on yellow posts in his gums. He says something in an incoherent *joual*, and with savage might swipes his flute across my outstretched fingers, then raises it and beats my face so hard I nearly lose consciousness. My cut cheek bleeds and my hands shake—my finger bones turn cold then hot, and for many seconds I fear he's broken my fingers: I can't feel them.

He raises the flute and aims for my collarbone but I back across the road and flee toward the storage place of my red coat. My head and hands throb but my breast has been struck the worst blow. My loneliness for his flute, for a comrade, for a moment of conviviality with another man of the street—all combine to strike grief through my chest, and as I stumble toward Nettoyeur Serge Daoust I catch my reflection in the Bank of Montreal window. I'm a crumpled stick-legged insect, a daddy longlegs swatted against a porcelain tub.

Sophie calls this kind of talk pure self-pity.

Why haven't I put my red coat on before today?

It amazes me how much more respect people award me whenever I wear it, though Sophie calls it unsurprising.

"They don't even know what it is," I remind her.

"They don't need to know. They take one look at its military spiffiness and there you go, you're a man they love to obey."

"But even police and guards in the subway, and officials at the government office when I try to update my *carte d'assurance maladie*. . . ."

"Especially those people! Surely you know by now that faced with a military garment bureaucrats are the most compliant of all souls."

IN THE ALLEY BETWEEN SERGE DAOUST and a garment shop for teenage girls I crouch behind a recycling bin and change into my uniform. Every time I put it on I congratulate myself on having chosen the plain version. No ostentation, or, as Sophie puts it, no bells and whistles.

Its plain frock tones down the gorgeousness of the red so that while arresting, it fails to incite fear or untoward attention or ridicule. Its subdued tailoring keeps the garment elegant and respectable as my coat of 1759. It's a classic design and I've always been proud of it.

I feel certain, as I smooth the creases from its having been sandwiched between the bouffant hoopla of ballgowns and the severity of hospital uniforms, the busker would not have dared assault me had I been wearing it.

The south edge of the city of Montreal opens onto what they call the Old Port, but the only old thing there, once you reach the water, is the bridges. The bridges are rickety. They are falling apart. I love the way the Champlain bridge sits squat and cantilevered over the water like an architectural mushroom, sturdy yet lightened by spokes and spans and strips that underpin its upper arc.

To feel the slightest bit human, I have to look at the bridges instead of at what city planners have done with the Old Port. They have covered it in cement: angled, vertical, stretching for officialdom. There is no place on this part of the Saint Lawrence River where a man can regain a feeling of nature. You have to go west for that, toward the Mercier Bridge and the Mohawks.

I fervently wish to find Harold again, he in his yellow clothes, me in this red coat: together we'd be like a caution light and a stop signal joining forces to halt my old sadness. Dare blues try and barge through such a blaze?

15 Umbrellas

THURSDAY, SEPTEMBER 7.
EVENING.
Mont Royal. Montreal, Quebec

AT NIGHTFALL IN THE TENT, Sophie seems unimpressed with me.

"What's the matter with you? You're jittery. You're unfocused. You haven't been to see Madame Bee at all, have you?"

"I went to buy a ticket but—"

"But but but. You didn't go and see her but you did something. What was it?"

"I'll go to see Madame Blanchard. Tomorrow . . ."

Is the old walrus on Sophie's tent moving? She's done something to its eyes so they find me like eyes in a portrait gallery, which I find disconcerting. She has painted, in the sea and around the walrus, some new small fish and weeds and flames of blue and green. I wish I could dive in. My coat glares in the half-light. Red is not a colour that merges with the walrus's colours. Red wants to subjugate other colours but here in the tent it cannot.

"You're preoccupied with something or someone—you have been since Tuesday—who is it?"

I fear that if I risk telling Sophie about Harold or Mrs. Waugh she'll want to know all the details and give a verdict before I've had time, myself, to decide how I feel. But if I don't come up with something to appease her she'll wear me out with her questions, well-meaning, all of them, but . . .

"I was thinking about my mother. Her pretty miniatures—"

"Henrietta?"

"She kept them on a tray to look at when she couldn't sleep."

"For God's sake."

"She did! She had a miniature shoe, an infinitesimal harpsichord and even an umbrella, though no one in England had a real umbrella then."

"They had. England invented bloody umbrellas."

"You're wrong."

"Babies in England are born with tiny umbrellas attached to their thumbs."

"When I brought an umbrella home from my leave in Paris I was the only person in Blackheath in possession of one. I was laughed at."

"A likely tale. Did you find that story in the library?"

"It's true! You know I still love umbrellas. Umbrellas have always struck me as graceful, multi-purposed. Do you not want my tales anymore?"

"I want you to get better. And for that, I need your tales to ring true."

"But can I tell you an umbrella story? I admit this is not mine, it's about a man called Ears, and I did find it in the library—I was searching under *M* for my old friend Sir John Mordaunt but I got waylaid by Maupassant: his story in which a man named Ears longs to buy an umbrella but his wife won't let him . . . it explains how I feel about umbrellas—I find them important and poignant."

"This is one of those times I wish I was a baleen," Sophie says.

"What?"

"Whales are blessed with natural self-forming earplugs."

"I'm not talking about ears or whales or their earplugs, I'm trying to tell you about a *man* named Ears."

"The lack of self-regulating noise intake is a basic design flaw in the human body."

"Sophie, hear me out? The man named Ears went to work in his office every day, carrying his pathetic, cheap umbrella, patched and so worn that his workmates made up a hateful song about it and chanted it cruelly every time he walked past."

". . . What were the words to this cruel song?"

"Maupassant didn't say."

"Can't you make them up?"

"I don't make things up."

"Oh. I see."

"The story, Maupassant's story, is that Ears begged his wife to hold back some of the housekeeping money to buy him a new umbrella, and she was so miserable she could hardly speak . . ."

"Please," Sophie rolls away and pulls the sleeping bag tight over her head, "spare me the miserable, nagging wife."

So, I keep to myself the heartbreaking tale of how Ears' wife finally allowed him to spend eighteen francs on a new silk umbrella, only to have a catastrophe happen the very next day: somehow, ashes from a cigar burnt a hole through his glorious new umbrella in the cloak-room while he slaved away on his sums.

Did a malicious coworker do this on purpose?

Maupassant did not specify.

Terrible consternation ensued, with the wife refusing to help in any way except by making a claim with the family's insurance company. The man at the insurance office tried to tell her they did not reimburse people for burnt umbrellas—she needed her whole house burnt down.

Ah, replied the wife—but we did have a house fire some time ago and did not report it: if you refuse to pay for my husband's umbrella to be mended, we will have no choice but to make that far larger claim . . .

And so on, until finally the insurance clerk acquiesced: she could have the umbrella re-covered in the best silk. And so she did, telling the repairman that money was no object.

This story immensely saddens me, and because Sophie refuses to listen I am left alone with it, as I am left alone with so many heart-breaking stories.

"Only your own story can cure you," Sophie mutters after a few minutes of silence. "Umbrellas have changed. Purple LED lights fly up and down their sticks. They don't cost half a month's wages and nobody patches them with silk. I told you to understand the past, not worm deeper in."

"But Maupassant's story is from 1884, a hundred and twenty-five years after my death."

"Get with the new."

"Might you prefer the umbrella story in *Howards End*?"

"Whose end?"

"E.M. Forster. Is the twentieth century up-to-date enough for you?"

"Never mind Howard's end, what about yours? Where is Jimmy B going to end up? You'd better get a move on or I'll be here until the apocalypse listening to him drone on about umbrellas."

"But *Howards End is* my story, or at least very like an important part of it . . . a rich woman with a luxuriant umbrella accidentally takes a poor man's decrepit umbrella home from a concert, and when they try to return the objects to each other it creates a doomed romantic upheaval nearly identical to the way I lost Eliza. . . ."

"Eliza Lawson? Again? Oh, Jimmy. I'm ready for you to leave if you can't do any better than this after all the time I've spent with you, trying to get you to face what really haunts you."

In fact, there has not been a September in the last eleven years when Sophie hasn't uttered this very thing. If I don't give her a grain of truth now and then, she loses all heart.

So. "I met a blue man . . ."

Blue, yellow . . . a story sounds true no matter what the colour, as long as there is a colour and the colour is pure.

"See? I knew you met somebody today. I could tell from your face, from your whole body. I knew somebody had you mixed up about time again. Harking all the way back to the invention of friggin' umbrellas. Pulling you safely away from here and now. How much time do you expect me to squander listening to pointless tales that only distract you from the truth?"

"It wasn't today I met the blue man. But I thought about him all afternoon. And it's true, he did get me thinking of time, going back and forth in time, instead of doing what you want me to do, like visiting Madame Blanchard."

"A blue man."

"He was all dressed in blue."

"A blue man from the desert? Are you finally talking to me about the desert?"

"Not the desert. The blue man was in the field behind our house in Westerham. I was playing with George."

"Oh." She slumps. "You and Westerham and Henrietta and George Warde. You and Eliza and England and king what's-his-name."

"He had a wool hat on, though it was the middle of summer, and he was hunched over but he had bright blue quick eyes, and he wagged his finger at me to c'mere. I tried to get George to come over with me but he wouldn't.

"'Would you like to know three things,' the man asked me, 'that will let you have the life you really want?'

"'Yes please.'

"'Good! You're a good boy. Well, the first thing is, you have to set a goal, and you have to make a little change every day towards it—that's called increments—you make an incremental change and you do it every day. Have you got that?'

"'I think so.'

"'The second thing is, if you had one pound and you doubled it the next day, and you doubled the amount you had every day from then on, how long would it take before you have a million pounds?'

"'I don't know.'"

"Damn right you don't know," interrupts Sophie.

"I can't remember exactly how many days the man said. He mentioned the number twenty-one. But I can't remember if he meant it would take twenty-one days of doubling to reach a million, or if the twenty-one days were the amount of days things remained slow but after which a stupendous increase exploded the numbers. I've never sat down to work it out."

"I know you haven't," Sophie says. "You never work anything out concerning money. Even the miserable lump sum Madame Blanchard shamed the Department of Veterans Affairs into sending you a couple of years ago, what did you do? Hey? Blew it on another useless—"

"It was exactly enough to revisit my birthplace, Westerham—I had to go!"

"Wolfe's birthplace. Not yours. You don't know where you were born, that's—"

"'I tell you this about the pounds,' the blue man said, 'in case you're afraid of money. You should never be frightened of coin. It is the foundation of everything men do. Everyone wants it, and nobody talks about it. It isn't just people who hide the fact that they want it—countries tell all kinds of stories to pretend they want magic jewels and magic kingdoms and palaces full of genies and spell-binding belly-dancers and even fairies and fish with scales made of silver and gold, but what the countries want is the same as what all the people want, which is money, and you mustn't be afraid of it or you'll miss the boat.'"

"Exactly!" Sophie cries. "Bring me that fucking blue man now. Where the hell have you left him?"

"Then he said, 'It's money that everything else comes from: Love, far-off enchanted lands, and all the things I've just mentioned, even God. You know how pretty church windows are, with all their lovely coloured glass?'

"I said I did. I was watching George, who was pulling his toy horse toward his house. It was nearly our dinner-time and my tummy was rumbling. Betty was making rhubarb and custard, my favourite."

"Jesus, Jimmy," moans Sophie. "What am I gonna do with you?"

"'Well,' the blue man said, 'even the churches, with their love of God, really underneath it all know about money and are always thinking about it all the time. You can't go anywhere or do anything big or grand or even good, without it. So don't forget that, it's the second thing. Now, what do you think the third thing is?'

"'I don't know,' I said. Remember, I was only a child.

"He bent close to me and said, 'You have to go back in time, not just forward. Do you know how to do that?'

"'No.'

"'It's easy. Remember the first thing I told you, about making a goal and doing something, some little change, an incremental change, each and every day towards it? Say incremental.'

"'Incremental.'

"'Good. Well, you have to cast your imagination forward now, to the point you're envisioning in five years, ten years, or however long it will be until that future day when your goal is within reach. Can you imagine you're there?'

"'I think so.'

"I was getting tired of him and I couldn't really imagine it, but I wanted to let him get to the end of his lesson so I could go home and play with my dogs and have rabbit pie and then some pudding.

"'Place yourself there,' he said, 'with your goal plucked and in your hand, in the future, and now, using that same imagination, look back in time and see what you must have in place a year before the goal is reached, then two years, and so on, so that you can see the steps from your future goal, back in time, until now. Once you have done that, you will know what to do along your way to get the life you really want. Now that's it. Now go, and have your good life.'

"And with an abrupt hand-wave like a magician completing his enchantment, the man in blue dismissed me. I wasn't dreaming, I saw it all clearly, and I remember him and his words better than I remember many other things from when I was very young—and I could smell Betty's pie and custard. He was gone, and I didn't think of him again except for a few fleeting moments today, when I guess I was thinking of someone or something that reminded me of him."

"Someone passing by on the street?" Sophie demands.

"Something or someone . . . it doesn't matter."

"Oh," says Sophie, "it does matter. I think it matters very much."

RED MAN

16 Madame Blanchard

FRIDAY, SEPTEMBER 8.
AFTERNOON.
A suburb. Montreal, Quebec

MADAME BLANCHARD WILL HAVE HAD her lunch by the time I arrive at La Residence Dernière Rose. Lunch is at noon, supper at five, bedtime at nine thirty. Wakeup at eight and a boiled egg with tea tasting of chlorine at eight thirty. By arriving in the afternoon I'll avoid having to interrupt her meal.

When I last visited Madame Blanchard—is Sophie right, can it really have been two years ago?—the nurses had moved her to a smaller room. At least she still had a window: it looked out on a golf course and poplars that waved their tops like overgrown woolly pipe cleaners. The dark trees absorbed light from the sky, while the golf course flared a hot lime, but her view was an improvement on that of her previous room that had faced the parking lot.

How eager she'd been to struggle with me around that gravel lot, gripping her walker, bent over it, determined to make the full circle, though no one had planted so much as a clump of daylilies at its border. For an English war bride to be without her garden is, I think, a cruel fate. A bell warned staff we'd gone outside. They seemed to ignore it. I had the feeling Madame Blanchard could disappear onto Boulevard de Salaberry and none of them would notice.

With her war-bride cheer she made her circuit as if enjoying a day in Connaught Park. Her high voice, her wispy hair and house-dress, and the loafers that did not sting her bunions—no one outside her tiny domain saw the woman I knew. For a glimpse of that, one had to be admitted to her room, with its lemon geranium, her ceramic dormice, made in her childhood home of Staffordshire, and books all over the floor. The staff was forever devising tricks to rid her of those books. Dust traps, they said. You'll break the other hip.

In her own house she'd tended gooseberries, brambles, and a weeping birch under whose branches I read all afternoon concealed from crow or gull or any human other than herself as she brought me something nice to drink. She remained obliviously English despite half a lifetime in the New World. Her rock garden. Her sage and onion stuffing. Neighbours had a little laugh about this behind her back. Now the staff at the home hardly noticed it. When a woman reaches her nineties no one sees what came before her diapers, her sleeping pills, the ghost-white cup-ring on her night table.

TODAY, SUZETTE CROUCHES OVER THE reception desk eating a whistle-dog from the A&W down the hill. A stink of liver bathes the corridor, it being Friday. Madame Blanchard does not eat liver. Instead she has the staff prepare her a chicken fillet.

"I'll see myself in . . ." I turn toward room 219 but Suzette waves no and the supervisor with striped hair comes out of her office.

"We tried to telephone," she says. I always have to surreptitiously check her nametag—Gisele Thunay-Dufresne. "What happened to your face?"

"Nothing." I do not feel like explaining about the busker's flute.

"Wait here while I get the correspondence we tried to send to you."

She retrieves three cancelled envelopes, all addressed to myself, two to the Gaspé postal box whose payments I failed to keep up after Madame Blanchard left the old house to be cared for here, and one addressed to the Mission this past June while I was not yet in the city. "We knew from your instructions that this last one was unlikely to reach you." She hands it to me. "But you gave us no alternative. We trusted someone there might know a forwarding address. I've warned you something like this might happen."

She flicks a lacquered nail while I open the envelope and take in its contents.

It is true that the time Madame Blanchard fell and broke her hip, it took a couple of months before I found out. The Gisele Thunay-Dufresnes of the world believe this to be neglect on my part.

But Madame Blanchard knew I loved her.

I remind myself, here on this tiled floor that emanates a pong of Javex through the liver odour, that this is what matters.

"Where . . . is there . . . Is it the Anglican cemetery?"

"She is not in a cemetery." Madame Thunay-Dufresne places a large brown envelope in my hand. "Here are her papers. We proceeded according to most of her wishes. I'll have to telephone the funeral service and ask them to courier the box. I'm afraid we'll have to transfer the courier charge to you. We've done all the paperwork and the cheque is in here along with the other papers. Really, we should not have had to deal with these extras. If you had been here earlier, we could have saved some of her knick-knacks for you. As it is, we have had to send most of it to Fripe-Prix Renaissance. You could have made better arrangements. If everybody did as you have done, we'd barely stay in business."

She clacks down the hall. Suzette plugs in the plastic kettle and stirs Nescafé and coffee whitener into a cup for me. Dabs my face with a cloth, cool and damp, removing the bloody encrustation.

"I'm sorry about your loss." She looks down the hall to make sure it's empty, then reaches in the back of a drawer to extract a small packet. "Here. I saved this."

In it lies the smallest dormouse from Madame Blanchard's collection, the one I used to hold while she read me British stories as a child. Is it even a dormouse? I become unsure. I have called Madame Blanchard's figurines dormice since I was little: but really, this one is some sort of unrecognizable meadow-creature with a longish nose. Might it be a tiny platypus? It has a tender aspect, and as it rests in my hand I wonder if Madame Blanchard asked Suzette to keep it for me.

I sit on a bollard in the parking lot and wait for the courier. He has to go in and have Madame Thunay-Dufresne sign for the box containing the remains of Madame Blanchard. The funeral home calls it an urn, but it's nothing more than a box made of waxed cardboard. It reminds me of the takeout Chinese food containers Sophie brings to the tent on Friday nights after she gets paid.

As I hold her remains I reflect that being with Madame Blanchard, even in her last years, always held some comfort for me.

Now her little house by the sea will change even more.

The thought of that house terrifies me all the way back downtown on the train with Madame Blanchard's carton on my knee. I know the house became unlike its old self eleven years ago, when Madame Blanchard had to move out of it. Already, then, its roof groaned toward the stones and pineapple-weed. But now her ashes make it irrevocable: I can no longer pretend I might repair that house, or repair to any time before it fell derelict. The house and Madame Blanchard fell apart together, leaving me no shield against reliving war in Technicolor, all night, every day . . . alone in that house sagging into its field of rhubarb by our crescent beach and taking me down with it. . . . Until, as August bled into September, I ventured down to the beach and met Sophie.

AS THE TRAIN CREAKS INTO Bonaventure Station I feel hungry—and am ashamed of the hunger. Why, when one is bereaved, do the animal humiliations persist? I feel starved, and want potatoes.

Wolfe's first potato was at his mother's house when he came back from Portsmouth at thirteen, thin, seasick and ashamed to have abandoned Cartagena, his very first campaign. I remember Betty made him a plate of magical whip—potato fluffed with milk. He'd never had it before. She sprinkled nutmeg on it. It revived him in a way he had not known food could do.

Is that truly what happened?

Even if Sophie makes fun, even if my memory is unsure, I can say with authority, if only from the times Madame Blanchard cooked potatoes for me as I came home from school, that a bowl of mashed potatoes with a square of butter swimming in the fork-tine furrows on top is restorative.

So yes, I am sure James Wolfe asked Betty to make this dish whenever he felt low. Later, when he returned from battle, she made him a nice dish with potatoes thin-sliced with gold edges in a pot, but it was his French cook, François, who transformed potatoes into medicine.

"Don't tell me," François said, eyeing Wolfe. I *hear* François saying it: "I see by your colour: *Je le sais exactement.*"

François concocted a red-hot soufflé that was not so much nourishment as revivifying inspiration. He made it when . . . I could hold down no other food, the worst time being when I returned from the torment of our aborted assault on that windswept island off Rochefort, not long before I sailed for Quebec. If François had not been present at Blackheath then, and had not made his potato soufflé, or if a craze for turnips or parsnips had overtaken the country instead of everyone going mad over potatoes, I do not know that my victory at Quebec could have happened.

> *François's potatoes steamed as I lifted their cover. The steam was blue and curled with swirling hoops over the chocolate hues of our dining room with its window looking out on my mother's garden that had a coat of new snow. I was glad she had gone to Bath. It meant I did not have to pretend robust humour. I was close to collapse. I found it shameful to return to England fresh from our army's cowardice at Rochefort and had returned to Blackheath to keep away from the glare and questioning. I wanted to bring down my fever with diachylum and sink my foot in the warm fur of my dogs and hide for a month or two. . . .*

RIGHT OUTSIDE BONAVENTURE STATION IS downtown Montreal's Le Petit Québec, where the poutine is cheap but good and does not have the artificial red gravy they give you at La Belle Province. At Le Petit Québec they give you squeaky cheese curds in gravy that's brown and thick.

I set Madame Blanchard carefully on the Formica table.

The server has red hair like mine, subdued by a hair net. His nametag says *Augustine.* So the French here still name their sons after Catholic saints! Part of me wishes that with such a name, the youth might have been destined for a more auspicious job.

A rack near the door has yesterday's paper languishing on its bottom shelf. I sift through it as I eat, looking to see if anything of importance has happened in the world, but someone has torn half the pages out. Still, what remains is hardly inspiring.

If I had to name my greatest disappointment regarding New French Britain, I might have to say it's the inconsequential drivel I read in papers purportedly published by the country's learned set.

On page four runs a list of every detour one must take to avoid construction on the Champlain Bridge:

> *Stay clear of 15 south from the Turcot Interchange from Highway 132. Stick to designated routes on Atwater and de La Vérendrye Boulevard to access the Bonaventure Expressway during installation of two modular trusses upstream of the bridge . . .*

Below this item a restaurant reviewer outlines the merits of scalloped veal over the Salisbury steak at his favourite diner. Things have not changed an iota from the coffeehouse drivel I used to read in London at Osinda's or the Cocoa Tree. . . .

It's the same with what I overhear in the streets. I eavesdrop on Montreal hoping I might hear its civilians discuss the latest findings in astronomy, or new perspectives on ancient philosophy, but they bleat the same small-talk I could neither abide nor understand in London of 1752: sports, weather, insipid flotsam sent on the wind by the latest political scandal—details petty and trivial and numerous as Sophie's froth-flecks on her painted walrus's sea, ephemeral. You'd think it all the most weighted precious stones, the way people bleat on. This fills me with chagrin and always has done.

On torn page fourteen, half a face resembles Harold's—but I know it's just me wishing I could find him again. I miss his cheerful yellow clothes. His was a motherly understanding. In the absence of both Henrietta and Madame Blanchard, might not one's best mother be a man? The bit of headline remaining under the photograph says *Man Apprehended After Exp*. . . . I recall Harold said he'd caused a small avalanche climbing Mont Royal, and wonder for a moment if he might have graduated to explosions.

Dejected, I walk to Rue Laurier and try poutine with lamb and pomegranate: then to Crescent Street for a mountain of sausage and mash. None of this is cheap, but the cheque for seven hundred dollars in Madame Blanchard's paperwork means I can afford it. I feel surprised the nursing home hasn't gulped every last cent of Madame Blanchard's account, but I suppose seven hundred is no big deal to Gisele Thunay-Dufresne.

Now I'm too stuffed to visit the place I found last year, where they grill coins of potato sliced so thin you can see through them. Instead I head to Dépanneur Tracy to buy Sophie's favourite potato crisps, a type made by Miss Vickie, or so the package proclaims.

I'm headed back up the Main when I realize I have Sophie's crisps and I have the brown envelope from the nursing home with my cheque in it and Madame Blanchard's papers, but I no longer have the box that holds her ashes. I've left her with my Styrofoam plate and plastic cutlery and greasy paper napkin littering the table at Le Petit Québec.

Has Saint Augustine saved Madame Blanchard?

I race back down.

"Augustine left," says a lad, dark-haired and painfully thin. "I just replaced him for the three o'clock shift."

The place is quiet after the midday rush and the lad takes a moment to open the trash bins and poke around with a spatula then a pair of tongs and even a broom. He wants to help but can't see my box in the bin: perhaps the bin has been emptied into one of the six Dumpsters out back?

I cannot bring myself to tell this boy, whose nametag bears the name of Jesus' earthly father, that my box contained beloved human remains.

"It's all right," I lie. "I'm fine. It's—thank you."

Outside I gulp a breath of rain and diesel. A pigeon cocks its head beside a puddle.

"The box did not really contain Madame Blanchard," I tell it.

Pigeons have eyes the colour of beer bottles. They have red, wrinkled, rubbery toes, three pointing forward and one in retreat.

"Her soul had already departed. . . ."

Her soul and her body have both departed: Three weeks ago, Madame Blanchard became smoke that floated above the city and now travels beyond it over the trees and fields and rivers and other pastoral features that ring Montreal. She has gone up into the air and become cloud.

The pigeon flies up into the letter *O* of Jean Coutu drugstore and settles comfortably among the pigeon-dissuading spikes someone has installed.

I have been unforgivably negligent—my heart thumps at the bottom of its cage—but strictly speaking I have not spoiled Madame Blanchard's flight out of this life. That flight began with her death, or perhaps it began with the burning of her remains. The ashes, I tell myself, were secondary.

Still, I feel so ashamed I can't return to the tent before stopping in at Les Ancêtres on the corner. I no longer drink to medicate my sorrows as a rule, but it takes me several pints and a fair amount of hard stuff to numb the self-recrimination.

FRIDAY, SEPTEMBER 8.
NIGHT.
Mont Royal. Montreal, Quebec

IN THE NIGHT, I WAKEN Sophie and beg her to return me to my mother.

"It's simple hypnosis, Jimmy Bee," she says, not unsympathetically this time. "I've told you how to do it yourself."

"C'mon, Soph. Without you I can't even find the doors."

I shut my eyes. Following Sophie's directions, I will descend hills and stairs until I reach the series of doors, all different colours. I'll choose one and walk through it, and slowly she will have me look up to see one of my ancestors. I regard Sophie's procedure as auxiliary to my own memories—when she puts me under I'm as if concealed on a theatrical stage, unnoticed by the actors.

"You're descending the stairs," she says. "Down another flight, then another. Descend the very last flight and go out the back, down the bank to the courtyard, down through the passageway with its closed doors, all the colours. Now . . . which one?"

I still smell our tent canvas and Mont Royal's night air, but I see the doors.

"Green."

"Open it. . . . So . . . where are you?"

"Snuggled in a soft, woollen cloak. My mother's face is looking down at me."

"Which mother?"

"My mama."

"Which mama?"

"Don't!"

"How big is your hand?"

"What? . . . My hand?"

"Raise it between your face and your mother's."

"Tiny. My hand is tiny. . . . Am I a baby?"

"I don't know. . . . Can you understand the woman?"

"I know how she feels. It comes through her eyes."

"What does?"

"She's sick of waiting. She waited a long time for me. My father's no good—he's old and he's not a good companion. She waited for me to be born, and here I am, but I'm not—" I feel unbearably sad.

"You're not what?"

"I'm not what she wanted. . . ."

My mother's loneliness is too deep for me to mend. I am just one baby. I look around to see if there are other babies who might help.

There are flowers outside my blanket, yellow in the grass, but no other babies. My mother's eyes are wet like big plums. I grow wary of the plums.

"What's happening?" Sophie's voice reaches me.

"She's only pretending to love me. . . . Really she'd like to go away, far from her baby. And she does. She goes inside the house. I'm still outside. She gets smaller through the glass, which I touch. I dislike how cold it is, and hard. I see her in the shadows doing solitary things."

"Like what?"

"Snipping dead leaves off her begonia. Writing letters. Pretending she doesn't know I'm here."

Silence. I can feel Sophie waiting.

"I'm shivering. The whole day goes past. When my mother comes back she says, 'See? You learned. I told you you'd learn.'"

"Have you learned?" asks Sophie.

"I don't *know*!"

My mother did this often.

My father never knew, and Betty wasn't with us yet.

My mother would leave me all day and then come back and whisper, "You're not mine." I tried to tell her I belonged to her and no one else—I cried with all my heart: I *am* yours! And she said, "Very soon you will not care about pleasing me, so I am not going to care about pleasing you. So there—live as your father's soldier-son, you little-red-dimpled not-mine."

Has Sophie fallen asleep? Half the time when she gives me an ancestral consultation or a hypnosis treatment she's the one who relaxes—I suspect she hypnotizes herself. I open my eyes.

Little-red-dimpled not-mine cannot fall asleep. He has wandered Montreal all day in his red coat and here he is tonight, still little and red, and once again he belongs to no one.

I turn to Sophie's painted walrus and whisper, "I need real help."

Sometimes when Sophie is pretending to be asleep, she will throw her voice like a ventriloquist and make the walrus on the tent wall speak.

"Before I died, I had hoped," I whisper, "that man as a species was moving—inching, to be sure, but progressing nevertheless—toward some greater purpose. . . ."

"A greater porpoise," mocks the walrus.

"I know I'm slight," I tell it. "I'm thin and insubstantial, I know that, but I wanted to do something big for England."

"Hmm . . . slight, yes. I see a parasitic whelk, a very tiny one, though it seems to believe in its heart that it is quite big."

Rain hits the tent and damp filters into the sleeping bag.

"I tried to secure new territory, a home for Britain's genius and evolution!"

"Right."

"I mean—you know religion's a delusion I never entertained—but I'm talking about the humanitarian soul of a nation. I hoped boys like Gus and Joe at Le Petit Québec—boys who became soldiers with me to gain a pay of mere crusts and breeches—I really thought the New World was supposed to give them a chance at a parcel of ground."

"Ground you figured nobody else was using."

"I gave ordinary boys a chance only privileged Englishmen knew before. . . . I believed a seed in these youths could, in the New World I won for them, become glorious as Milton, or a second Cromwell. . . . But the rich squash them here, just like they did at home! Geography transforms itself—or I thought it would—into psychological space, into freedom for the mind. The point of my efforts was that ordinary Englishmen might possess this land and flourish on it. . . ."

"Excuse me," mutters the walrus, "while I regurgitate this clam breakfast into your tricorne."

"Instead, I find the old, weary bondage. I never claimed to be altruistic. I knew if we didn't annex the New World, the bottom would fall out of England's economy and ruin us all."

"No more cucumber sandwiches."

"But surely, a secondary good coming from our empire should have been that a youth having any spark might thrive here. Yet the poor toil here unexalted as ever. As for the well-provided, their banal crowing echoes the clang of trussell on planchet under every New World moment: a relentless strike of metal into coin."

"I'm sorry, I'm half-asleep. . . . Did you say something about the Second Coming?"

I give up. Rain patters on the tent.

Rain understands me. I welcome it in this place where all softness or questioning . . . all poetry or intelligence, has drained into the ground.

17 Watermelons

SATURDAY, SEPTEMBER 9.
MORNING.

The Riverbank. Montreal, Quebec

THIS MORNING, CIVILIANS STROLL the riverbank in rumpled pants—they saunter past me now. A man who tells me he's from British Columbia nods at me on the way to his daily swim near the sewage outlet, possessions bundled on his handlebars. He's one of few men around here with hair longer than mine.

"The water's great," he hollers.

"I know it."

Various dogs leave their owners to sniff my trousers. What a small but all-infusing joy it gives me to rub their forehead indentations. There is no denying my September pilgrimages have been a lonely business.

Beyond the chokecherry bent by last winter's frost stand slabs of rock that serve as the kitchen furniture of a man I often see wearing a fedora. He's not here today, though he has left his tablecloth folded in the grass alongside his transistor radio. It strikes me as tender that no one has stolen the radio.

Is my uniform, too, just another costume—like the swimmer's dreadlocks, the itinerant's moth-eaten blazer, the dog-walkers' neoprene tights? Are we all one solitary traveller?

I break through a straggle of goldenrod and sumac and penetrate to the wild river-edge.

Beneath a maple scored with graffiti, I stare toward my old Quebec.

Looking downriver is for young people, who unconsciously follow the water as it flows toward their unknown future. Daydreaming while looking downriver fills a youth's heart with mysterious anticipation. But when you've lived through long experience—my mother told me this and now I know it to be true—you automatically gaze up a river, toward the water's source, its past. In sympathy with where the water has been you remember all you have been and done.

I turn my face upriver, away from Quebec City. Can Wolfe, can I, really bear to return there? Sophie mocks me, but she isn't the one who must do it.

What if there is a museum on my battleground selling little red-haired dolls made in China with plastic mould-seams running down their sides?

What if Quebec City has no record of me at all? It wouldn't be the first time I've been thus disappointed.

Perhaps officials at the Plains of Abraham have hired someone who looks like me, someone who might do a passable job of portraying General Wolfe for my death-anniversary in a few days. Some student offsetting his tuition costs while he prosecutes a degree in history or political science or even some branch of the arts.

In recent years I have had little trouble finding freelance positions enacting military roles at historic sites for cash. These kept me going while I waited on my mother's never-ending letter-writing campaign for the release of my military pension. God bless mothers. But I've made more money as a fairground beer-tent busboy than any military mother has ever won for her son's war service.

Since 1760, my birthplace of Westerham has held an annual dinner with battleground theatrics in my honour. Sophie finds this hard to believe, but I eventually convinced her. In 2015 I travelled back to England and attended undetected even while dressed as myself so I might apply for the position of dramatizing what the brochure called my "pious and immortal memory." I didn't get the job.

"How could they not hire you?" Sophie marvelled. "You are the image of James Wolfe, and you actually believe you are him."

I bought this uniform from the classified section of a British recruitment magazine called *The Locker*. It was the best I could manage and I spent nearly a hundred pounds on it that I'd won from Boum-Boum Larose in a game of poker at the Bucket of Blood. It's far from the real uniform any Redcoat wore in my Quebec campaign, but it is better than the costumes of some men who get jobs on battlefields during important reenactments. Some of those fellows . . . I have to look away.

I found Westerham overwhelming that year I attended as myself. I shied away from the Wolfe statue with its well-meant inscription. I'd barely entered our old house—it had become a museum preserved with our bee skeps and even my canteen with my old spoon still in it—before I realized the building had grown a new soul. Its alien smell forced me outside. I retreated quickly to my camp near the festival fields and darkened my hair with walnut oil. Then I signed up not as Wolfe but as Ruadh Mackay, a lad I slaughtered at Culloden.

There were tents and a hog roast. There were choirs and dignitaries. There was even a ballet.

I endured the spectacle of a lout named Tim playing myself, too short by six inches yet at least two stone stouter. Instead I earned less than seven pounds an hour standing in for a Jacobite soldier in a skit put on by the Royal Society of Medicine, the College of Surgeons and the Society of Apothecaries, who wanted to compare medical care on battlefields now and in 1759. Then some woman named Mountjoy commandeered a team to set watermelons one after another across the lawn outside my beloved George Warde's house.

I have nothing against watermelons.

There were hundreds perched on their ends and prevented from toppling by the use of string and dowels from the U-Do-It hardware shop on the main road. My job was to fire a musket and demonstrate for the surgeons, and for a straggling audience of grandmothers and aunts and children and their schoolteachers, how musket balls split the watermelons, which stood in for human flesh, so that red pulp exploded, spurted, oozed and dripped, melting in little piles and globules on George Warde's meadow in the ruthless sun.

At Dettingen and on other battlefields I had seen the human remains those watermelons were meant to resemble. I could have told the watermelon clean-up crew that their job, not the musketeers', was the most realistic part of the exercise. You scrape up the remains of a shelled soldier in much the same way: you collect the pulp off the ground with a spatula fashioned out of whatever stick or spoon or stone comes to hand, or you harvest your buddy's innards with your palm. You don't want to leave him there. You could stuff what's left of his pulp into your canteen, and I've done it. That old spoon in my canteen has gathered the sacred remains, reeking in the sun.

Seeds. We spilled watermelon seeds all over that Westerham field. Slippery and living, they sickened me more than did seeing the sweet mottled rind and blood sugar-pulp explode. I've seen my comrades hit the ground the way those seeds sank in the dust. Men dying in war are seeds: they cast themselves into bog and dirt. Sand yawns and men grind into it, every dying fighter animated, planting himself, frenzied, digging to stay alive. Seen from a height the men are tiny, wriggling, animate seeds, shoving themselves in the living ground. At the stupid Westerham thing I wanted to scream the difference: that the watermelon seeds are alive! The dead fruit yet bore surviving seeds: some would sprout new life that year but soldiers' seed stunk dead in our blown-off balls.

If I were not a disciplined man I could have murdered all the spectators. I could have taken the ladies in their straw hats and strangled them with their scarves.

After I witnessed the Westerham watermelons I became more afraid of how men might remember me than of how I might have been forgotten. If my British countrymen grieved my soul with such displays, what might I find in Quebec where, let's be honest, no one cares for me at all?

Henrietta Wolfe once wrote a letter in which she outlined how much she loved me. She addressed it not to me but to the man who was my superior during my Paris leave. It must have amused the man, perhaps even irritated him, but he put it down to motherly sentiment and passed it on to me without comment or censure. I have seen it in the digital catalogue of one of the museums that preserve my memory: someone must have ripped it out of my pocket on the battlefield while they were taking the scissors to my hair:

My dear Lord Bury,

When my son departed England I saw you and explained how I love him. I was in mid-explanation when you dismissed me and I realized you had wearied of this woman's complaints: you assured me all parents love their sons alike. I grant that many do love their sons very much.

> But not as I love mine. I am nothing like his father in temperament and neither is he. I am in my son and my son is in me. I bleed by any blade stropped in a room where he dwells. Cold wind near him blows my skin like the membrane enclosing peeled onion or egg: the cloudy layer silken under the carapace.
>
> If he perishes I will with joy abandon my own so-called life: I'll clench and break beyond this wooden agony into freedom. So summon my son to death, if is your plan for him, but know that in doing so you condemn his mother to the same bliss.

My mother was wrong about the bliss of dying. A lot of people are. People think death is an end, a comforting oblivion, and I wish with all my being that it were.

ALONG THE RIVER COMES A WOMAN practicing a single line from a Chinese opera over and over. Her ruffle-eared spaniel snuffs up to me, its paper-thin tongue quivery and sunlit. I bend to pat it and its joyful drool soaks my pant leg. As they walk off I spy a different woman approach with a yellow retriever.

The yellow dog fixes her brown eyes on me, and I recognize her. She is not wearing her service dog vest but instead has on a blue collar with pink owls on it.

"Excuse me," I say. "But is that not Harold's dog? Is this not Veronica?"

The woman stops to let me and the dog reacquaint ourselves. Veronica is now a civilian, whereas I have put on my soldier's coat.

"I told Harold he'd have to find someone else to walk her after next week," says the woman. "If she was shorthaired I wouldn't mind. If she was a Weimaraner or a coonhound . . . I sweep up enough goddamn hair at my salon—yours is nice though, if you'd brush it—ever think of selling it?" She hands me her business card: Sylvie Lauzier, stylist. "I'd give you forty or forty-five for it."

"Why can't Harold walk Veronica?"

"Psh—Harold!"

"Is Harold . . . has there . . ."

"Haven't you seen him on the news?"

"Where is he?"

"*Bavette de boeuf*'s on sale at IGA," she says. "I gotta run." And as she hurries off, she flings a few indecipherable words about Harold, words that sail past me and fall into the ever-listening river.

I SIT BY THE WATER on a cushion of flattened reeds. The river chants its choppy flopping sounds as a tanker drifts past and sends ripples.

This part of the Saint Lawrence is a plashing-spot for gulls and the odd goose or heron making its way to Parc des Rapides. When I ask it things I once asked its selfsame body farther down, between Point-Levis and Quebec's fortress, I find today's river is a mute sibling of that talkative one of old.

Why, river, are you silent?

I studied you, and you taught me. Why will you not teach me again? I studied you and your banks. I found things out. I did not take your silence for an answer!

I read your current every night as my soldiers slept.

I sat among rhubarb and cabbage stalks of that old *habitant* whose house I'd seized, and requested that you inform me.

Has time diluted your power?

Your body in those days taught me to be quieter than a vole, more mercurial than eel or smelt. I smelled your weeds and hid my red coat under a rock and stole by dusk in underclothes dim as submerged stones.

That river told me of Montcalm. It reported Montcalm in deep mourning for a dead daughter . . . but which daughter? Beloved Mirète? The letter did not say if he'd lost the one he loved most. And Montcalm was himself unwell, having succumbed to a sense of doom even greater, perhaps, than my own habitual melancholy. Bad vapours are one thing: seasickness and dysentery and all that. But to lose Mirète . . . ?

I listened, and in listening became the river's own. I became a droplet in the river. That river carried me swift and fluid and noiseless past sad, dreaming Montcalm, to the secret beach at Foulon.

Anyone could see the beauty of Montcalm's house from the shore—he had rooms galore, and in them, every comfort: cruets made of crystal, full of vinaigrette with chives chopped into it, even snippets of the mauve flower. He had a basket of slippers, whereas I walked the floorboards of my one-room farmhouse in the socks I had worn on the ship—not that I complained or am complaining now. I just want to point out that he had the comforts of home, or at least of hospitality: he was a guest in the home of a wealthy local man, with all the blessings and perks.

The biggest thing of all, and it affects me yet, is that I was cold.

I was cold to the bone and I couldn't get warm no matter how many fires I lit in the kitchen, or how close I sat to the embers. I was and remain solitary, and that makes a coldness in the heart that can turn into disease if one is not careful, and in myself I believe it has.

Some people might think I'm deluded in imagining I can pay Sophie to hold me close and feel the relief I'd feel were an unpaid lover to radiate heat. I pay Sophie and people think—my mother would certainly think—that nothing can alleviate the icy touch of cash changing hands. But Sophie does a good job.

Montcalm had slippers and he had fine sheets and despite his sadness and his love-letters to his wife he had a woman who fetched him wild strawberries folded into whipped cream from the cow she kept in the back yard. He had a window-seat on the landing and used to sit on its fine brocade with a blanket on his knee and his book of poetry, different from mine—he told me during one of our brandies that his was an anthology. He liked dipping into a variety of the finest minds between games of Goose with Marie-Louise, the little slave Vaudreuil loaned him.

Montcalm had a daily life—all the French did. We were in their homeland as invaders, encamped and temporary, while they had all home's comforts. No wonder he did not want to come out and fight—it would prove a great inconvenience.

The way it feels to be near a fire but unable to warm yourself is this: you feel inside your body a bruise like the rot inside a bad potato. All you want is the housemaid to come with her sharp little knife and cut out the black rot—the potato would have a chance then. But the dark spot, like the rest of the fruit, is alive, and has its own growth and emanations. It causes an ache, a dank pain heat can't reach. The spot is made of dense dark matter far from the sun, and has its own bitter energy. We think cold is an absence of warmth but we're wrong. It is a present and energetic fire, and I knew this as I kept watch outside Montcalm's lovely house, so much more a home than my commandeered farmhouse at L'Ange Gardien with its poisonous foxgloves and the tiny radishes that burned hot while I crunched them cold.

—

TODAY THE RIVER TELLS ME NOTHING. It gives me no hint as to what has become of my blind yet not-blind companion, Harold in yellow, who I suspect understands me better than any slave, or prostitute, or strawberry-bearing lover, or even any mother. Perhaps it is because Harold, like myself, has been unable to see properly for so many years.

It is September 9, and I must face the fact that I have not yet done what I came to do: see for myself the Plains of Abraham on the days leading to my own death-day. I have to face the truth that Sophie is no help to me anymore. She goads and threatens to abandon me if I spend my eleventh September in Montreal without making that journey to Quebec City. What will you do, she says. Go and moulder again in the place where I found you, where fog and juniper claw across the bogs?

No, the one I need now, the one who understands, is Harold.

Did Harold say he'd go with me to the Plains of Abraham? I think he said that.

But where's Harold now?

The woman minding Veronica knows. . . . And the river and I both heard what she said, but only the river caught it. Why can I no longer trust it to tell me anything? I lean in again to listen.

18 Finding Harold

SUNDAY, SEPTEMBER 10.
AFTERNOON.

Hôpital de Verdun. Montreal, Quebec

"I LIKE NOTHING MORE," Harold says, "than placing myself at the sweet mercy of people who seem quite normal."

In the main corridor at Hôpital de Verdun he reclines, knitting, on the gurney I contrived to nab so he won't have to sit on the only chair—one with a broken, jagged seat—in the waiting room. An orderly left an old man on the gurney after nurses summoned her to the elevator, and the old man leapt off it and raced to freedom.

"How did you find me?"

"Yesterday I met the woman who walks your dog."

"I have several dedicated caretakers for Veronica—was it Sylvie?"

"I lost her card—she had a pointy face and a lot of hair. She offered to buy mine."

"That's Sylvie! She makes wigs."

"She told me you'd been on the news."

"Have I really?"

"I wish she'd mentioned you were at the end of the broadcast."

This morning I jeopardized my sanity watching the news program in the library: soldiers with their heads blown off, families pacing the tarmac, sons and daughters lowered in flag-draped coffins. I became dizzy, a peril for tall thin people: that thing happened in my ears where the inner bones go awash in a pounding rush—whoosh! Stallions trample my head. Sophie calls it hypervigilance but it's only my common-sense approach to the eternal unexpected. I ducked under my carrel. I cowered, whimpering, reaching for the knife I keep in the sheath I stitched inside my red jacket's arm. The librarian eased me back into my chair and gave me a glass of water. I sat dutiful with headphones on as the anchorman went on and on.

"Was I the funny bit they keep for the end?"

"You were after an advertisement in which a retired sportsman claims to keep his legs strong by resting them on a vibrating disc."

"Guy Lafleur! What an honour to be on the television after him—greatest scorer in the history of the Montreal Canadiens. What did they say about me?"

"They said a man lay down among the raspberry bushes in the First Nations section of the botanical gardens."

"It's true."

"They said he took a nap in the shade."

"I did! I fell fast asleep."

"But not before removing all his clothing and stacking it at his feet . . ."

"I'm afraid that's true as well."

"To the consternation of the Heirloom Marguerite Preservation Society, who came upon him without warning after having travelled by coach from Bowmanville, Ontario, for their annual afternoon tea and garden inspection."

"Was that who it was!" Harold laid his knitting down. "Now, I'd wondered that. I was under the impression they were specifically there to look at orchids. I'm sure one of them mentioned a cream coloured orchid with red spots. But you're saying it was marguerites?"

"I think so . . ." The anchorman's mirth bothered me. *The ladies did not press charges*, he smirked, *but they did alert garden staff who had the nude man apprehended. He is known to police and has been placed in custody pending investigation*. . . . I felt like penetrating the screen and wiping that dimple off his face.

"Marguerites," Harold marvels. "Isn't it amazing how the brain fastens on certain details, and not always the right ones! But how did you know I was here?"

"This is the third hospital I've been in today, looking for you."

THIS MORNING I BOARDED the Metro at Berri-UQAM and rode uptown to the fancy prison on Boulevard Rivière-des-Prairies to ask if a blind man named Harold, who was no longer blind, had been sent here.

"What is his *nom de famille*?" The receptionist chawed green gum. Did all Montreal officials sit behind partitions and expect one to talk to them through half-moon holes so low one had to bend one's knees and become like a six-year-old?

"I do not know it."

"*Tabarnouche*, if you don't know his name . . ."

A sign on the partition said *Respect Uniformed Personnel*. I thought for a split second that it said *Uninformed*. Then I remembered I was in my uniform. Were we all as uninformed as each other?

He scratched cherries and bananas off a couple of lottery tickets.

A lank-haired woman in the waiting area said, "Maybe they threw him in the lockup." Her bulging purse was covered in studs. "If he's harmless."

"His name's Harold. Maybe you saw him on the news?"

"I only have Netflix."

"Harold isn't a criminal."

"Neither is Jean-Maurice!" said the woman. "Jean-Maurice is completely innocent."

"Harold may have committed a small error in judgment . . ."

"Jean-Maurice wouldn't squish an ant."

"Harold's was a simple mistake such as might be made by any one of the street people around the Y or the Mission . . ."

"I'd say they've put him in the lockup or the Douglas. But they won't tell you unless you're next of kin."

I managed to convince the receptionist to hand me the washroom key, which was chained to a shoehorn in the shape of Santa Claus, also in his red coat far from home. I wiped down my collar and dampened a wad of paper towel. With this I refreshed my face and cleaned my shoes. Then I took bus 67 to the police station on the corner of Rue Angers. I left my uncertainty tied to a fire hydrant out front. I stood tall and told the attendant that as a British army general stationed here for the month of September to take part in tactical exercises I needed to contact a suspect individual whom police here had also deemed of interest. The attendant did not want to tell me anything but he ended up rummaging online for the file in question and muttering that Harold had been taken by ambulance to one of the hospitals.

"Which hospital?" I asked. But by then the man had regained himself, and said he was not at liberty to tell me.

ABOVE HAROLD'S GURNEY HANGS a sign warning, in French, that wait-times cannot be predicted and anyone becoming belligerent will be prosecuted. The bloody bandage around Harold's head seems to have dissuaded staff from kicking him off the gurney but does not press them to slow down or check on him as they hurtle down the corridor. The chaos reminds me of Culloden.

"I don't mind waiting," he says. "I quite like being still for hours."

Harold knits and knits, forming tight circles like webs made by an industrious little arachnid. I discover he loves talking about himself. It turns out that on his one night in jail he staged a peaceful protest—they had not allowed him to knit—and he was beaten up by a Buddhist monk.

"He harmed me by accident."

"But you said he came down hard on your head with a tray. . . ."

"It was an accident of the heart. My philosophy on knitting made him snap."

"Why was he in there in the first place?"

"He'd ignored several injunctions." Harold touches his sore head. "He was banned from going into pet stores."

"How many stitches did you say you had?"

"Stitches." He laughs in his ruminating way that suggests he is reminded of things too odd for me to understand—I can see how he might have infuriated the Buddhist.

"You mentioned some astronomical number . . . what's funny about . . ."

"You said the word stitches just as I was counting stitches."

He knits and I sit with him, and in the seven and a half hours it takes for someone to finally attach an electronic monitor to track his brain signals he manages to run out of things to tell me about himself.

"So, you, Jimmy," he turns to me. "You're a career soldier. A bona fide lifelong military man. An inter-generational warrior." Unlike Sophie, Harold appears to have no trouble at all with my having been born in 1727. He does not disagree that I might have been adjutant at

Dettingen and aide-de-camp for Hangman Hawley at Culloden in 1745, whereas Sophie snorts at the very mention.

If a person knits as you speak of the past, you can become mesmerized. As the yarn unwinds from its skein your memories naturally unfold to their full length. I tell him about my fierce adoration of George Warde, and about the strange love between my mother, Henrietta, and myself. Harold listens without judgment, his soothing line of wool unspooling and purling round his needles. I tell him how Hangman Hawley made me hammer up gallows at his tent-flaps to hang the lad Jonas who romanced the laundress Hawley fancied, then he hung a fourteen-year-old who forked the glob of suet Hawley had his own eye on.

I start to say something about loving and losing Eliza—I've been talking for over an hour—and Harold says, very politely, "You mentioned her, I remember . . . but . . . tell me again about losing your brother." He says this with a frown as if he hasn't quite understood. I recall telling him last Tuesday in Chinatown, at Magic Idea, about losing Ned after Dettingen, about having to write home and tell my mother how I'd distributed his effects. . . . A letter it cost me tears to write.

"Tell me again about the box of your brother's things," Harold says. "The one you sent home to your mother."

The bravest moment in a big brother's life is not the instant before his own death in battle. He foresees that the moment he enlists. The brave part is when he sees limbs blasted off a boy down the line and doesn't know if they belong to Ned, or Elwyn, or whoever his beloved might be.

"I saw the blood of the loveliest boy soak in the stones," I tell Harold. "I ran to see, but the head was torn off—the head was a bag of blood, a burst football rolling till it smacked into a rock. His blood congealed in a tide-mark on that rock. And the rock belonged to land I knew would never be home to any of my people now or down through history yet to come."

"But this was your brother? It was Ned?"

"Nobody could tell me who it was."

"But your brother died, and you told me you sent his things back home. . . ."

"Yes. Ned died."

A dead soldier's little world fits in a tin box. What a shrunken world it is: a tin around its cube of air that in a few years no one will disturb. My brother's amulet! I thought it was made of wishbones and delicate bones from inside fish-heads, but when I looked close they were the cochleae of a child he'd shot through the eyes. We killed anything that spoke no English. Woman, child, dog, no matter. The woman who stole at night to the river to lather herself in starlit soapwort . . . we shot her as well. Anything that fluoresces in the night and is not English, you must doubly kill.

"And you sent that sad little box to his mother?"

"I did what you'd do for any mother. You get rid of the macabre amulet. You replace it with his dog tag, his phone, his memory stick. You write the tender note proclaiming her younger son, the younger of all fairy-tales, an honest and good lad who lived very well and always discharged his duties with cheerfulness: *He lived and died as a son of yours should—all his friends miss him, and our Colonel made me promise that I'd assure you of his particular concern. Elwyn was an excellent soldier, and if I ever appear to laugh again, or to have a good time in my life, it is because time—a traitor—always lessens the degree to which a bereaved heart swells in sorrow. . . .*"

"I see . . ." Harold pauses and clicks his needles as if in some curious deliberation. "I thought you said your brother's name was Ned."

"It was."

"And some of these things in the box of Elwyn . . . they were Elwyn's things, not Ned's, am I right?" Harold puts his knitting down and touches my tattoo. His hand is warm and I wonder if his continual knitting has permanently heated it. "Elwyn's things aren't from your old battlefield, are they? They aren't from Scotland and they aren't from Quebec . . . they're things a soldier might leave behind in modern warfare."

Harold resumes knitting. He knows as well as I do that past, present and future are contained in a single length of yarn.

My tattoo is coloured like his wool, but duller, since ink fades and Harold's wool is new, or is perhaps not wool at all, but something from a dollar store, made in China out of petroleum.

"Modern warfare" is such a contradiction in terms. All warriors descend from a single, ancient Council of War forged at the dawn of manhood, when standing stones mimicked the thrust of our sex and we coated ourselves in vestments so insubstantial they became symbols. Our true garb has always been the tattoo, and mine's a beauty, bearing my warrior-name and pierced by a sabre that will forever stand straight even if my body should crumple.

19 Nobody

SUNDAY, SEPTEMBER 10.
NIGHT.

Mont Royal. Montreal, Quebec

WHEN I RETURN FROM THE HÔPITAL DE VERDUN, rather late, Sophie asks, "Where've you been all day? Who were you with?"

Sophie disliked it last year when I befriended the young woman nosing around the park to document facts about marginal and homeless citizens for the census. Sophie couldn't believe that the woman, Sarah, had dutifully noted down my name as James Wolfe, son of Edward Wolfe and Henrietta Thompson, born in Westerham, England. I got confused about my birthdate and Sarah replied with understanding that for many homeless people such was the case. Sophie rolled her eyes as Sarah recorded that I was a soldier currently out of work, unmarried to woman or man, and childless.

"I stopped in at the Mission. My copy of Gray's poem came." I don't feel like telling Sophie anything about my day with Harold, and it is true that I did pick up my book, though it was a disappointment.

"And?"

"I had a hard time getting it open. The box was cemented! I injured my thumb ripping the end. Here—look."

"What?"

"It appears to have been woven out of laundromat dryer lint by robot spiders or silkworms, and the first page I opened tore under hardly an ounce of pressure. A drop of tea spilt on this book would cause the entire thing to dissolve."

"Watch your disappointment," she says. "You let it have too much power. Poetry lives spoken in air, not written on paper. But I'll admit . . ." She fingers the sad volume. "This flimsiness is disgraceful. You're almost better off getting the ebook."

"I've memorized the poem," I remind her.

Where does a poem exist when unspoken and unwritten yet committed to memory? I imagine its words afloat: letters invisible, vowels inaudible—a vapour unseen and unheard that yet infiltrates the soul, like love, like my memory of Eliza or George, less substantial than fragrance but outlasting death.

Rain patters on the tent.

"Why am I seeing twin cactuses over your head?" Sophie demands.

I don't feel up to questioning her visions just now. "I've no idea."

"One has eyes all over it—eyes covering the whole cactus: big open eyeballs staring as hard as they can. The other one's covered in spikes. Long, lethal spikes—it's afraid. . . . What the hell are the cactus twins trying to say?"

"They're your vision. How should I know?"

"But they're over your head. The one with eyes, it's starting to overflow with tears. Every eye on it is a river of grief. *You're* a river of grief tonight. Why?"

"You know there are a lot of reasons why a man like me might feel sad."

I have not told Sophie about Madame Blanchard and do not want to admit that she died before I had a chance to say goodbye.

Much less can I confess I've lost her remains through negligence, through inattention or preoccupation. . . . Sophie is always accusing me of these things.

"This rain reminds me of the night I saw Eliza Lawson's wraith come to me in a vision on the seas!"

"Stop it. You need to come back into the present."

"But I plainly saw Eliza! I've told you, she sailed through the constellations and her hem snagged on Orion's dagger over my ship the night she died—I got no sleep on that board under my smudged porthole . . ."

"Please."

"No! I watched Orion straddle the North Atlantic and wished I had his nonchalant tilt. . . . English manners had unfastened from me like pea-tendrils from a trellis! I'd forgotten how to relate to men in any civilized way. Whenever I set sail my belly spewed sustenance and instead of food I absorbed rain, wind and weed-stink. You know this! You know I remembered how to command men, but not how to command myself—how sick I was of retching into my old friend, the too-small tin pail. . . ."

"I bet that made a nice splash and a pretty tinkling sound, like a bell, and I suppose right after the bell you saw your dear Eliza, dagger-snagged . . ."

"Hanging against the star-hunter as if she were his little sister—how small she looked! Her dress was like the rosy inside of a shell sequined with herring-scales. She stared through my porthole. I knew Miss Lawson was dead and I needed no telegram. I already wore a black armband after my father's death—it was easy to pry my porthole open and drag the mourning-silk through the starlight as Eliza scattered her Valentine sequins down on me."

"Valentine?"

"We had departed Portsmouth for Quebec on the *Neptune* on February the fourteenth."

Sophie chaws her stick of beef jerky from the Dumpster.

"Eliza was my mind's guide. She was my inspiration and my self-knowledge. She was and is my every true vision, my every signal. There was nothing sublunary about her."

"Sub-what? What the hell?"

"Have you not read Donne?"

"Er, no?"

"*Dull, sublunary lovers' love, whose soul is sense* . . . 'Sublunary' means under the moon, accompanying other things that also exist under the moon . . ."

"Seal-flipper pie?"

"Things that can be felt, tasted, touched and smelled . . ."

"Narwhal? Army boots? Hard-boiled eggs?"

"Things whose soul is sense . . ."

"You mean you and Elizabeth Lawson didn't feel each other. You didn't touch each other. You didn't smell each other. Did you even talk? Or were you locked together in some sort of extraterrestrial sacred silence?"

Sophie chooses this moment to let off a noisy fart that reeks of today's vat of chicken korma the Bombay Restaurant donated to the Mission. I have to untie the tent flap and stick my head outside. "Are you saying," she persists, "that if Miss Lawson had grown old and you saw her next week as an old woman on a park bench, you'd still fling yourself at her feet?"

"Old?"

"If her shell-pale gown's in tatters and she has varicose veins and has grown extra-large ears and a humongous nose . . . you do know people's ears and noses never stop growing?"

"Could you please not . . ."

"You'd love Miss Lawson the same even then?"

"I'd—yes."

"There's one just like that who walks her Pomeranian every morning down Parc Avenue and plonks herself under the lion statue and takes her dentures out to suck a banana. She used to be an ethereal beauty like your woman. Her daughter's with her sometimes, a younger version of her with identical bone structure. I'll show you next time I see them. You can let me know which one is sublunary, who sends you over the moon and who leaves you lying under it cold and dead as an avenue of unlit chimneys."

Sometimes I wonder if Sophie envies or resents women who are delicate and who do not work as janitors in homeless shelters and who have heart-shaped faces and do not swagger around in steel-toed work boots. Instead of arguing with her I lie listening to the night sounds of the park: leaves rustling with that first papery dryness beginning to take over their summer-green softness. The rummaging squirrels, and the soft, heavy raccoons thumping toward their night-market: the rubbish bins lining Rue Olmsted.

Sophie is right. I sometimes use my thoughts of Eliza, and the sadness they bring, to veil other, more recent kinds of sadness. The ones Harold understands about me now. My wretched losses, recent losses that have no gauze of time to soften their edges. Losses caused by my own mistakes. How can I have lost everything?

AS SOPHIE SNORES, I RECALL how behind Madame Blanchard's house whispered a grove of spruce, and in that grove grew timothy hay and in that hay spangled Louis, Lolly and Madarin. I used to go and talk with them—Madame Blanchard made me carry bread in my pocket so as not to get carried away by the fairies as her real-born son had been when she and her Canadian soldier were first married. She did not like it when I came home and told her about my fairies, did not like it at all, but Madame Blanchard was never the kind of foster mother to burn my arm with the stove damper or clip me around the ears with her wooden spoon. This was in summer, and I was alone a lot.

Our stove sat under the beam painted with shiny CN-train paint and hung with a copy of *The Angelus*. All the kitchen chairs had the same paint because Monsieur Blanchard brought it home free from the station when he was done his shifts. He stole it, all the conductors did. They all stole paint and they all died on the railway one way or another—after Monsieur Blanchard was gone, Madame Blanchard and I had the house to ourselves. I played with Louis, Lolly and Madarin while Madame Blanchard went to council meetings—our town council had no men in it, all women, because what man wanted to manage a pot with no money?

At my first school dance the other boys picked girlfriends—Gérard Cormier and René Vaillancourt pursued Emilie Callaghan. I was not very interested in girls then either, at least not in getting them behind the Coke machine and kissing them, though I did sit with them on Wednesdays when Madame Blanchard gave me money for hot chicken pie. I liked talking to girls a lot better than boys.

I did not run to the front of the class the day soldiers brought the tank and guns, though I was glad the soldiers had come: our blackboard had a terrible new math problem on it that I did not think I'd ever decipher—I remember cadet recruitment came as a blessed diversion.

They brought fifteen rifles—and they let us take turns aiming them.

I aimed mine at my sunflower in our biology corner. When the other boys aimed theirs at Miss Cranton I felt sick even if she was not my favourite teacher. I wished I could swivel the guns away from her but you don't do that to Gérard or René or Alphonse and Elzéar Huet or you end up with a face-full of gravel like the peanut bits in an Eat-More bar.

No.

What attracted me were not the gun barrels, nor the tank the soldiers rolled up to our classroom windows . . . it frightened me: a faceless, mechanical grasshopper. Nor was I enthralled or intrigued by the soldier who did all the talking, though he wore red and gold gorgets and had his photo on page one of the Gaspé *SPEC*. He promised college, with our fees paid by military scholarship. All we had to do was sign and get our mothers to sign. There was no need to fear we might not measure up—there was state-of-the-art training in Bagotville and Valcartier. We all knew about these camps. Brothers and cousins had packed their bags after *secondaire cinq* and boarded the Valcartier bus and kissed their moms goodbye.

Mothers have it hard in a situation like that.

Mothers have the wrong status to go interfering in a soldier's life when that soldier gets infected with romance. Mothers know they have no say: they are women, they are roses on the wane, they are the past generation. They've begun looking upriver to the source instead of downstream to that thrilling unknown. They are not beloved, and if they were—if some mother was strangely beloved by her son or daughter with a rare and heartbreaking intimacy—the child would still clamour to be one with the vivid stream snaking out of the village.

Madame Blanchard picked up the phone when she read the note saying the recruiters were coming. I heard her tell the principal he might as well invite the Pied Piper of Hamelin to our village. He must have asked her to repeat this, which she did a couple of times before hanging up gently and looking sadly out the window at our rhubarb and our blackcurrant bush.

I did not protest when she made phone calls like this, or when she visited the school to complain. When you are a foster boy from away, when you are spindly and pale, and you like talking about books with girls, you are already far from any hope of gaining approval in our village. Already boys shouted at me in the schoolyard, "*Va-t'en, criss de tapette!*"

The recruiting lieutenant outlined what would be in store for us glorious sons and daughters of Bougainville and Percé and Port-Daniel–Gascons. We'd amount to all a youth could hope to be or become or give. There would, he said, be a lot of giving: an extravaganza of elevated sacrifice. We'd learn the meaning of living, not the mundane meaning for which rural youths so tragically settled. And so on.

His heroic rhetoric was not the element that won me.

We were close to the start of summer holidays, about to be unloosed to reclaim softball bats in a blaze of hawkweed. We were to go trout fishing in La Rivière Malbaie, and climb that precipice shadowing the over-fall where every boy in Bougainville worth his life would jackknife down to the cold green pool below. It was not a wide pool and not always deep enough: once in a generation someone sliced his skull and released brains full of fresh algebra into Minnow Gulch.

The mothers said no. They spent wretched time beside the toaster, picking a shrivelled leaf from the coleus plant, scratching dried maple syrup off the kitchen table with a thumbnail. Don't go, don't dive in Minnow Gulch like Stéphane Durocher. Don't come home from Afghanistan in a body bag like Guillaume Macdonald.

Mothers invoked the dead names, but no one listened. It remained each mother's lot to flap her gums in the wind.

Madame Blanchard was a very good foster mother, almost the same, in every respect, as my real mother.

"Those *jumelles*!" Sophie shouts, suddenly awake just as I am about to fall asleep. "Your cactuses! I know their names. Their names are Discernment and Fear—when the eyeballs on the first one, Discernment, have properly grieved, the tears will flow down and water the second. Then all its spikes—I see them unfold—they're bound to flower brave and unafraid."

Trust Sophie to bring up the notion of fear and bravery now, in the small of the night, just as I begin to feel lulled by the sound of raindrops tapping the taut orb of our tent. I snuggle down into our rumpled old sleeping bag. I do not feel one little bit like leaving by morning's first light. But the time has come.

20 Babies

MONDAY, SEPTEMBER 11.
EARLY MORNING.
Mont Royal. Montreal, Quebec

I WAKE WHILE IT IS STILL DARK, to hard rain and one of my lonely fits. I have to meet Harold at dawn—yesterday they finally cleaned him up at the hospital and pronounced him fit to go home with a new bandage on his head. Between my flute-bruised cheek and his bandage we're going to look a fine pair on the road to Quebec. Damn this damp cold. If my shoulder sticks out of the sleeping bag, I can't tell the difference between the air and the chill of my own dread. My twisting wakes Sophie. I lie still, trying not to annoy her, concentrating on our tent with its seams and folds, transparent as all the fragile shelters we raise to enfold ourselves: our cocoons, our membrane-wheels. . . .

"Go back to sleep!"

Our tents, our veils and parasols . . . What exactly did I write to Henrietta Wolfe upon discovering umbrellas in Paris? I have seen that letter somewhere recently—yes—the words are coming back . . .

Dear Madam,

The people in Paris use umbrellas to defend themselves from the hot sun, and something of the same kind to secure them from the snow and rain—I wonder a practice so useful is not introduced into England, where there are such frequent showers, and especially in the country, where they can be expanded without any inconvenience. . . .

How my mother scoffed at this!

I have never understood her resistance. Why would she—a sensible Englishwoman—scorn something so useful, given how much rain fell in London and Blackheath?

Granted, she had no sun and the Parisian way of shading one's face from the light simply did not apply to the English. But rain! Why did my mother not even consider enjoying such elegant respite from our nearly constant rain?

I hear her now: "Anyone foolish enough to raise half a silk balloon over his head every step he takes would certainly be the laughing stock of the whole country for being so unfit and cowardly as to be scared of a raindrop."

Am I really scared of a raindrop?

Despite my best efforts, Sophie remains awake and annoyed: "Have you not got some sort of bedtime prayer to calm yourself?"

"You know I never pray. I don't believe in incantations. They remind me of the elaborate grace intoned by the bishop in the big priests' house where Montcalm persuaded me to dine during one of our Sundays of truce. The bishop had twin Indian slaves who'd tried to run away and he'd taken an iron and seared each one's shoulder with a fleur-de-lys, from which pus oozed at the scab edges. The bishop devoured three roasted snipes. Now there's a bird with a song worth hearing."

"Is it in the morning you're leaving?"

"What makes you think that?"

"Usually there are a few of your socks lying around, but there are none to be seen now."

Our tent might be damp and even mouldy but suddenly I wish I did not have to leave it.

"And your toothbrush is no longer on the flat rock. I'm inside out with fatigue here, can we just . . ."

"Are you saying you're going to miss me?"

"Also, a letter came today for you at the Mission. I have it here."

"Where's the flashlight?"

"Look. We both have an early rise . . ."

"Can't I read it? Who's it from?" I hold it up to the filtered lamplight:

JW
Hôtel Le Priori
Rue du Sault-au-Matelot
Québec City

"I dunno. Maybe James Wolfe finally got sick of you impersonating him and has written from his death-scene to tell you to stop."

"I need the flashlight!"

"Read it in the morning! I'm perishing with fatigue."

I lie sleepless until the appointed hour.

Around five in the morning I hear someone outside the tent. I draw out my dirk and hold still. I poise the blade and it occurs to me that before I depart for Quebec City I should slice the canvas and cut around Sophie's painted walrus and fold him up and take him with me in my pocket. She painted him there for guidance, hasn't she said as much? She's always implied the walrus might have a teaching for me, but I have heard nothing from it yet that did not in fact come out of Sophie's own mouth.

As I raise the knife Sophie barks—can the woman see in her sleep? —"Lay it down!"

"I was only . . ."

"Asshole. Haven't you stolen enough, with your knives and your guns and your bayonets?"

"I thought you said the walrus was meant . . ."

"The walrus is not yours for the taking."

Again I hear a noise outside the tent. An interloper gropes through the tent flap, and as I'm about to slash at him I glimpse his face—he's the clerk who served me and helped me listen to the *chansonnier* Gilles Vigneault, and then held me in a vice-like grip at Archambault's music shop. This fellow slithers into the tent on his belly, mud streaked all over him.

"Do you recognize me now, Jimmy?" he says.

I know he is talking about a time before Archambault's. And I remember now that he is always the soldier who comes after me here, that he is another young man whom Sophie helps. I look at his tattoo and remember how to decipher its arabesque calligraphy, but this does not mean I can tell you his name.

"Jimmy always imagines he's the only one," Sophie says.

When I slip behind the tent to recover my medicines I take a last look at Sophie's walrus, whose form, lit by the park lamps, is opaque when viewed outside the canvas, as opposed to transparent inside. I have not looked closely at the walrus from out here before. I incline my ear to his head and listen somewhat pathetically to see whether he does not have some wise message of farewell. His face moves and I realized it's Sophie's face I see pressed against the fabric from the inside.

She aligns her eyes with the walrus's and mouths, *Listen to your own goddamn animals.*

THE RAIN DOESN'T LET UP as I make my way down to Saint Catherine Street, checking the spines, fabric and handles of last night's umbrellas discarded in the trash bins.

There's always a good reason an umbrella has been abandoned, but a few still look promising. It's a mercy nobody knows me as I try out the trashed frames: I triumphantly glide a ring up its pole only to have the silk wheel float off and sail into a lamppost.

At Casse-Croûte Diane, where we have agreed to meet, Harold listens to me with a curious, crackling reception—as if knitting needles were a kind of radio antennae.

Outside, tied to a pole, is his golden dog.

"I'm still not sure I want to hitchhike," I begin. "And you've brought Veronica?"

I have my pack containing water, apples, a couple of tins of beans, last night's letter from JW in Quebec, my envelope of papers from Madame Blanchard, and my extra underwear. After our Breakfast Special Number 4 we walk past Gare Centrale—we'll soon reach Victoria Bridge and after that the clover-leafs and the non-pedestrian nightmare of overpasses and turnpikes where Harold seems cheerfully prepared to lift his thumb.

"Veronica will be an asset, not a liability, you'll see."

"I don't know if I can stand the noise and the air whistling off transport trucks. . . ."

"You'll be all right, especially in that jacket. It counterbalances my dubious bandage. You can hang back off the pavement altogether if you want, and leave me and Veronica to do what we do naturally."

Harold says hitchhiking is something that fits particularly well with what he calls his skill set. He can't remember what happened yesterday, or even five minutes ago, unless he crayons a symbol of it in his notepad, but he seems capable of feats that give me anxiety.

"Remind me about your hitchhiking skills?"

He loves this question. "The first plus is that I'm very good at appearing non-threatening."

"I guess knitting helps?"

"I can't knit and hitchhike at the same time!"

Harold has rules about the way he does every single thing. I imagined that a person might easily knit and occasionally stick out a thumb on the roadside, but now I realize that for Harold, this would be impossible. Both things cannot be done at once, since neither hitchhiking nor knitting is as simple as I might have imagined.

"In Jamaica you put your thumb like this . . ." He makes an aggressive lunge, jabbing his thumb groundward, body craned forward. "You're telling the driver, essentially, *hey—you have the wherewithal to own wheels and I do not, therefore you're obliged to give me a ride*. You wouldn't do that here."

"No, indeed. Someone might run you over. Or bash your head in."

He regards me as one might a charming three-year-old. "Perhaps it's not that rough. But you're absolutely right, it wouldn't be culturally appropriate to hitchhike like that here. Here you have to be much more inquiring. You hold yourself like this . . ."

"I guess I can see how you can't simultaneously knit."

"Exactly." His entire body has become a most polite question.

"You have your thumb and body held high away from the traffic, yet are hesitantly asking if, perhaps, there might be some chance of assistance?"

"That's it!"

In his eyes, I am an astute three-year-old. "I still don't feel I can do it."

"Do you not? Really?"

"If your first required skill is that you appear non-threatening, I am at a disadvantage. I like to present myself at my full height. I like to travel armed. The thought of appearing weak . . ."

"Remember the driver is in control. They are driving the car and this helps them."

"But the other side of that is—you give away your power. How do you keep out of danger?"

"Right." He looks into space. "A lot of people think there is more danger and violence, more lack of safety in the world than there really is. I know that I had a terrible experience when I was a child, but, since then, I've found people, on the whole, to be extremely kind and willing to help. I've hitchhiked in five countries over fifteen years and never once felt unsafe—well, maybe once, but it was nothing serious, and I had a talk with the person and we reached a place of safety quite easily."

I think of all the missing hitchhikers on the news, decapitations and rapes, victims buried alive along roads to and from nowhere. I feel tempted to point out that maybe he has no fear because he is quite a large man . . . but Harold is such a *not*-man—so open and soft I fear if I point out his size or his maleness he might weep. "What would you do," I say, "if you got in a car and found it unsafe? If you felt you were vulnerable?"

"You mean if the driver turned out to be dangerous?"

"Yes."

". . . I'd do the same thing I do in any situation, whether the person I'm with seems bad or good. I don't look at who the person has become. I look at everybody as if they are the same, because they are, in a way, to me at least. Bad or good. Rich or poor. Male or female. It doesn't matter."

"Everyone? Millionaires? Bullying tycoons? Thieving corporate bosses? Torturers?" I want to add things. Many things I have seen or done. There is no end to the butchery and cruelty I've been a part of. I suspect Harold is aware of this.

"All of them," he says. "Even the man who raped me when I was little."

"You look at them how, exactly?"

"They were all babies once. I look at them as babies."

"No matter what they've become?"

"No matter what. I babify them."

GREEN MAN

21 JW's Letter

JW
Hôtel Le Priori
Rue du Sault-au-Matelot
Québec City

SEPTEMBER 8TH, 2017

Dear James, or perhaps, dear Jimmy . . .

May I call you that?

Yesterday I took the train from Montreal to Quebec City. As you can see from the letterhead here, I've booked a room at Hôtel Le Priori, a chic little place near the funicular in Quebec's lower town, with exposed brick and a brushed metal sink shaped like an ice cream cone. There is an air freshener in the hallway that I had to surreptitiously quarantine.

I have been studying James Wolfe's letter to his father in which he explained how his shortened leave affected him. I made a copy of it at the Fisher Library and have it here with me now. I have read and reread it . . . so now I do see how James Wolfe might come back to visit in 2017. And I see, Jimmy, believe me, how you feel Wolfe has chosen you.

To his father he wrote that everybody knows how hard it is to get a bit of time away from the army, yet no one allowed him to seize what little freedom he could. You've given him, haven't you, that opportunity he feared might never occur again?

It has also occurred to me—and forgive me for not having understood this sooner—that James Wolfe was always a young man. He was never *not* young—thirty-two when he died. In the work I am writing now, he remains young in physical appearance but he is old, really—as you know. Forgive me for appearing to separate Wolfe and your own self, but know that I understand—coming to Quebec City has helped me understand—that, in you, Jimmy, Wolfe has come back to a Canada in which both he and Quebec have grown older.

An important part of my own quest, through getting to know both Wolfe and yourself, is to ask what it might be that remains after one's youthful illusions fall away. Forgive me for having looked into a few particulars about your recent past—I managed to glimpse the name on your library card at the Fisher, and, from there, I was able to find out about your military record in Afghanistan. I wonder how you manage at all, back from there, encountering a world that, for you, has utterly changed. I fear you find no loveliness here at all, though I hope there might be something in civilian life that can cheer your soul.

Tomorrow I plan to further explore your Plains of Abraham. My old friend Raymond, who lives part-time in Quebec City, walked the plains recently and calls them "desolate and beautiful all at once." When I met my editor recently and told her I was getting to know Wolfe, she said, "Do you like him?"

I'm not quite sure how I feel or what has happened to me, as I have followed your story.

Tomorrow when I go and walk on the field where the culmination of Wolfe's life and death transpired, the plains will be hemmed in by modern Quebec City. Last night, hungry after an afternoon of wandering around, I walked the lower town's alleys and found them lined with little shops and galleries, and strung with fairy lights. It is late in the tourist season but couples walked the cobblestones craning their necks at this and that, their satchels and purses bouncing off their hips. I ate a hot little vegetarian pizza at ten o'clock on the *terrasse* of a gastropub at the bottom of the steep rise to upper town and heard a lot of English, though I'd expected to encounter mostly French. Tonight the moon, still nearly full, hangs like a festive lantern above the town.

I phoned home yesterday after checking into the hotel and my cat-sitter was watching a movie about time travel. He said the film made it seem as if we already possess, or almost possess, the means to travel back in time. It was that skillfully done. Later, sitting with my artichoke pizza that had a delicious charred crust and thinking about the Wolfe you and I have both come to know, the Wolfe who died in this same place two and a half centuries past, I thought, yes, we do possess the means. Through the letters of Wolfe, not via memory, as you seem to have experienced, but through a kind of listening through time—I've heard him. I know I have. Not in the way you've heard him, of course, after the desert, after your own war. But still, through reaching with all my inquiry into his words, I've met him, or I've met . . . perhaps through my having met you, Jimmy . . . his warm presence.

This morning I walked from Hôtel Le Priori toward the Plains of Abraham. I scaled the winding hill around the funicular, walked past the Chateau Frontenac with its extravagant architectural peaks and cornices, and came upon a monument thrust straight into the sky: on its side stretches the name WOLFE, facing upriver toward the plains and the colony. I thought: was it deliberately made in the ugliest possible British style, phallic and unadorned, without a swirl or any French curve at all? Then I looked at the other side, down which stretched the word MONTCALM.

I sidled up to eavesdrop on a couple standing with their private tour guide. "This monument," said the guide, "is the only one in the world dedicated to two warring generals."

Each general's name occupied an opposing plane of the white shaft, sharing one pillar but never able to see each other, each facing resolutely away. Even an onlooker could in no way see both names from a single vantage point.

"There was a lot of debate about the language in which the plaque should be written," said the guide. "No one could decide whether to engrave it in French or English. So they wrote the words in Latin."

The marble plaque is yellowed, discoloured, as if someone has held to it a torch or stained it with urine.

Dear Mother, I see Wolfe writing in a letter he then crumpled and discarded, *let me go.*

Dear Mother Country of Britain, let me go to the beauty that is France.

Dear Old Mother, let me go to all that is France, all that is New.

I walked across grass looking for the Plains of Abraham Museum. I saw a toddler with a plastic shovel planting bulbs in a tulip bed, watched over by his mother, who wore a Parks Canada Staff uniform.

Over by the stone fortifications a man said into his cellphone, "Bar codes can be printed with a regular laser printer on any of your products."

I heard jackhammers and beeping trucks backing up all around the plains, from the main road to the docks, and in the green centre floated conversations, bicycle bells, and odd, fluting notes of passerine birds.

Around the ruined stone citadel on the plains stretches a moat with signs: *Chute: Danger of Falling.* There is serious construction going on: men in hardhats with jackhammers burrow rubble out of casement holes. I had no idea where the museum was, its signs having petered out. The construction racket was horrendous and reminded me of what all the history books say about sound on these plains—that the battle was deafening. Was it? Is that something, Jimmy, that you know?

I encountered a couple who had ascertained there was no museum where I was headed: they sought it, too. We stopped near an interpretive sign about the Ross Rifle Factory, Cove Fields and Arsenal Laboratory. Then the man spotted in the distance the orange sign, *Plains Museum*!

The plains really are beautiful, as my friend Raymond has said. They are not flat, but designed with curved paths, and stretch over hills and rises with trees on them. There is not a feeling of stretched-out desolate flatness as at Culloden: this does not feel institutional, but feels like someone's homeland. The land is feminine and hummocked and curvaceous, not angled, linear, masculine or English at all.

The lines of land against sky rise and fall, dip and breathe: it might be a battlefield but this land is still alive.

The land tells me the French were far from vanquished.

Can I say it's almost as if Wolfe has never been here at all?

I continued on, then, into the museum. An employee at the desk provided me with a little map that showed, on the far side of the plains, a path—the very path leading up from L'Anse au Foulon that was taken at night by Wolfe and his army to surprise and defeat Montcalm; a path that has remained obscured by rock and overhang and forest for the 257 years since Wolfe climbed it at four o'clock in the morning in silence and stealth. The path has been revamped, said the clerk, so that for the first time in history you can walk on it and see it for yourself.

"When did it open?" I asked.

"Two weeks ago."

Jimmy, I walked to your L'Anse au Foulon path. In fact, I have walked all over Quebec City and have been persuaded to look at the history of this place in a mysterious new way, a way that moves me to tears.

My heart broke in the museum over the French colonial soldier's overcoat. It has its tails turned back at front and rear so that the corners meet in a little bow-shape at the soldier's sides. The coats were made of cloth woven in Marseilles. It had a blue collar and cuffs, but was mainly of greyish-white wool, with eighteen wrought pewter buttons down the front. Once he put on the coat, the French colonial soldier also donned a hat trimmed with silver lace. This did nothing to prevent him from being mistreated or killed by his own superiors if he complained, or his wife complained, about the bread made with ground peas, or the rancid horsemeat that he had to eat, provisions being scarce for all the ordinary men, though the French officers and corrupt governor Vaudreuil and his henchman Intendant François Bigot dined on roast game and brandy, imported Gruyère, goose legs, olives and honey.

But it's those jaunty upturned coattails that sadden me, secured at such a proud slant at the thigh, as if the coat has been imbued with power to stride all by itself, untenanted, in a New France made for earnest young men, ever hopeful for their futures, ever starry-eyed about a soldier's life and worth.

It came to me then, that every monument, every object in the plains museum, every rose and bleeding heart nodding its head in the Joan of Arc garden bejewelling the Plains of Abraham, every citizen and every ship and bird and fish in and on the river, attest to the continued life in Quebec of the people of Wolfe and Montcalm, standing on the same ground but, like the names on the plinth overlooking the river, never seeing each other.

But enough of this. It is time to read myself to sleep. Last week, I went to Atwater Library and borrowed a battered green copy of Erich Maria Remarque's *All Quiet on the Western Front*. I'm sure, as a great reader yourself, you know that Remarque's birth name is Erich Paul Remark. His protagonist, named Paul, draws on the author's own story of fighting on the German side in World War I. There are scenes in this book, of loveliness or anguish, that I know will be seared in my imagination for all time. It is another firsthand account of war that has impressed on me the truth that we are in all time at once, that history is now, that we are in an eternal struggle with power and aggression.

Among the unspeakable horrors Erich Paul Remark makes speakable because of his precision and his humanity, he writes this about his soldiers' camp on the moors:

> But most beautiful are the woods with their line of birch trees. Their colour changes with every minute. Now the stems gleam purest white, and between them airy and silken, hangs the pastel-green of the leaves; the next moment all changes to an opalescent blue, as the shivering breezes pass down from the heights and touch the green lightly away; and again in one place it deepens almost to black as a cloud passes over the sun. And this shadow moves like a ghost through the dim trunks and rides far out over the moor to the sky—then the birches stand out again like gay banners on white poles, with their red and gold patches of autumn-tinted leaves.
>
> I often become so lost in the play of soft light and transparent shadow, that I almost fail to hear the commands. It is when one is alone that one begins to observe Nature and to love her. And here I have not much companionship, and do not even desire it.

He then goes on to describe the miserable pathos of the Russian prison camp adjacent to the moor, where the enemy's starvation distresses him so much that he breaks his own cigarettes in half so as to slip them through the fence.

We both know how Wolfe loved birches.

With my warmest regards,
Genevieve (Jenny) Waugh

22 The Ravelled Sleave

MONDAY, SEPTEMBER 11.
LATE AFTERNOON.
Quebec City, Quebec

A SOMATIC WEIGHT HANGS OVER Quebec City as Harold, Veronica and I tumble out of the Volvo of our driver, a Mrs. Lovage who kindly allowed us to squeeze among several buckets of rhubarb and some sheet metal with which she planned to fix her chimney in Portneuf-sur-Mer. I cannot, at first, understand how so much golden loveliness hangs over Quebec's streets, it being the second Monday in September. There are no drifts of blossom and no new bright leaves—in fact the mornings came in cold all last week in Montreal, as I nuzzled cold-snouted with Sophie, chill creeping into our bones. But Quebec City, a day and a half before the anniversary of my battle, is heavy with sumac and late roses. I'll have to undo my red jacket and tie its sleeves round my waist in order to walk my old hills.

Harold has paperwork: there is a health office on Boulevard Saint-Cyrille Ouest where an official is updating his medical care card, and he wants to visit the office of the registrar of births to find his mother's death certificate which, he says, will let him access five dollars a day that he is not now receiving as part of his government cheques—it has something to do with his mother's years of work as a teacher in La Beauce.

"All the government offices are here," he says. "We both need to go and get our files updated." He insists the government has not been paying me my due. He says I'm entitled to more than the pittance owed an uninjured veteran: three hundred dollars a month extra, which I have not been receiving. "You should be on the program called social solidarity," he says, "for persons whose capacity for employment is severely limited—trust me, I know the ins and outs of that."

In his notepad he has written down enough errands with stars jotted beside them to keep him busy for months, with a special Quebec City section. There's a wool shop on Rue Saint-Jean where a woman he met three years ago in Tulsa promised to give him a skein of discontinued pea-green silk. He has a fourth cousin whose friend inhabits a cellar crammed in one of the higgledy-piggledy alleys between the Grande Alleé and Abraham's Heights: Harold has scrawled the address in his notebook as constituting a possible couch to sleep on. Finally, he has a bone to pick with a program officer named Yvette Leblanc at la campagne sur la santé mentale on Rue Jacques-Parizeau.

We agree to meet at eight thirty on the morning of my anniversary, September thirteenth, on the stools at Dépanneur Bonenfant where coffee's fifty cents and the toast is complimentary. Harold and Veronica will sleep at the flat of his fourth cousin's acquaintance and I will sleep on the plains.

I meander downhill after Harold leaves me, ending up in the lower town, the centre of which holds the chapel that stood when I arrived to lay siege: Notre-Dame-des-Victoires. It sits humble and handmade by the people, not by a pope or by powers that have made church a thing I mistrust. In 1759 I nearly destroyed it. But now I stand in its vestibule and weep.

A Spanish saint, Genevieve, stands in the chapel holding a

basket of loaves no bigger than my baby fingernail. These breads, offered for a dollar to pilgrims, have an unexpected effect on my emotions. It's as if, stumbling into the sanctuary almost by accident on a tide of weariness, I have collided with a holiness I denied all my days as a soldier. It is not a holiness in which I can believe, but in which someone else might.

In the nave hangs a time-buckled painting of a fishing barque, crude and small on the sea: Mary, Joseph and child-Jesus float over it in a glowing cameo I'd normally dismiss as unsophisticated, but the tenderness here in Old Quebec's central square unravels me—where is Harold with his knitting needles? The Holy Family trembles.

I run out, and into a shop that sells knobs of bread and salami ends labelled *loup-marin*, which I remember as the locals' name for preserved seal meat. I buy a slice for old times' sake and move into the square to eat it under the bust of Louis XIV. I am hoping to revive myself, but Louis's onyx curls cascade over the cobbles. His youthful grace taunts me with the reminder that, contrary to Mrs. Waugh's observation, I have never been a young man.

In this centre of the jewel of Quebec I'm stabbed by a longing to see my death-mate, the French counterpart to my generalship, the beautiful, sad Marquis de Montcalm, but I do not know where his body has been laid down. Last time I saw him he was leading the charge that would end in his own death. Surely he must lie in a vault within walking distance.

It has been my custom to ask a taxi driver for this sort of information in any strange city, and Quebec certainly feels strange to me now, layered with scenes of war and peace.

I glimpse—peripheral, fleeting—my Highland warriors, collapsed on the ground like fruit fallen among the living, who yet dance lithe up the narrow streets.

A taxi halts to let two old women out into the square and I slide into the back seat to inquire after Montcalm's whereabouts.

The driver has not a clue of whom I speak.

"Montcalm, the Marquis . . . "

"Qui?"

"He is famous—died in battle here above us on the plains two hundred and fifty-eight years ago this week, surely you know?"

"He is dead?"

"Surely there are plans to commemorate that very battle here—the day after tomorrow? It's . . ."

The driver regards me with barely concealed irritation. He does not know what I am talking about. I depart his cab and vow to ask someone in the streets what has happened to Montcalm.

Montcalm was more beautiful than I am: he was like his name, *calm mountain.* I secretly compare my nervous, starved spirit—hungry wolf, lone wolf, scrawny and smart, quicker than the calm mountain but not held in nearly as much affection by my country or by his.

Part of me loves Montcalm.

I turn up a lane whose name I recognize—Rue du Sault-au-Matelot. The afternoon sun is too bright and I keep to shaded parts. I pass an exquisite jeweller whose windows display filigreed silver, moonstones and sapphire. I linger at the window of Jacques Vaillancourt, Ébéniste, to admire a chair carved from cherrywood fluid as a glass of Guignolet. I pass geraniums in window boxes identical to geraniums whose petals fell like drops of blood in my hair in Paris. I finger hand-tooled boots on a sill, and want a mille feuille and a pain au chocolat.

The hill turns laborious. I see from below that the plains have been planted since my battle with numerous copses of many kinds of concealing trees.

I feel a familiar exhilaration as I climb, passing the funicular and the grand and monstrous Chateau Frontenac and the very cacophony of construction that Mrs. Waugh referenced in her letter, to where the plains' main gates hang open on the Grande Allée. Young men kick a soccer ball on the grass. The plains museum bears canary-coloured banners.

I see that the plains have been incorporated into the life of this place—I had not expected that they would become part of the poetry of daily living in Quebec: in the sunken garden named after Joan of Arc, two lovers slice tomatoes releasing musk in the air and the juice runs down the young man's forearm, which he licks. A bowl of silence lies in this garden, around which noises of the city rumble and push. Someone—a man named Fred whose bust bears a gossamer-glittering web spun from his nose to his ear—has redesigned the plains, so they lie no longer sere or even flat, but undulate: warm hills planted with every manner of beech and willow able to grow in New France. For this *is* New France: nothing British thrives here—unlike Montreal which has succumbed to so much British influence, an influence I have been trying—god help me—all my born days to outrun.

I come to an apple tree under which two *marmottes* share small, rosy crab-apples with gentle, animal goodwill, oblivious to me, in the spot where a young Redcoat fell—I see the youth crumpled there now, white-faced and bloodless, his hair the russet of mine, as was the hair of so many young Jacobites. It was for them I stopped covering mine with the white wig.

The smaller marmot appears to look into my eyes and I have the horrible insight that my dead Highlander's soul has roamed the plains, has leapt into this animal and now beseeches me through its eyes. Who is this departed boy and why can I not settle on his name?

"*Ned—*"

But in this body gape wounds my brother, Ned, did not suffer.

Ronnie? Ronnie of the drum, the Highlander I knew in Culloden!

Or did Ronnie drum for me here? Certainly Ronnie was one of the Highlanders who followed me through more than one battle. . . .

This body is certainly not Elwyn's, is it?

I hate that I can barely picture Elwyn anymore, his face, the sickening mutilation after the pounding he got in that shithole—not here—did I not lose Elwyn here? Surely it's in fact Elwyn I see lying here, on the plains. . . .

I have seen so many dead boys.

It occurs to me that the younger marmot is trying to communicate with me: "Yes but no," say its eyes. "You have it right that I hold this young soldier's soul for safekeeping. Come back tonight when no one else is here, and I'll divulge to you his name."

The marmot is real and warm and I know the boy is not. Or I'm fairly certain he is not. . . . I am seeing a figment and not a man. Still . . . The other animal, the larger of the marmots and—I think—the older, concentrates on an apple at the entrance to its burrow and gives me no word, only a calm gaze that I also feel in some part of me I am meant to recognize. A marmot, I remember from my biology and Latin classes, is a mountain mouse.

Listen to your own goddamn animals, Sophie said.

I HARDLY SLEPT LAST NIGHT—I need rest and shade.

I climb the plains to the trees, which reach in a swath of loveliness all the way toward my Foulon. I know where to rest, where to dream a cooling dream that'll take me out of this fever of the plains with their tour buses, soccer players, and the red-and-orange kite that sways loud as a blood moon, loud as my Redcoats. The modern sky hangs lurid and cruel as the palette of George Townshend, that worm among my brigadiers, the one who mocked me hardest.

Historians have not divined my army's most potent weapon.

Generals of losing armies have never known it.

I search here under the sacred shade of ash and maple for that spot on the plains where I bade my men do the thing that won our battle. I bade them obey me, yes. I bade them each take a mouthful of smashed snails for their dysentery. I bade them carry gear by the hundredweight over the Foulon: muskets and cannon, more poundage than a man can carry unless he's possessed. I bade them move silent as phantoms. Did I threaten deserters with scalping by my own hand? Yes to all of it. Did I forbid them to pray in my presence, invoking instead a supra-divine cunning? I did. But none of these things gave us our edge that slew the French.

No one knew we were here.

We were so exhausted we hardly knew it ourselves.

I timed our ascent so that in dawn's glimmer no Englishman would err and shoot the red coat of his brother. But dawn was not my secret.

When we attained the Foulon cliff—after we deceived the sparse sentries with our very good French, after we sweated under our loads and tricked the owls of New France into not shrieking our presence—we got to the edge of the plains, a mile and a half from where the battle would explode. Then I drew my secret sword.

I have said inferior commanders do not read Xenophon or other philosophers of war, but had they done so, such studies would have failed to tell them what I know from my blessed country of poetry, realm of genius, divine part of man I have found nowhere near a church.

I commanded my men to lie down on the plains and go to sleep . . .

. . . the innocent sleep,
Sleep that knits up the ravelled sleave of care,
The death of each day's life, sore labour's bath,
Balm of hurt minds, great nature's second course,
Chief nourisher in life's feast . . .

I locate that blessed hollow now! Under a family of new willows I lie. Just as I bade my men lie down in 1759, before our enemy woke.

I sensed then, and I feel it even now, that these new trees on the plains are far lighter in spirit than the oak and wych elm that surrounded our Scots camps at Culloden. Culloden's assault on my reason began with tortured roots and waterlogged bark.

Owls screamed as they gathered loot. I was eighteen. I hid from men so as to recover from the horror of Culloden's slaughter but I hadn't bargained that a kestrel would sail toward me, murderous. Pewter light etched the creature's beak, its all-knowing eyes, its wing-parts and talons. I discerned how mechanical a falcon is, how fiercely it zeroes in on its bloody intent, its flight never joyful as men imagine flight.

As soon as Scotland knew me for a warrior, that land unsheathed its brutal genius; faces appeared in its every root and in all the moss, conniving where to suck rainwater, where to lay the next silt layer. Unlike this place, Scotland leaves nothing to leisure—land in highlands and lowlands alike is not given to ease. It gathers freshness and a kinetic clarity that has no kindness in it, only eerie attention, greedy to suck a man's marrow, and his brain as well should he recline in the moss too long.

A soldier need not be slaughtered for the moss of Scotland to invade him. Simply lying down for a rest turns him into occupied territory all the rest of his days.

When I was eighteen I never confessed to my mother what befell me in Scotland—I hid the haunted dereliction of my mind from her, and with my father I stuck to military news: how he loved comparing my situation with campaigns of his own though the two bore no resemblance, his mind and mine being like the minds of two men who are wholly unrelated.

If I wrote to my mother of ancestral presences I called them evanescent as the sheen on a pigeon, and never told her how phantasms loitered shy until I'd slept weeks amid ruins and standing stones far from English conversation.

I've pretended never to anguish. I mocked any man among my soldiers who became afraid of the spectral realm, accusing him of weak conscience and an overblown imagination. To no one did I admit the outlandish presence of malevolent enchantments whether we bunked in roofless chapels or in shattered coal cellars—the whole of Scotland is laid bare to rain, frost and mischief. From its rocks and roots rises the green man enwreathed with oak leaves. Half man and half animal, he guards Scotland from soldiers like myself not through cannon or grapeshot but through driving madness into our intellect.

In Scotland I kept seeing the green man's face not only over pub doors but in the woods. Any time I asked a local about him I was met with a blank unknowing, a secret stare. To sleep in the Highlands for a fortnight with no roof was to forever dread the green man's influence over my mind.

Culloden! That's where my regiment had the drummer named Ronnie. And I *did* bring him here with me, to Quebec—I'm not remembering incorrectly. . . . Ronnie did not use a regulation stick but tore a branch from whatever tree would yield him one. He told me such a stick spoke for the land and meant the land would not treat us as invaders. After Culloden he formed a habit of finding a stone seat with a vantage of many miles, and he drummed with his naked hand and cocked an ear to the drum as if it were talking to him.

I sat with Ronnie in the Highlands, lured by that drum. I was used to thinking of a drummer as practical: a way to keep men apprised of one another's coordinates in fog or in artillery smoke—his drumming an audible sign to keep us from scattering.

The first thing Ronnie did when we arrived in the New World was make his own drum out of the skin of a deer he'd shot, and wood from a cedar he cut after lightning struck it. He let me sniff the wood and it emanated deep sugar. On Île d'Orléans he lifted the drum to my ear as he hit it and I became aware that its vibrations were more than sound: they reverberated and entered my body as a man enters a woman. The reverberations dislodged my own bad vapours. Warmth suffused me where all along had dwelt my old remorse. And I realized the function of drums in battle is this: to infect soldiers' blood with the fleetness of the wild animal and strength of the tree that fashioned the drum.

"Sound it to me through this temporary slumber," I asked Ronnie as we lay on these plains to rest before our battle, and he laid me down to sleep better than any apothecary's concoction. It's a wonder I woke in time.

But wake I did.

I never woke up on any day better or with more courage than I did from that half-hour sleep on the thirteenth of this month in 1759, my men slumbering round me like maidens before we rose to slay Montcalm. I'll never forget the thrum of Ronnie's drum in my sacrum.

I wish it sounded in me now.

23 The Foulon

TUESDAY, SEPTEMBER 12.
MORNING.
Quebec City, Quebec

MY DESCENT OF THE FOULON path feels strangely gradual and I realize some sort of machinery must have been employed by the parks people to gentle what was far steeper of old. The gentleness irritates me, and I can hardly believe my eyes when I come to a juncture where earth gives way to sinuous pavement that inclines by such tiny degrees anyone at all might ascend or descend without becoming out of breath. I halt at a lookout equipped with a guardrail over massive riverside tanks, noisy cranes, transport trucks, and endless traffic speeding along Boulevard Champlain.

A woman in a business suit appears to instruct a gaggle of well-dressed men on some point about the scene below and I inquire, "What's in those great round containers down there below the boulevard?"

"Those are the grain silos of the Old Port of Quebec."

The silos possess the imposing dereliction of industrial edifices from the early twentieth century and I feel the strange dislocation of time wash over me again—the sensation has become familiar though I do not love it. I expected this old port to be modern yet it looks outdated, while this—my old climbing-route up the Foulon—has become spanking new. It was *my* place, the scene of my feat of imagination and risk. But it is unrecognizable, utterly modern: a serpentine beast rising in a fashion alien to me. It no longer belongs to my memory, but to a strange, collective understanding shared by this official and her entourage in their impeccable clothes. These are men I have seen paying to have their shoes rendered agleam at shoeshine stations between gates at airports.

"I see the silos are old," I tell the woman, "but this . . ." I fling my hand toward the sinuous trail, "the path, the guardrails, the little plantations of seedlings . . ."

Brave tufts of leaf glow new and alive, too baby-green for an autumn day. The greenery forms small islands among mounds of raw and unnerving rubble—wounds in the landscape, made by backhoes and specialized incline-busting front-end loaders.

A placard stands near us with the figure of Montcalm painted on it, and a quotation, apparently uttered by him though I never heard him say it: *Defeat is the ordinary price of being the weaker party, but being taken by surprise—that is truly woeful.*

"The placard," I say, "the path itself . . ." The woman waits, and I sense I've interrupted an important information session. "How new is it?"

"Very new," she says. "If you go over to that bend and look down, you'll see the best part. Yes—just over there . . ."

A feeling of desolation engulfs me.

I silently name the doll-like cut-outs tied to chicken-wire that has been stretched over the escarpment: effigies of my soldiers cut with a jig-saw from some sort of space-age shining board designed to withstand weather: Gunner Wendell Macpherson, eighteen, out of Bonnyrigg. Stanley Black from Coldstream. Bramwell Taylor, seventeen, his fingers previously blown off by a bottle rocket the French filled with tar and lit, yet Bramwell climbs the bank faster than I ever could because he has lashed his wrist to tines he hacked off his bully-beef prong.

My men glitter flat on the escarpment, faceless silhouettes, clambering dolls without the third dimension even dolls should possess. Those not sunlit gape dark like holes cut in the landscape where I positioned them. Is that Ronnie, clambering with his silent drum . . . a scrap of two-dimensional puppetry!

I flee the woman and her entourage and descend the new Foulon.

A crone in a covered ruby scooter decorated with a silver balloon slobbers an ice cream cone as she retraces my glorious ascent. A cyclist hurtles down, his helmet the carapace of some exotic fly, pink zigzags emblazoning his tights. The asphalt is harder through my soles than the root and shale I climbed to defeat Montcalm.

I come to billboards bearing artists' renditions of my battle. They depict me as Brigadier Townshend did—a cartoon—a poncey, wispy, tiptoeing lightweight, my pointy little nose in the air like that of an insect or a hummingbird. My nose and my sword vie for status as silliest proboscis. Here on these boards, as in Townshend's sketchbooks, which I know have been preserved, I am ineffectual, effeminate, inept—not to be seen for a moment as anything remotely resembling a war hero. My spindly limbs akimbo, a face that simpers, "*Mother, ready me a dish of tea and a currant bun—my battle was a dizzying dance and I fancy something sweet.*"

Should I care that the woman with the silver balloon must believe Townshend's cartoon?

I was never vain. I don't waste time reacting to pettiness in others and my own failings are big, not small. Pettiness on my part is not the reason Townshend hated me.

The letter he concocted our night of the Foulon, minutes before we made our move, was nine lines long but can be paraphrased in two:

Sir—

Why haven't you told me what the hell we're doing?

The truth is, I confided in no one.

It is astounding how a seed-speck of insight flies straight into the heart of one's enemy if you let a spark slip to the wrong man.

But the Foulon was my only chance. It was a crazy chance. It combined sheer impossibility with hope's sole glint. It was a plan too desperate to entrust to anyone save myself.

That is the difference between myself and a man like Townshend. I am a man who can keep my own counsel and bear the resulting murderous loneliness, and face every consequence, whether success or failure. Risking failure has never been, for me, a problem. I look on it as life's consummate thrill—wagering all for the sake of one doomed chance.

I grabbed the only chance I had. It was perfect. It was a point of precise illumination, a flash of clarity in a world of imperfection, a world sad and disorganized, broken and incomplete, as I am. What small-minded cartoon by Townshend, however long-lived, can obscure such an instant?

Now, as I descend the new Foulon, I resist any temptation to dismantle or deface his cartoons.

I stand on the riverbank, its pack of industrial cranes and containers groaning and crashing between myself and Point-Levis from where my army levelled Quebec to rubble. I walk the edge of the horrendous industrial zone in the traffic-din on the road named after Champlain until I spot the tip of Île d'Orléans, and next to it the white cataract of Montmorency Falls whose waters have been crashing down those rocks incessantly every minute and second over the two and a half centuries since I last saw them. It was a mystery to me as a boy to think how waterfalls did not run out of water: surely they must run dry even if they came from some mountain pond fathoms deep. I used to ask my father about this, but he never answered me directly or satisfactorily, and I don't think he knew the answer, for he was not a man I could imagine ever, out of mere curiosity, following a mountain stream to its source.

But I have done it.

I followed the waterfall behind our house in Westerham—up its chute and along its thin stream into the hills. The stream widened but not very much, then narrowed to a trickle that ran for miles. I followed it thinking that at any moment it would dip and widen into the lake that must surely be wide and deep. But instead of widening into a lake, my childhood stream thinned to a needle of silver and then, under ferns and peat and shale, disappeared in the ground. I had not known underground springs existed, invisible yet apparently inexhaustible, unnamed and awarded no credit for having fed the waterfalls below.

Now, at the bottom of my Foulon, I am weary. Here is another billboard bearing a caricature of myself: I read a portion of its caption, written to explain my Foulon victory, but can read no more once I ascertain its tone: I won not through any virtue or discipline of mine, but through accident, *par hasard*—sheer good fortune that overshadowed Montcalm's misfortune and his abandonment by a France that cared nothing for her colony but left it orphaned, neglected and unprotected, able to be taken by even an ungainly fool such as myself.

Now Quebec sees me as ridiculous and who am I to argue?

How graceful she is, the City of Quebec—like Paris. Its heights and low areas stack atop one another like a city in an intricate dream.

Dear Mother, I want to write—but where have I put my pen and paper?

I want to describe that jet-black bust of Louis XIV in the square, unlike any English monument, hardly a monument at all—more a curl of night-ocean scooped with loving hands and bestowed on the street. You can glide past it as a bird over the wave.

Dear Mother, J'adore all things French!

THERE WAS A NIGHT IN New France when I foolishly forgot to guard the distinction between myself as a general and as a man. I let my personal longings get the better of my actions, which is something I hardly ever do. Whenever I do it, I come to regret it bitterly.

It was July 1759, and I couldn't stand the mosquitoes another second. The bogwater with its carnivorous jug-leafed plants. The stink of my men. The relentless stringy beef, bowel chaos and toe fungus. The cloying incense of Canada's sticky fir buds. The goad of her white-throated sparrow's song sharp as spruce pins.

I'd imprisoned the French, not anticipating how inhospitable their land would become without them in it. The lonely quiet became unbearable. There is nothing of comfort to me in a Canadian wood and I cannot live in it. I know this now beyond doubt, and it might be my only certainty regarding my Quebec fantasy. But at that time I was still under the colonizer's spell.

I forgot myself and sent out invitations. I commanded my officers to bathe and to wash their clothes, and invited the women prisoners of New France to a soirée in my tent.

I had the sutlers break out the marzipan and confits, and our cook dug a pit for a pair of lambs Niall Mackison had risked his neck fetching from a cliff on Île d'Orléans. I ordered my last pineapple sliced and studded with barley sugar and laid on a trestle. I borrowed French glasses from Montcalm himself. I did all this not out of kindness to our prisoners, though I was always pleased to cause any woman happiness, but out of my own longing. I wanted an illusion of Paris and I got it. There were gowns, coiffures. We lit the great tent with candles. I played my flute, and a little songbird—a miller's daughter from Isle-aux-Coudres—sang "Partons, la mer est belle" and "Vive la rose," and we all danced.

Sophie never believed this story. She ridiculed it until the phantasm, illumined and gorgeous, faded from me.

But it all comes back to me now. And the story is true. I sent the invitations on my best ship's paper and I thought the women would be glad to get them. It was a stupid mistake. Have you never let your enthusiasm for a venture cloud your judgment? I asked Sophie. Have you never been surprised and hurt when others do not share your love of some particular, lovely enterprise?

The women of New France came. They'd bathed, and had done the best they could with a few scraps of ribbon and muslin. I tried not to stare at their weird little hats, or to inhale as I danced near their decayed teeth. I did not mind overlooking the incapacity of colony folk to reach the level of European sophistication. Some of the prisoners were dressed in well-made garments their servants had stitched with imported silk. It was not too primitive or outlandish a scene.

The problem was, I forgot that every last woman among them hated me with her whole heart.

Their hatred billowed out to my tent walls until those walls strained like the engorged gut of a lord who has filled himself with a lifetime of rancid mutton and ale. I could hardly breathe. Much as I imbued my face and my every gesture with civility that night, I intercepted nothing in return save barely disguised derision.

Remembering that derision renders me downhearted now, especially among these disdainful caricatures populating the new Foulon.

Where has my old Foulon gone?

Under the high sun—is it already past noon? —I see, beyond the billboards and the path and the cut-out effigies of my men, a wild and unchanged part of the cliff!

Does it know me?

I move closer and see that the landscapers and the designers of history have their limits: they have not altered the face of the cliff beyond one small area. Above me, dark against the bright sky, looms my real Foulon, and I resolve to climb it once again instead of going back into the city by the manicured path.

My boots cause little avalanches on the escarpment and I think of Harold. I think: the last time I did this climb, I had company.

My coat drags in the dust and I become thirsty. I feel more worn-out than I did in the pre-dawn of my death-day: daybreak then felt exhilarating.

I am weary from all my travels, the weary afternoons with their futile suns.

As I scramble back into the trees I'm grateful for their cool darkness. I feel respite as I reach the trees and grab their roots—their roots are fingers of dear ones who have missed my presence.

24 Who Am I in the Night

TUESDAY, SEPTEMBER 12.
NIGHT.
The Plains of Abraham. Quebec City, Quebec

WHEN I WAKE IT IS to see in the forest a lurid stain from sodium lamps in the port below. My trees muffle the industrial rumble, but the woods' margin still suffers the port's racket, an extra layer of hollering from workers repairing a massive vessel that bears no cargo save passengers. I peep through foliage to see its name in the lamplight: *Empire Summit.*

The Plains of Abraham at night are more sympathetic to my eyes than in the day—I wander to that place where I saw the marmots and the wraith under the apple tree, was it yesterday? Was the lad Elwyn? No—Ronnie? Was it here—yes, here are the fallen apples, but the fallen youth has disappeared.

I lie down where he lay, fancying the damp grass might retain a drop of his warmth, but night vapours sink into me. I lie on a few sour little apples hard as stones, inedible—I could use their juice, were there a single drop.

Beyond the field spangle Quebec's lights—churches and apartments and office buildings, even a sky-high restaurant that revolves, glittering, over the city. Here in the lonely field I feel a cold worm under my fingers, an icy wet slug, a spider crawling over my face, and the moon, luminous but uncommunicative sailing over my head, waning as she did during my siege. I have always thought the waning moon resembles a lozenge being sucked, and its one indefinable, dissolving edge makes me uneasy, unlike the sharp crescent of a new moon, or that perfect edge when the moon is full.

I hear a shuffling near the apple tree—shadows shift and I make out the outline of the animal I saw yesterday, but instead of gathering apples it watches me. The second marmot hangs back at the entrance to their den. I feel compelled to make no movement or sound. I'm not scared, but I imagine one of them could jump and bite my face. I've had many a rodent lick salt off my cheek in my bunk on the *Neptune*, and one or two have bitten me while I slept.

Sometimes an unaccountable sadness comes at me from out of nowhere. There are innumerable reasons to feel broken-hearted, but which one is at play during any given bout of broken-heartedness? Sometimes I can't tell.

"Why look at me?" I ask. "You're just an unimportant little animal." I can't see its eyes but I feel them. "Did Sophie send you?"

A scrap of cloud stretches threadbare over us. There is a French word for it, when the cloud-cover stretches and breaks into chaotic little floaters, the way my men lost formation and scattered into ineffectual pieces of scarlet on the day of my battle—am I the only one who requires precision of formation in combat: an alignment of line, plane and colour in a most sacred kaleidoscope? A kaleidoscope that goes beyond symphonic sound, beyond artistic genius, and into the realm of maps and nations and of entire countries sewn together in the ultimate creation that is our human purpose and destiny—the whole globe is a general's aim, his symphony, his masterpiece. The object at stake in his work is no abstraction, but is the only reality he possesses.

I have taken comfort in the blessed peace of the choreography of war.

I see that choreography now, rising on this misty field under the waning moon.

All around me in the grass arise my lads. But it isn't lads a general sees during the fight: what he sees is the beauty of tactical structure and geometric precision. The calming harmony of military strategy. The form and metre of soldiers taking their places as the general has ordered them to do.

I watch it rise out of the mist around me now—the aesthetic harmony of lines, columns, formations of infantry combatting not only the men of New France but also the adversaries of boreal swamp and bog that encroach on every attempt to carve a town or village out of this damned wilderness.

Around me materialize the sharp, beautiful red coats and guns and hats and bayonets against the rise of hill and hummock: this field breathes like a woman waiting for us to fall.

But we don't fall, for we planned, mathematically and artfully, this scheme, the visual field, the planes of line and colour, just as my favourite painter, Jean-Antoine Watteau, planned his *Festival of Love*—a scene so similar to these undulating plains I feel I've entered it.

Was not my battle a festival of another sort of love?

Do people think a butcher hacks away at a cow without devotion? No! He follows a map of utmost precision, slicing rib from breastbone, unwinding intestine from curled bud, lifting brain from skull into brine with his slotted spoon, each tool fit for its task.

Or the war is music.

For, as Handel has his lines and spaces into which he must slot, finally, a set of musical notes—half notes, whole notes, quarter notes: an arsenal of fractions whose intervals and lengths can stretch into timeless space or become exquisitely small—so a general must compose his score, his symphony, his musical gift for the king.

My brigadiers gathering around me in the mist complain I am indecisive!

Would they dare interrupt Handel at his composition desk? Have they not noticed paper crumpled knee-high around the composer as he charts new variations, not out of vacillation but out of his quest for perfection?

The field peoples itself before me. I watch from my place under the moonlit crabapple, its strange little animal standing over me—silent and soft, as if he can somehow protect me.

Am I remembering my old battle, or are these new variations?

Notes sound at the composer's command. Do my brigadiers and other detractors suppose me rigid or unreasonable? My orders have been few but necessary. I don't deny I require obedience even while I change my mind. Do people suppose I am only a man speaking? How many times do I have to explain that a general is not merely a man?

No. Just as Handel erased, obliterated and changed the line-up of notes in his perfect compositions, so a good general must have cooperation from his brigadiers, and from soldiers down to the lowest ensign . . . not as a matter of human rank or personal superiority, but as a question of life-giving symmetry. Without the fidelity of the lowest sixteenth-note, the whole symphony is lost in cacophony.

Harmonious alignment with the highest English principles is everything to me. It is why a man who elevates his personal appetite, one who cannot control his impatience, his loyalties or his morals, is beneath my concern and cannot expect protection under my care, as long as I remain a general.

Men have a talent for mocking the tilt of my nose and chin, but no inkling of the exquisite dance of choices I entertained. It is not true that I changed my mind. My mind, in a single moment of focused contemplation, contains more possibilities than other men might conceive in a thousand days if they changed their minds every hour.

I see combat's game-pieces move in infinite combinations. This is not changing my mind. It is, rather, a consummate warrior's steadfast meditation.

The warm-blooded marmot sits on the grass inches from where I lie. I ask, "Where's the lad I saw lying here yesterday, that wraith in the bright afternoon?"

The animal regards me.

I name my Highlanders, starting with Ronnie, though I know this lad wasn't Ronnie. . . .

He's the one you refuse to name.

Has the marmot said this? He is staring at me so quietly now. He regards me with an attitude I recognize: calm and disconcerting, challenging me.

"Sophie," I ask again. "Did Sophie send you?"

Do I ask this aloud in the night? Or does the animal play with my thoughts the way Sophie did?

I check myself—Sophie has not sent the animal. The animal lives here all the time. If Sophie has sent anyone, it is myself. Hasn't she said, over and over again, I need to face the plains?

On this turf where the unnamed Redcoat lad lay this afternoon—am I lying in his blood?

The marmot sits humble and apparently insignificant, but self-possessed as if he owns the plains, or at least holds great status here. He commands his place on this hill like a landowner disguised as a servant. He listens as I cast about to anchor myself in time and place.

I mistrust that moon's soft edge: to me the moon-blade is the edge of time itself, and when that edge wants sharpening I cannot know where I'm moored.

"Who was that lad? I half recognized him. . . ."

The marmot looks at me with what feels like considerable pity.

"He lay here," I insist, "yesterday in the afternoon, right where I lie now, then he sank away—he was one of mine, wasn't he? You told me to come back at night and you'd tell me his name."

Not one of yours.

Is it the animal I hear, or wind in the crabapple?

Or do the Plains of Abraham themselves possess a voice?

We hold him in safekeeping, as we safeguard all the lost.

Have I spent too many nights with Sophie and her walrus and her teachings so irrelevant to a man of my brutality?

Is the marmot not both silent and insignificant?

Let us hold safe the spirit remains of the lad, our red-haired Wolfe . . .

"You think he is yours!" I exclaim to the creature.

And of the beautiful Montcalm. And of the undetermined number of Amérindiens anonymes *and British and Scots and Acadians whose blood is here with that of Wolfe, whom you wish to be but are not.*

The plains and their animals and their wind and their whispering tree fall silent.

"If he's yours," I say, "if you hold Wolfe in your safekeeping, and he is not within me and I am not him, then who am I in the night, lost in September on his Plains of Abraham?"

Do the plains call me by that name I've feared since I heard the taunt in my Gaspé schoolyard?

Va-t'en!

Criss de tapette!

De fieffés imbéciles!

Get lost, Jimmy Blanchard.

25 Deathstalker

WEDNESDAY, SEPTEMBER 13.
MORNING.
The Plains of Abraham. Quebec City, Quebec

THERE ARE SO MANY THINGS to forgive. Some are heinous, others small.

The last time I saw Madame Blanchard, she said, "I hope you'll forgive me about the onions."

"What onions?"

"The onions I used to fry every day as you were coming in from school. I wanted it to smell nice and homey for you, coming in. I never knew what I was going to do with the onions from one supper to the next. I started doing it the day you came home and said supper cooking in other boys' houses made your mouth water. Fish cakes, caribou cakes—Madame Rivard and Madame Brunet were always cooking delicious things. I just wasn't that kind of mother," said Madame Blanchard. "If I had been, you might not be so skinny."

But it was not the things Madame Blanchard was or was not that drew me in on recruitment day at school.

Neither was it the rifles, nor the lieutenant's enticements, nor the mechanical grasshopper squatting on the schoolyard dirt, glittering in parts but cavernous, a matte-dark foreboding in its manifold niches and inset grooves and important compartments, hundreds of these, folded or punched into the dark metal as if by manipulations of a robot genius. You could hide secret messages in any of a hundred niches or slots or little cubes of space. You could stick money in there, coins folded up in paper money. There were places where you could stuff a couple of bologna sandwiches for later.

The tank was a geometrically crumpled mountain of latent power.

I was very interested in it.

But the tank was not the element of recruitment day that won me. I was essentially unwinnable—I wanted books and solitude and would have been content to spend the summer of 2003 lying under our wild crabapples like this one here on the Plains of Abraham, except they were spring crabapples on that day, gnarled and interlaced and newly wind-robbed of the blossom clusters that dressed their gesticulations like insane gypsy brides.

But the visiting lieutenant had a young soldier with him—a boy from Luscious Bite—that's how I heard the name of his village. Imagine a place called that, I thought, and this boy had come from it.

I searched for the outport with that name on maps of Quebec and the world that Madame Blanchard had Scotch-taped over our woodstove. Days and weeks after the general left town with that boy I looked, and never found it. I never knew until Elwyn wrote it on my hand for me two years later that the name was Lushes Bight, a tiny place, almost never found on any map. But Elwyn had a map that contained it, and I saw it with my own eyes on the northeast coast of the island of Newfoundland, a coast even more desolate and lichened and brine-encrusted than my Gaspé.

These plains are bucolic in comparison.

How long have I slept under this September crabapple?

Under my head, my envelope of papers is dew-damp and so is Wolfe's coat.

There was a morning when Wolfe was a child of . . . three? Four? Maybe five or six. He was in a trance brought on by the multitude of petals on the apple tree outside his bedroom. Their scent was faint, yet it invaded him—I smell it now—every pistil and stamen was surrounded by lit pollen. His mother, Henrietta, shouted up the stairs, summoning him for some task to do with his shoes. . . . I forget whether she wanted him to put them in the hall or give them to Betty for cleaning. . . . They were his blue shoes with real brass buckles. He put the shoes away, or he did something with them, and when he returned to his lit-up blossoms, the tree drooped, a sudden storm slashing it—and he saw the petals all stuck like dead moth-wings on the grass.

THE PLAINS MUSEUM HAS OPENED. I go in and wash my face in the public restroom, then ask the attendant my question: Will there be a reenactment of the battle of the Plains of Abraham here, today? To mark the anniversary?

I point at my coat. "I have experience participating in such events."

But the attendant, a young man, florid of face and having a strangely baby-like, milky expression, replies that there will be no such thing.

I press him. "Today is the thirteenth of September, is it not?"

"Oui."

"I know it's not—I mean, Quebec City is hardly, I suppose, going to celebrate . . . but . . ."

He lets me go on like this for some time before pulling a paper from under a stack of loose-leaf and perusing it with apparent reluctance. "There will be, today, at one o'clock, a reenactment just outside the main door. . . ."

"Oh?

"On the meridian between the parking lot and the plains."

"Really? Is there any chance I might—could they need someone to play the part of . . . of General Wolfe?"

He looks down his nose at me and says no, this thing is a foregone arrangement planned for educational purposes and is out of his hands—he knows nothing more about it than what he has already told me. In fact, he is not sure if it will really happen.

"But if it does, then you think I'm too late to be hired? Perhaps, if someone fails to materialize . . . I could step in as a last-minute *remplacement*?"

"*Non*—if it happens at all they will hire nobody. It is not a paid event. It is educational."

"Might there remain any work to be had in . . . in setting up for the event? I have resorted, at Wolfe's birthplace in Westerham and in other reenactment sites at other times, to this kind of . . . auxiliary role—anything to be part of the proceedings. . . . I see there are no chairs outside—perhaps you have folding chairs you'll need carried out? For the audience?"

"*Monsieur.*" The man appears disgusted—perhaps my attire is not as smart as I have imagined. "There will be no chairs. There will be no audience."

With that, he stuffs the paper in his pocket and disappears to a back office through whose doorway I spy a whining photocopy machine and a tantalizing pot of coffee. Disheartened and repressing a wish to protest, I exit the museum and the plains themselves and head down Avenue George-VI and zigzag the descending alleys to Dépanneur Bonenfant to see Harold.

—

HAROLD ATTACKS A HOT DOG, all-dressed with the condiments peculiar to New France, his needles and wool parked tenderly beside his plate. I order an *eau-de-vaisselle* coffee and ask how he slept.

"Like a baby! And you?"

"I was troubled . . . there was fog. I slept under a tree that reminded me of my childhood. I kept veering between . . . here . . . and . . ."

I place my dew-damp papers from Madame Blanchard's nursing home on the Formica. The cheque made out in my name for the little bit of money she had in the bank—$754.57. Her list of medications and so on. Receipts from the nursing home outlining what they did with the rest of her bank account. Her letter to the Department of Veterans Affairs, so similar to the one Henrietta Wolfe wrote to the prime minister of England, asking for justice regarding her son's military pension—then the papers pertaining to Madame Blanchard's guardianship of me.

I show Harold a document dated 1987. "Here's the one with my birth mother's name on it after they found her stoned at a tavern on the beach in a town whose name they've obliterated with a black marker." I first saw this document just before Christmas at the age of eleven, searching Madame Blanchard's bedroom to find out if she was hiding a Sears guitar.

"Your birth mother?"

"They found her turning her purse inside out for the lotto machine while I screamed alone in the bedsit with my foot caught in the crib slats. The social worker omitted all the names of people or places, leaving only the name of the bar: La Taverne . . ."

"That narrows the field!" Harold resumes his knitting.

"And the first name of my birth mother: Noémie."

Harold focuses on twirling together strands of yarn where his wool has split.

"I know I *told* you my mother's name is Henrietta Wolfe. . . ."

"And so it is." Harold calmly peruses his stitches and runs the yarn through his fingers. "Henrietta. Yes. . . . It's a lovely name."

He still sports his yellow shirt, very clean, much cleaner than my red coat. I wonder if he has a habit of visiting laundromats, and how he manages to live rough as I do yet remain fresh as a chrysanthemum, such a light yellow.

"You believe my mother's name is Henrietta?"

"It most certainly is."

"Though this paper plainly states that I'm Jimmy Blanchard?"

Harold doesn't even glance at the paper. Instead he reads into his wool as if it is helping him understand me. "Of course."

"You understand that I'm actually . . . in truth, I mean in very essence, I'm James Wolfe?"

"I do. I understand it very well."

"And not just . . . a nobody."

"Of course not."

"Every schoolboy in Quebec learned all about Wolfe when we were small. But none of the other schoolboys responded the way I did . . ."

"They were very likely firing chewed paper pellets at each other."

"For me it was, *Get lost, you fuckin' fag! Ai, moron! Enlève-toi d'icitte!*"

"A lot of us well know that scene."

"I was nobody and nothing. *Un* bébé lala!"

Harold lays his knitting in his lap and gazes toward the shelved tins of Habitant pea soup and *ragoût de boulettes* and the Vienna sausages that have not come from Vienna.

The cook in the corner kitchen in his paper hat tosses a fryer-basket full of *frites* so crisp they rustle throughout the dim shop.

From nails hammered down the side of a shelf dangle packaged rubber gloves, bathing caps and fly swatters. One high shelf holds a concentration of things I find incredibly useful and can never seem to get my hands on when the need strikes: WD-40, duct tape, steel wool, glue. I'm tempted to get up and have a closer look, but Harold says, "You became Wolfe as a way of honouring the parts of yourself no one else saw . . . and . . . it's not as if the real Wolfe minded . . . he was waiting to be found."

"For a very long time!"

"Found, known, loved. Understood . . . and from what you've told me—from everything I've heard you say when you speak from his position—Wolfe longs to stop being such a high-profile figure. He wants to see how it feels to be . . . well . . . to be you. Someone unknown. Unheralded. It's in—what's the poem you said he carried everywhere?

"Thomas Gray's 'Elegy Written in a Country Churchyard.'"

"He longed to be a nobody just as you longed to be a somebody. It's a hilarious piece of justice, really, because in the end . . ." Harold counts his stitches and lays his incomplete circle on the counter and smooths its bumps.

I finish his thought. "I used to be so envious of him . . . I used to imagine James Wolfe had more control over war than I did. . . ."

"But your ranks differ no more than markings on that deck of cards over there on the counter: who is the joker and who the king?"

"As Jimmy Blanchard I certainly didn't have the power to reward men under me with extra pay or a word of praise, because there were no men under me. Hell, I wasn't even Jimmy Blanchard—I had no way of knowing who I was, and still don't."

I thrust the wretched foster care papers across the counter. They fall on the floor and I don't bother to pick them up.

"For all I know I could be related to you, or to Sophie, or to one of the boys Wolfe saw fishing in the river Etchemin. I could descend from a Gaspé fisherman whose nets Wolfe shredded in 1758. I could be a complete nobody. I've never found out. Madame Blanchard was no help. She cared only about beauty. . . ."

"Beauty?"

"Well, I never saw anyone else's mother trek down to the beach and take her shoes off on laundry day—a fine Monday of warm wind and sun—and walk the sea-frill where the hard stripe of wet sand shines, and pick up a pocketful of quartz and green glass and bits of bone-white pottery she called willow-ware decorated with pictures of the very ocean waves that had smoothed and broken its pieces. She laid these on the white windowsill and she filled the milk jug with flowers other mothers yanked from their cabbage gardens with rusty trowels. She did not play cards at night, nor take the bingo bus, nor watch *Days of Our Lives* on the television in the afternoons, and she despised it when I signed up."

"Do you feel you let her down?"

"I don't know how she felt—all I cared about was the boy, Elwyn, who the lieutenant brought to our class. The lieutenant pointed out Elwyn's insignia: a chevron—and boasted that Elwyn had completed a course in weapons management and threat response in Longueuil and was about to leave for service in Afghanistan. In June. The very time we would all be enjoying the fruits of peace and good government in our lovely meadows."

"Elwyn wore a chevron?"

"I liked the chevron's grace but I'd never been seduced by flags or fancy uniforms before, and I did not think I'd be any good at polishing my shoes. Elwyn had a glittering starburst that kept flashing on his boot-toe as the sun glanced off our classroom's window frames."

"Elwyn's boots dazzled you!"

"It was none of those things that drew me. It wasn't the dazzle. It wasn't the boots."

Harold knits thoughtfully. "So what was it?"

. . . It was the fourteenth of May, and robins had come back to our cove, and we were all watching for the moment when we could pick fiddleheads and devour them twice-boiled to get rid of the bitterness. At our house Madame Blanchard melted pats of real butter on the greens instead of margarine. I had seen two dragonflies and harvested most of our rhubarb. Now here was a boy, Elwyn, all dragonfly, all robin, all burgeoning newness of strong, sour, wild rhubarb, having a face whose beauty pierced through me clear and sharp as an arrow of geese flung home from the blue. . . .

"Where have you gone?" asks Harold.

Where have I gone?

When Wolfe saw his first battle at Dettingen at the age of sixteen he looked in the mud and found headless men, bodiless arms flung from horses, the ancient death-grimace on face after face. He grabbed the dead faces and looked in their eyes—were any of them his brother? He found his brother Ned-not-Ned again and again . . .

"At our shithole Ghundy Ghar," I tell Harold, "that hill rising out of the poppies like a filthy boil, I hunted for Elwyn exactly as Wolfe once looked for his brother Ned. But afterwards, Wolfe repaired to his tent, alone, for two whole days. I didn't have that luxury, not one day, not even an hour or a minute—not a second, even now—after watching Elwyn crawl in the dust trying to find his arm. . . ."

"Elwyn, whom you loved?"

"With his arm blown off he looked like the scorpions we hunted at night. Our gunner, Mavis, used to slice their legs off and sprinkle them on his meal pack. He had the maimed victims race each other, the side with legs thumping and dragging the amputated side. We called it the Mangled Assassin Olympics. Elwyn looked like one of them, dragging himself toward us: one side raising itself unnaturally high with each lurch, and the armless side, the left, and he was left-handed—dragging with a horrible judder. I was freaking out because he and I had made a deal: one sees the other permanently maimed and we finish him off."

"But then you couldn't."

"You quickly redo the math when it happens: an arm missing might not be all that bad. He can do things with the other one. Choose knife or fork. Ruffle the dog. Hold me in his remaining arm while we sleep. Elwyn and I had three arms between us and yes, I loved him."

"Why could he not run?"

"The Afghans were a few hundred yards away—Elwyn should've had no problem running to us—but his every move was pinned to the mud and stones because he was searching, he was asking where the fuck did my arm go.

"I'm gonna fetch him, I told Mavis, who was busy unjamming his C7 in his boxers and a pair of flip-flops he'd made of duct tape and packing foam from a shipment of Tim Hortons vanilla dip with sprinkles. We had eighteen doughnuts each that day.

"The Afghans started flinging grenades and mortars and we had a new problem appearing at the east side of our position: I saw we were in for a Taliban swarm we'd failed to expect.

"She's overheated—Mavis slammed his gun and racked the slide—she's gummed up. . . . Dust was always jamming our guns and the jury was out on whether we needed more lube or less. Nobody could agree. Mavis was about to load a new round when Tippet and Galbraith tore out from their cover and hammered the ground between us and the Taliban for what seemed half an hour but was only, I'm told, nine minutes.

"But in that nine minutes I lost sight of Elwyn and that was because, as I saw when I finally walked over to where he'd been crawling in search of his arm, he'd rolled over into one of the dried-out gullies left all over the place by a combination of long-gone rains and ever-present wind. He fitted right in there like he'd been top-loaded into that all-dressed steamie you just ate.

"If Elwyn hadn't been unarmed and destroyed and half buried in that natural-looking, gravelike hole, he might have been a little bit interested in my telling him that for those few minutes of crawling, he lumbered just like one of Mavis's handicapped scorpions.

"Like I said though, I did not have two minutes to grieve Elwyn.

"You become a body and then you become remains and when you're finished your five seconds of being remains you're shucked into that unreal realm of glory in which we're all supposed to have believed from the start of our deployment. The never-never land of departed souls, more significant dead than when we farted or slept or gulped pineapple ham rations and masturbated together. Departed, we attain an importance reverential and unreal and in the past tense which is always somehow fictional.

"I didn't have two minutes for grief, but I did ask Mavis this: What's the name, the species, of the scorpions in your night races? He told me the word but I handed him my arm and said, Shut up and tattoo it. When he was done I said, Great. Glorious. A big, long crazy wild Latin name, Elwyn would've loved it."

Harold reads my arm: "*Leiurus quinquestriatus* . . . Is there an English translation?"

"That's the first thing I asked Mavis. What's the common name? He said, I'll tattoo that for you as well, but I said just tell that one to me. And he said it's Deathstalker, lemme add it on for you, and I said no, don't tattoo that on me, I want to keep that name to myself.

I wanted to whisper that one at night to Elwyn. I wouldn't have it written. I wouldn't in any way expose it to scrutiny beyond that of my own private remembrance.

"I might not know my own real name, or the name of my original hometown where the woman called Noémie gave me up to social services, but I knew when I came home from Ghundy Ghar I wanted to look out from Madame Blanchard's landing, past Cap-d'Espoir to Anticosti and the North Atlantic then Newfoundland where Elwyn spent nineteen years of his life without my having an inkling he existed. If I looked long enough I saw him in the fog.

"I'd stay and I'd watch and I'd drive Madame Blanchard nuts, not doing anything, not cutting firewood or helping around the house, hardly recognizing her except to sit and eat cod and potatoes she'd leave for me with a plate turned over it on the stove. She wanted me to go to the city, to Montreal, to get help. Finally, in the middle of summer 2007 when her own health gave out and she had to go to La Résidence Dernière Rose, what was I to do? I paced the floorboards, stayed up all night, didn't eat properly. I started remembering more and more about James Wolfe, how no one understood him the way I did, not even in school when I was a boy, long before I knew anything about a real battlefield."

"You felt you were the one who really knew him," replied Harold.

"Yes. I spent the whole latter part of that summer alone in the house thinking of him, comparing myself with him and falling far short, at first."

"You felt yourself a lesser soldier than he was?"

"Of course. Next to James Wolfe, James Blanchard of B Squadron really was a nobody—a twenty-one-year-old redhead nobody from Bougainville."

"So being James Wolfe made you a somebody."

"I lay on the daybed with my eyes shut, willing Wolfe to help me, to impart something of himself to me, make me more like him. I spent July and August begging him for that. Then September came and I was forced to venture outside as the nights were getting cold and I'd no more fuel for the stove. I climbed down to the beach to find driftwood and that's when I met Sophie, working in Germain Medosset's van."

"And by that time, Wolfe had become part of you."

"Without having come to know the heroic Wolfe as I did through that lonely time, James Blanchard would continue to be just another ruined soldier trying to find his way back home. Sophie calls it my dead-end delusion."

"Hmm."

"You don't call it that, too?"

"I don't call it anything like a delusion," Harold says. "I call it the heaviest possible dose of reality."

26 Bright Game

WEDNESDAY, SEPTEMBER 13.
NOON.

The Plains of Abraham. Quebec City, Quebec

"I FOUND OUT A LOT of things about you yesterday when I was walking around town," Harold says, swiping a half-eaten brioche off an abandoned plate as we pass a café *terrasse.* He folds it in his cloth handkerchief and pockets it despite Veronica's nose-quiver.

"About Wolfe?"

"Yes! About James Wolfe in his days as the general."

He leads me around. It is strange, having him show me the obelisk bearing my name opposite that of Montcalm's, the marquis facing downriver and Wolfe eyeing the Foulon. Just as Jenny Waugh wrote to me, the monument has a Latin inscription:

Mortem virtus communem
faman historia
monumentum posteritas dedit

"I believe I understand it," Harold says. "After all, Latin and English have a lot of the same roots . . . *Their virtue gave them a common death, and fame gave them a common history, and this monument, well, they'll both have to share it.*"

He leads me to a beautiful library where, up some cordoned-off stairs behind a balcony rail, stands a foreshortened statue of myself pointing past the stacks of books toward some undetermined goal.

"The librarian told me," says Harold, "that a couple of butchers made the original shortly after you died, and mounted it over their shop, where people pelted it with rotten fruit and knocked it down onto the street so many times they had to make this new one. Even this one got stolen and carried around the world in a boat and stuck in front of an English pub until someone mailed it back here. To get it in the crate they had to hack off that pointing arm—you can see the mend. . . ."

"He's very short," I complain.

"He is, isn't he. I guess when you're a butcher you're not much of a sculptor and maybe you don't really have enough wood. So the librarian told me that after the Falklands War an Argentinian student burst in here and flung a Molotov cocktail at you and set five hundred books ablaze and the staff had to throw you out the window into a snowbank to save you. So *someone* cares. . . ."

We meander along the Grande Allée and I very much like the tasteful monument to myself in the spot where I died, in front of what is now a beautiful art museum, even if the monument has been blown up and replaced several times and bears traces of a great big red X through my name where rebels have obliterated it and city officials have gone at it with some sort of remedial acid wash. Not far from that monument is the very wellspring from which I received a drop of water as I lay wounded. On the plains behind my monument lies the exquisite sunken garden dedicated to Joan of Arc where I sat for a while yesterday, and we go there, Harold and I, to share his brioche with Veronica.

"Don't think," says Harold to the dog, "you're going to get brioche with real butter in it every day. That's not good for working dogs. You have to have your avocado oil." He fishes in his pack for a handful of the Working Friend dog food he never fails to provide: he showed me, with some care and pride, that on the label it promises twenty-nine vitamins, no additives, 18 percent protein and a patented oil made from avocados and glucosamine, for dogs over the age of nine. For two weeks after the bag has been opened, Working Friend promises to stay tender.

But the brioche is dry and I wish I'd fished a bit of water from my death well and stored it in one of the Perrier bottles lying everywhere. Late roses and Jacob's ladder have begun to glow bright as the plains develop a cold mist, silver sun-dogs retreating over Point-Levis across the river.

I sense drumbeats through the fog.

A young woman carrying the fleur-de-lys strides past us, purposeful, her pigtail swinging behind her hat.

"Excuse me," I say to Harold as he fiddles around in his pack searching for a wet wipe, "but did she not look to you to be dressed exactly like le Marquis de Montcalm?"

But the woman has disappeared into the fog, headed for the museum grounds.

"His blue coat, his red vest and golden stripes . . ."

"I really don't know, I didn't see . . ."

I rise and Harold follows, past Joan of Arc on her beautiful horse, past willows and a little boy pulling his wooden toy truck behind him on the mown grass. We walk down to where the French and British armies have begun to assemble. As the museum attendant warned me, there are no folding chairs. The armies gather on a traffic meridian as he predicted. We have to stand behind a line of parked cars to watch as the woman who is Montcalm readies her troops:

"Assemblez, ligne un! Assemblez, ligne deux! Assemblez, ligne trois!"

A second young woman joins her. Is she—can she be—today's Wolfe? She has a blonde pigtail and a beautiful replica of my Redcoat uniform, much grander than the original one I wore for the battle, and far cleaner than the version I have on my back. I wonder where she got hers. How is it that you can buy a replica of my coat made to fit a small young woman? I suppose that if she is affiliated with the museum there must be a tailor somewhere who has sewn the garment to her specifications.

The armies line up in a completely unbelievable way. Four tour buses pass through the road in the plains above. Construction racket clamours in the city at my back. Cyclists ride past the armies, uninterested.

The female General Wolfe and all her soldiers yell everything in French, before suddenly breaking into *God save the Queen! God save the King!*

Joggers prance past the proceedings. Japanese tourists walk past without stopping to lift their cameras. Harold and I are the only spectators and I fear someone might ask us to move along as there is no place for us and we are in the way. But we might as well be invisible.

After twenty minutes of preparatory theatrics, Montcalmette and her soldiers commence their fatal march toward my men, who—and this is somewhat true to the way it happened—do not move a muscle until the French are within shooting range, and then, with a volley of shot, the French collapse on the field.

There is a minute of indecisive quiet, in which a huddle of other persons begins to budge from the meridian's edge. Can it be . . . yes . . . they indulge in a simulacrum of Mohawk war whoops as if from some cartoon . . . they tend to the injured French soldiers then encircle and kill the remaining Redcoats.

Montcalm and Wolfe are the correct age—Wolfette is about twenty-five.

But the soldiers . . . the soldiers are all between eight and eleven years old.

After the enactment, Wolfe and Montcalm peel their surcoats off and spread them on the grass, and take Tetra Paks and granola bars out of a cooler for their students, who sprawl over the battlefield and await their school bus.

One of the children lies on the grass reading a book separate from the others, and I would like to see which book she has chosen—it's a thing I do on the train, on the bus, on a bench in the park, whenever I see someone reading. Though reading is a solitary act requiring privacy and quiet, I feel bound to other readers by an invisible thread of words, a kinship without speech. I suppose this is one of the things that made my schoolmates laugh at me and I wonder if this young child's schoolmates taunt her in the same way.

"I wouldn't mind," I tell Harold, "getting a bit closer to see what that child is reading . . . just out of curiosity."

I wonder if her book will protect her. For some reason, despite all that has happened to me, I still hope reading might help somebody. But her school bus arrives, and I hear in the melee that she and her classmates are bound for Rimouski, four hours northeast of here across the Saint Lawrence—halfway up the coast to where I have lived all these years in the old wooden house of Madame Blanchard. Perhaps once the children come of age their well-meaning teachers will invite a young soldier to their classroom with an invitation to die in the wars now being born.

As the school bus leaves, taking the children's voices with it and leaving lonely the sounds of jackhammers and distant sirens, Harold, Veronica and I walk to a small memorial stone in the distance, next to which someone has planted a sapling. The plaque honours Montcalm: this is the place where he received his mortal wound on this very date, yet there is no one to notice but the three of us. Like us, the Marquis de Montcalm has become nobody.

"It's because he did not win," says Harold. "There lies a sadness around Montcalm that will never go away. But," he reaches for his knitting bag, "*sadness* isn't the right word, now, is it? Maybe the public emotion around Montcalm isn't sadness at all, but ignominy. People avert their faces from him, and from you, both of you turned to stone and clothed not in glory but in a disease infecting body and psyche of the New World. No one can deny it but neither will anyone admit it. Instead we go on teaching the children our bright, empty game."

Harold retrieves wool out of his bag, sits under Montcalm's memorial stone, and knits.

"You like knitting this much?" I ask. In the time I have known Harold, he's left a trail of holy circles with almost everyone we've encountered: ticket takers at the Metro stations, a policewoman manually operating the traffic lights at the corner of Rue Jacques Parizeau and Rue de la Chevrotière, the cashier at Dollarama.

"Even people who've known me a very long time," he stretches the phrase so it hangs like a soft reproach in the air, "think I find it relaxing."

"And you don't?"

"No! It's not at all relaxing. In fact, it's quite the opposite. You've been on many a battlefield, so you know."

"What has knitting got to do with battlefields?"

"I'm firmly of the opinion that every meeting of the United Nations, and every war fought on every battlefield, should have a person present who is devoted to knitting."

"In the midst?"

"Exactly. But not concentrating on the knitting—instead very much engaged in the talks or in the conflict." He fishes from his pocket the chain on which hang his keys and his folding scissors, and snips his wool.

"Are your scissors a part of your equipment like my musket or my dirk?"

"They most certainly are, as is my yellow attire."

"I was wondering how many of those yellow shirts . . ."

"I have quite a lot. I was in Orillia working as a caregiver and I had a little bit of money and saw them on sale in a shop, and I bought eighteen of them. They were ten dollars each."

"Eighteen?"

"It's important for a knitter to wear high-visibility gear."

"Instead of camouflage gear?"

"Absolutely. Knitting is an important part of the world's healing process, so it needs to be seen. We use the idea of knitting all the time to talk about this. We talk about bones being knit or mended after they've been broken. We talk about knitting relationships back together after they've been torn apart. And my knitting is another way of bringing that healing about. And it takes time. I'm talking about sitting at an important meeting or in the battlefield for three or four good long hours of deep knitting. It's hard work."

He glistens with sweat thinking about it. I see he is talking about real exertion.

"I'm engaged," he says. "I'm part of the proceedings. I'm not concentrating on the knitting. In reality, I'm not knitting at all."

—

I LEAVE HAROLD BEHIND ON the plains.

I turn back once, to see him knitting at the foot of Montcalm's stone. Harold said he will stay on the plains throughout this anniversary day of Wolfe's death. For me he will loop the yarn around his needles while the ghost of my battle unfolds. In his golden shirt, looping the green yarn, he is the living image of Mrs. Waugh's mysterious second tarot card: the two of pentacles, the one neither she nor I understood.

All this day and night of the thirteenth of September, Harold promises, he will remain on the site in my stead, brightness beaming off him in the midst of the battlefield. Smoke and fire, drums and death-screams will not obscure him. I leave him, high-visibility Harold in his yellow sweatshirt, seated on the grass knitting to the heartbeat of Ronnie, my not-yet-fallen drummer.

I climb down from the plains, their incline now so gentle, their embankment lazy and easy as the herring gull gliding in air currents over the Saint Lawrence River. I hear her needle-thin cry flung aloft and raining down on me this admonishment: *Climb on, General Wolfe. Don't involve me in your memories and your regrets—I'm above all that.*

I follow the path of the school bus driving the students of Rimouski home: the bridge, the highway, walking and hitching ride after ride.

Vachon cake truck—

Nun's red Yaris—

Drifter's nicotine-stinking wagon—

Beer truck to the junction—

Back to this unmarked stretch on my Gaspé, between L'Anse Pleureuse and Manche-d'Épée without an ice hockey arena or even a road-sign warning motorists to watch for moose. No human is here to watch me reach the place where I leave James Wolfe behind.

Too soon, I approach signs of my return to life as Jimmy Blanchard: vetch leaves turning brown in the ditch, goldenrod high and going to seed, fireweed with its hot purple feathers waving overland to the estuaries.

27 Stolons

WEDNESDAY, SEPTEMBER 13.
EVENING.
The Gaspé, Quebec

A MAN CAN BE IMPORTANT yet completely misunderstood.

He can be remembered in bronze or in stone or only in the wind, yet all memory is a failed mirror.

Here come the barrens . . . hills stretch into the distance, snow on their round tops: rivulets fill the land's crevices and cleavages.

So many things are the same between my two lives as I walk this road linking villages whose fishing nets Wolfe ripped and burned, toward my own forgotten village.

I have surveyed moor . . . desert . . . does the terrain's name matter? Land outspans army and king. It outlives us, and will outbreathe us. Does the year of any given campaign—Dettingen, Culloden, Quebec, Ghundy Ghar—do its dates mean a thing? I dig up human bones everywhere—no matter where we fight a war, that land holds bones in it from previous warriors. I dig them up, shovel sand to pile on rock to pile on more sand, bones falling on me, pile 'em higher to make cover.

Shovels are the same throughout time.

Alone, I dig femur, sand and clavicle; I dig stones and myriad little bones of someone's feet, delicate and connected and graceful as the armature of birds. A man might spread his fingers and toes and rise up out of the land having become avian, become weightless, become mobile and all-seeing.

But nowhere have I been more alone than I was in that peeling saltbox after Madame Blanchard had to leave me eleven summers ago. As summer ended I burrowed under quilts she had made in her healthier days: her pink one with the green rose leaves, or the orange zigzag number with the crocheted edge like symmetrical seaweed or a scallop shell's crenellated hem. I kept La Grignotine Louise in business buying their Chef Boyardee spaghetti and meatballs as well as mini ravioli because of the pop-top tins that do not need a can-opener and can be stacked on the bedroom floor, there being no heart in me for getting up and descending into the root cellar to face potatoes with their malevolent and overwhelmingly populous stolons, active in the otherwise comforting dark. The stolons, white and probing, turn into ghost-fingers that would like me to join them underground.

The stolons await me now again—I sense them already in this foyer to my solitude. Here the land lies, grasses sing under the wind's voice, earth makes love to wind's touch, the ground is pierced and made lonelier by cries of geese and crows—nothing is more fearsome than this land's power to annihilate a man all by itself.

And a king believes he has subdued it?

At last I have stood on Quebec's famous battlefield and know it ludicrous—as with all the other battlefields I have seen, or Wolfe has seen, or Elwyn DeMaldaire or George Warde or any other soldier has seen—ludicrous to call the land owned, conquered, taken by one small group of men who do not even plan to stay on it.

Heaven help me, here comes the chasm, the boiling fissure of the Spout!

Its geyser rises, a pillar with its exploding silver head just waiting for me to succumb. Who hasn't wanted to fling himself on it and descend—what a rush it'd be, what a way to go dark, down with the herring and the seals. Weeds and brine and water-music then nothingness, no pain . . . why have I made it wait?

What waits for me at Madame Blanchard's empty house?

Alone last February I kicked my way under the frozen tarp covering the cut spruce in the yard. Alone I sharpened the axe to make splits and start a fire.

Alone I slept late and retired at five o'clock and felt a pounding in my ears like the sea. Alone I climbed the stairs to the landing and tried to look out toward Elwyn's homeland, tried to imagine that he had returned there, though he has not; tried to picture him eating breaded chops with his sister and mother, a dessert of homemade bread slathered in clotted cream and jam.

Alone, I cried in the creaking bed under whose iron frame sits Madame Blanchard's willow-ware pisspot that has quite a nice English scene on it. Alone, I read, or tried to read, old newspapers and *National Geographics*, and, always, my beloved history books.

In corners of Madame Blanchard's house has grown a black mould—not an onslaught; mere lines, lacy and delicate. I find it pretty, like frost ferns, only dark. Mould enjoys the chill, it likes aloneness.

Alone in that house I gathered my stories about the English hero Wolfe under my covers and gleaned more about him than I'd ever known as a boy. Wolfe, who for so many, like Tippet and Galbraith—those thugs of my childhood now working in the oil sands—remains a forgotten antique. Anything not in the books, any gap in his letters, occupied my solitude until James Wolfe's days transpired again with golden clarity in what has otherwise been Trooper James

Blanchard of Squadron B's fog of . . . is it envy? Is it, as Sophie claims, depression? Or is it that yearning all soldiers like me feel to act, to matter, to make even a tiny difference in this world?

I guess Sophie thought that once I walked the Plains of Abraham I would return to normalcy, to being Jimmy Blanchard, perhaps even be able to have an ordinary life with her, working together at the snack van in summers, going to Montreal for the autumn and winter seasons, with her working at the Mission and me, well, she always had the notion that I could, if I pulled myself together, qualify for a subsidized bedsit and find a half-decent job like hers.

But my plan has always been different. My plan was that I might, like Wolfe, finally sleep. I believed he and I were destined to become one man on this same road. And I planned to fling my breast here upon the Spout and fall, in triumph, to join him.

I've managed, over eleven Septembers, to coax myself right to the edge of this Spout, balance on its ledge and hover over the column of spume so that it soaks my face. Years ago I couldn't get this close. People say there are some who, upon reaching a ledge like this, would involuntarily hurl themselves over it with a compulsion that has nothing to do with suicide—but I am not that kind of man. My reluctance to balance here has been precisely because I know that I've always planned to fall.

How many soldiers get to choose this dynamic a grave, one that never stops rising and falling, heaving, breathing—calling out in the voice of loud waters to a coastline where all the birds, all the hares and partridges, the caribou and snowy owls and voles and seals and whales, hear the cataract's lament? Men in the desert don't get this grave. Elwyn will never have it. Montcalm and Wolfe have not found it. This is the one consolation being an ordinary soldier wins me. My own rushing waters, constant as the brook flowing from the Westerham hills behind Wolfe's boyhood home, loud as the falls at Montmorency that Wolfe heard each day of his siege . . . I get my own, personal, ever-gushing geyser of sorrow.

Do not think I haven't longed for this. It was to be my reward upon visiting Wolfe's Quebec battleground. Alone, gloriously alone, I could have done it. Do not think I don't have it in me.

Across the chasm, patient and golden, sits my companion.

Harold told me to keep her for as long as it takes.

He has given me instructions on how to live with Veronica as a workmate, how not to spoil her industry or her training.

Have you ever sat across the chasm of death and looked into a working dog's eyes?

I haven't seen anything close to that gaze anywhere except on the battlefield itself, in the eyes of a brother soldier, each prepared to die for the other.

Harold has given me Veronica to accompany me while I clean up Madame Blanchard's house and sell it. He has loaned me her bottomless understanding.

"How do you think," he asked as we parted on Abraham's Plains, "I came to understand who you really are?"

They call her a seeing-eye dog, he said, but she will show you what can't be seen except by fathomless observation.

He gave me her green leash and red harness.

He gave me her snow-boots and her bag of Working Friend. The salmon-flavoured one, her second-favourite next to the flounder and other wild foods that I will be able to feed her through the fall and into February, there being no shortage of fish and hares in our cove.

I have always loved dogs.

You can sell a Gaspé house to Americans these days. You won't get much for it, hardly more than twenty thousand if you're lucky, but someone will love that house, if only in the summers. Someone who's never had to live in it alone with Ghundy Ghar.

The hills become massive and snow-bedecked, the sky bigger, the sun lofty overhead. More rivulets. The round-topped hills give way to tableland hilltops, flatter, and clouds catch along their edges. All the lines of the earth are sweeping, undulating—rich, dark browns and tans and the reddish-dark heath-shrub, and always water glittering, snaking, or standing in little puddles in and around the pockets and creases and bog-veins of the terrain. Steep inclines, but with gentle, sweeping hollows.

Veronica—are you with me?

OCTOBER 5, 2017

RUE DROLET,
MONTREAL

Dear Jimmy Blanchard,

When you and I met, a year ago at the Fisher Library, I was, I confess, ready to dismiss you. I tried to concentrate on Wolfe's letters, on the man who died, in 1759, on the Plains of Abraham. I did not, at first, take into serious consideration the idea that you might have anything to add to my understanding of an English general who belongs to history.

Forgive me. I have finally met Monsieur Hippolyte Choinière, the handwriting expert!

He went on Tuesday to spend the morning perusing the following original documents in the archives at the McCord Museum:

- a letter Wolfe wrote to a Mr. Weston on December 29, 1741, when Wolfe would have been fourteen years old;
- a letter written at age twenty-eight from Southampton to his Uncle Walter on September 15, 1755, four years before the siege at Quebec;
- Wolfe's personal, handwritten Quebec journal, lost for many years, written during the siege, out of which Wolfe

is said to have torn some of the pages complaining about
his insubordinate officers. I believe this may be the journal
to which Heather Forest at the Thomas Fisher Rare Book
Library referred when I first visited her.

I met Monsieur Choinière beside the glass archive doors as he unlocked them with his security card: he presented a joyful, enthusiastic countenance. We went for lunch at a sushi café around the corner and spent several hours discussing his findings.

I began to divine that his work runs along two threads and that his main work now, which takes him to Poland and Paris and South America and China and other places, is the forensic work of authenticating handwriting in cases of disputed fraud. His other line, that of psychological analysis or personality assessment of a script's author, was prevalent throughout the seventies: large corporations used to hire him to read over the CVs of job applicants and offer his opinion on the best candidates, and the employers hired or did not hire accordingly. This psychological or graphological aspect, which I wanted him to do for the handwriting of Wolfe, is not so much in demand as it was. This only made me more interested in it. I liked the idea of Monsieur Choinière dusting off and exercising his psychoanalytic skills on James Wolfe's behalf.

Still, there was a forensic gleam in Monsieur Choinière's eye: apparently the authenticity of Wolfe's Quebec journal, the one that resides at the McCord Museum in Montreal, has been disputed. He showed me an article from *Le Soleil* of July 12, 2009, headlined *Les mystérieux journaux du général Wolfe.* It described how there are two other existing documents that claim to be Wolfe's original: one in the National Archives in Ottawa, and the other at the Royal Military College in Kingston. He would go, Monsieur

Choinière told me, to see if these journals would confirm what he already suspected after his perusal this morning. He did not believe the McCord had in its budget the means to pay for such an investigation, but he would do it because he believed it had to be done.

The sushi restaurant had the only quiet nook in the neighbourhood, which is full of noisy eateries with Formica chairs scraping the floors amid a cacophony of McGill students hollering over their falafels. I ordered an avocado roll and Monsieur Choinière requested salmon sushi that arrived bearing a very pretty translucent scattering of roe. We asked for Perrier. We slid the sushi aside and arranged his knapsack and papers, and my notebooks and pencil stubs and my pencil sharpener, across the table from each other.

When, a few days ago, I explained this rendezvous to my next-door neighbour, Lilliane, she asked, "Have you checked his credentials?" I replied that I was not worried at all about Monsieur Choinière's credentials: as far as I'm concerned, if a person wants to devote his life to the analysis of handwriting, then I believe he is sincere and has something of interest to say, though it might appear unusual or even improbable to some. Now I took delight in Monsieur Choinière's face, which brimmed throughout our interview with an overflow of *joie de vivre* that made him appear youthful, though he told me that as long ago as the mid-1960s he was employed as a social worker three hundred miles north of Edmonton.

"How did you go from being a social worker," I asked him, "to becoming a handwriting expert?"

He replied, "If you knew my aunt Iris, you would understand."

His aunt Iris, he said, had possessed a *ceinture fléchée*—the traditional woven fur-trader's belt dating from Wolfe's century—and would wear it every year in the Carnaval de Québec parade.

"She was red-cheeked," he said. "She was one of these people who you look at, and you want to smile. With her you knew you would have fun."

Iris was a nurse and a schoolteacher but during a time when Monsieur Choinière rented a room from her in his early twenties, she took a correspondence course in handwriting analysis. "She had such magnetism," he recalled. "She saw that I'm very curious—and I was interested in her mysterious course. With her firm voice, she told me, 'Hippolyte, you would be good at this!' And that idea stayed with me."

I had been wondering if his name was really Hippolyte, as it had appeared on his emails to me; now the answer delighted me.

Through a succession of social work and Children's Aid jobs in the North and in Muskoka and other places, he continued to study handwriting. "My sister was going to Haiti," he said. "She'd bought a blue convertible Volkswagen and she said, 'Come with me to Miami and keep the car and drive it back home.' On that trip I stopped in every library: Florida, the Library of Congress, University of Toronto. . . . I rented rooms and studied on my own."

He went to California and to France to learn more, and in 1976 he attended an international congress of handwriting experts in Paris, as an independent participant. "I knew who I wanted to meet," he told me. At the conference were all the heavy-hitters of handwriting analysis: syndicate vice presidents, forensic graphologists, foreign correspondents for *La Graphologie*, a handwriting analysis journal published from 1871 to the present day. He had read all their works. These people invited him for cocktails and he eventually became a correspondent for the journal.

"I have a complete set of every journal they have published

since the beginning," he told me. Since then, his handwriting analysis work has taken him to Tanzania, Belgium and Chile. He has testified for international penal tribunals and entered the archives of Carl Jung with a concealed spy camera.

Now, over our sushi rolls, he began to tell me his findings on Wolfe.

"I'm a movement translator," he said. "Handwriting is frozen movement. The page is the stage. My work is to animate that life on the stage. I am meeting the person.

"I'm asking questions of the page. My first question is to ask what is common to Wolfe's time and what belongs to him personally. For example, in the letter he wrote at age fourteen in 1741, even within the restrictions of that age, I can see what we call the *pastosity*—a muddiness—that means he was probably, as a teenager, discovering his own sexuality. It's unexpressed but present. Later it's the same with some of his emotion. He shows a conflict between being sentimental or emotional and being a man of action. With select people he can be affectionate. The feelings are there.

"His environment, in the army, is not the place to express his feelings. Within him I can see that possible ambivalence between feeling and thinking. It's like somebody who has a coat of armour. In nature you have the porcupine. Don't touch it! But then, the meat is so tender. It's the same with Wolfe.

"Did he idealize his lovers? With this type of personality, if he comes too close to the real person he's afraid of his own emotions. Psychologically, he is not really in touch with his emotions. We see this with the priest who loves the Virgin Mary—he channels his emotions there, and she won't challenge them. He expresses his emotions through reason."

Monsieur Choinière explained that in Wolfe's handwriting there is equilibrium between form and movement. While his fourteen-year-old handwriting is closer to a "copy-book" rendition of schoolboys' handwriting of that age—with, for example, flourishes on the letter *D*—it nevertheless betrays personality and is congruent with his later writing.

"It's angular, and it has irregularities. I see the strong influence of his environment—he's not a hippie of his time: he will fit in with society, but with enough individuality to be his own man. He's a man of action. What strikes me is the overall organization of the page: he can see the global aspect of things, yet at the same time is taking care of details. His punctuation is all there on the page.

"He has, in handwriting terms, a good degree of tension: a good mixture of tension and release. We score on five degrees of tension and Wolfe has three, which is best for a man of action, a good equilibrium. If it was too tense it would indicate he was scared. Too relaxed is not good either. His score is the best number for someone efficient. As a general this is crucial: in organizing the whole as well as the details, he has good judgment."

Monsieur Choinière invited me to ask him questions I might have about Wolfe, so I said, "Would you say he has a sense of devotion? Not in a religious sense, but more in the sense of persistence or adherence to a cause?"

Dear Jimmy, you might be interested to know that it was at this point I suddenly realized Monsieur Choinière and I were speaking about Wolfe in the present tense.

"Yes—devotion and a sense of purpose," he told me. "No hesitation. Firmness."

"I'm also wondering about the dichotomy between his ruthlessness—he's brutal in his burning of hundreds of homesteads up and down the Saint Lawrence, and he tears the nets of poor fishing families in the Gaspé though he knows fish is their only livelihood, and there are all the people he's slaughtered—yet he thinks of himself as principled and believes himself visionary. He envisions and hopes for a North America more enlightened than England. How has he reconciled his brutality with that vision?"

Monsieur Choinière considered this for a moment. Then he said, "There are principles of his time that he'd adhere to. The goal is all-important. He's not a diplomat. It's not a question of good or evil. How did he feel? In his Quebec journal, at the ends of the lines on some days the text went in a downhill direction. Direction follows the mood of the day. The handwriting is connected, but he puts capital letters where they shouldn't be. He has a very logical, practical mind—these people are action-oriented—but at the same time, when someone like that is stressed, the opposite emerges; the feelings, the emotions are there, though they have been contained."

I asked, "What about his brother Ned's death, and the death of his lover, Eliza, and the hard time he had when he first saw the butchery of battle at Dettingen? He went into his tent for two days and couldn't come out. He would feel emotion then the feeling would leave him and he complained to his mother that he was numb."

Monsieur Choinière nodded. "There are modulations: at the base of his writing there is vulnerability and emotion, but the global aspect is self-control, which is what will be seen in everyday life. But these people, if you can manage to become intimate, earn their confidence, that's when you realize their tenderness."

"What about his love of poetry?"

"He's a man of principle, socialized as a child soldier. Poetry is a socially accepted way to channel his sensibilities. His regular way of thinking is reason. We see, underneath, intuition and feelings. It's there. Some people are cold-blooded men of principle. We see in his handwriting that Wolfe is not cold-blooded. But he was socialized as a child soldier. Still, one thing that puzzles me," said Monsieur Choinière, "is his relationship with money or material things. It would seem money was important for him: he could give, but he had a need for security. I see this in his letter *s*—he put more emphasis on the letter *s*, and usually *s* has to do with money. Psychologically he's more anal than oral, more concerned with keeping than with giving—keeping things to himself. But then, being a man of principle, if he was to give, it would be through principle.

"He has also got what we call foxtails in his handwriting. When he comes to the end of the page, his writing is cramped in the right margin: he doesn't want to cut what he's doing. He wants to do everything in the same, uninterrupted line. He has trouble cutting off or changing a course of action.

"He knows in advance where he's going, and he doesn't stop. The letters are connected—they are even hyper-connected, especially in the Quebec journal. Also, we can talk about initiative. His letter *t* is on the ground, and the *t*-bar is on a 45-degree slant. We see this in people who can be impulsive, but because of the spatial organization of his writing on the page . . . he steps on the gas pedal, but then he brakes, using reason.

"In other words, his first response is to be impulsive, but he has enough self-control not to do anything he would regret . . . unless he is tired, or very ill, or has been drinking wine."

After we had discussed Wolfe's psychology, there was the matter of the Quebec journal and its authenticity. "I don't see any intrinsic signs of forgery," Monsieur Choinière told me. "If you try to forge, you write more slowly . . . like following in someone's footsteps. There are, therefore, tremblings, or breaking-points. I look at general features and small details. There are idiosyncratic gestures that a person doesn't even know he's doing."

He would go, he said, to Ottawa and Kingston, to look at the other documents claiming to be the real thing, but he believed he would, in time, prove that the journal we had read at the McCord Museum in Montreal was the journal Wolfe wrote during the difficult days you and I know about, Jimmy—the days of doubt and mutiny, illness and loss, loneliness and dejection, and the pursuit of a vision seen by turns as heroism or despicable folly.

We finished our Perrier and shared a pot of green tea. Monsieur Choinière had spent the whole morning in the McCord archives animating the frozen movement of Wolfe's hand. Now he told me, "It's like I was meeting him in person, doing an interview with him. I see him moving. . . . His writing is slanted and angular—I see him like this. . . ."

And Jimmy, at this the handwriting expert rose from his seat, raised a hand holding an invisible sword, and lunged across the sushi café, his body slanted and gangling. He suddenly became the figure of Wolfe himself—awkward yet determined and elongated, although Hippolyte Choinière is in fact quite small and round and not forceful-looking at all. It was as if his hours of studying and contemplating the handwriting of Wolfe had allowed Wolfe to briefly inhabit him.

As soon as I gasped in recognition of the man I have studied so long, Monsieur Choinière laid down his sword and re-inhabited his own frame, and sat down again on the other side of our teapot.

Finally, dear Jimmy, I asked Monsieur Choinière the question you have probably been wondering about: how did the handwriting of James Wolfe compare with yours, in the letter you were kind enough to let me share with him—the one about Wolfe's lost days?

I thought you might like to know Monsieur Choinière's exact words, so I wrote them down in my old friend, Forkner shorthand, so as to be certain not to miss a thing.

"Forensically speaking," said Hippolyte Choinière, "the handwriting styles of James Wolfe and your friend, Jimmy Blanchard, are worlds apart. But from a psychological handwriting analysis point of view, the documents might have been written by the same man."

Dear Jimmy, I will close, and attend to my own papers. As you saw, at the Fisher Library, I am not very neat, and between my photocopied research materials and my own notes, you can hardly see from one end to the other of this little apartment, papers everywhere! I have been writing draft after draft of the story of a man called James, yet I hardly know if I will ever be able to do him justice. So I intend to press on, through the winter, hoping to have some sort of coherent manuscript in time for the new year.

I am not sure where to send this letter. I hardly think it will last through the snow at the gazebo in the park, and you aren't at the mission at this time of year, I know. I guess I'll just leave it with the mission wrapped in a copy of my manuscript when I finally finish it, so that, should you choose to return, you might see what I have done with your story.

My sincere regards,
Jenny Waugh

ACKNOWLEDGEMENTS

I THANK MY FAMILY, FRIENDS and colleagues, especially the following, without whose advice and support I could not have created this work:

My agent Shaun Bradley, my editor Lynn Henry, Anne Dondertman, Pearce Carefoote and staff at the Thomas Fisher Rare Book Library at the University of Toronto, Anne Collins, Amanda Lewis, handwriting expert D. Gauthier, Jean Dandenault, Martin Dandenault, Juliette Dandenault, Esther Wade, Daniel MacNee, Hawthornden International Retreat for Writers, Dr. A. Nitpicker, Heather McNabb and staff at the archives of the McCord Museum in Montreal, book designer Jennifer Griffiths, Angelica Glover, Michael Winter, Barbara Wight, Nancy Hall, Janet Blachford, Shelagh Plunkett, Alice Zorn, Susan Gillis, Elise Moser, and Ross Rogers.

And I thank you, dear reader.

KATHLEEN WINTER'S NOVEL *Annabel* (2010) was shortlisted for the Scotiabank Giller Prize, the Governor General's Literary Award, the Rogers Writers' Trust Fiction Prize, the Amazon.ca First Novel Award, the Orange Prize, Canada Reads, and numerous other awards. It was also a *Globe and Mail* "Best Book," a *New York Times* "Notable" book, a *Quill & Quire* "Book of the Year" and a #1 best-seller in Canada. It has been published and translated worldwide. In 2014, Winter published an Arctic memoir, *Boundless*, which was shortlisted for the Hilary Weston Prize and the Taylor Prize for non-fiction; and *The Freedom in American Songs*, an acclaimed collection of stories. Kathleen Winter was born in the UK, spent many years in Newfoundland, and now lives in Montreal, Quebec.